Passion
&
Drive
Change the world!

THE MAN OF
CLOUD 9

BY
ADAM DREECE

ADZO Publishing Inc.

Calgary, Canada

ADZO Publishing Inc.
Calgary, Alberta, Canada
www.adzopublishing.com

Printed in Canada

This is a work of fiction. Names, characters, places, and incidents are a product of the author's imagination. Locales and public names are sometimes used for atmospheric purposes. Any resemblance to actual people, living or dead, or to businesses, companies, events, institutions, or locales is completely coincidental.

Library and Archives Canada Cataloguing in Publication

Dreece, Adam, 1972-, author
        The man of cloud 9 / by Adam Dreece.

Issued in print and electronic formats.
ISBN 978-0-9948184-3-0 (paperback).--ISBN 978-0-9948184-4-7 (kindle)

        I. Title.

PS8607.R39M36 2016   C813'.6   C2016-903824-6
                                         C2016-903825-4

2   3   4   5   6   7   8   9 2017-03-13 73,619

DEDICATION

To my wife, who has been on this crazy adventure of life with me for over twenty years. She listened to the wild ideas and ambitions of a crazy long haired guy in university, proposed a second date after I crashed and burned revealing my awkwardness and complete ineptitude at the first one, and inspires me every day. No one could have a better companion and partner through this journey.

And special thanks to my amazing beta readers, especially Shannon, Stacey, Sarah, Chris and Randy who went through multiple versions and pulled no punches in helping me make this book what it could be. You guys are amazing.

CHAPTERS

CHAPTER ONE
A GOODBYE

"Few people know that when the solar flare burned the middle states, Niko nearly abandoned his dream. Imagine that for a moment. There would have been no NanoClouds, no hero bringing about an era of innovation, no one reminding our broken nation that it could heal. We would have stayed in the shadow of the past, instead of rising and casting our own." Phoebe took a steadying breath and smiled. The crowd waited patiently.

"I got to know Niko," she continued, "right after the Flare. He was so passionate about this vision he had. And each and every day he was urged by those in authority to drop it. His life would have been so much easier if he had, but he wouldn't, he couldn't. That's not... wasn't Niko." A sorrowful laugh escaped. "Not at all."

She gripped the sides of the old podium and stared out at the enormous crowd. There sat captains of industry, heads of startup companies, press, politicians, and friends. She still couldn't believe she'd been asked to give the first speech.

She pushed her long, curly black hair over her ears,

revealing more of her beautiful square jaw and the sadness that soaked her from soul to her mocha-brown face.

She looked at the front row. She smiled at Tass, a younger woman with a topknot of dark hair. For so long, the two women had acted like rivals for Niko's attention. Why had it taken Niko's death for them to be able to find common ground?

Phoebe glanced at the silent cameras-drones as they floated about, broadcasting the funeral to hundreds of millions of people around the world. She closed her eyes and took in a breath of the warm and welcoming summer air.

"For days, the news had been filled with stories about the raw power of the destruction, about those who had been evacuated from the coasts decades before or who had escaped the Great Quake of California, having once again lost everything. It didn't matter that the best minds had seen it coming over a year ahead of time and that everyone had been safely removed because it was yet another opportunity to tell tales of destruction and despair. It almost tipped Niko over the edge."

"But somehow," she said, glancing at the woman with the topknot, "he held on to his dream. It was a privilege to see it first hand in the early days, as that almost extinguished spark of innovation became a roaring fire. And then, to be there at the end, despite his broken body, to see his passion and fire still burning as brightly. There won't ever be another Niko Rafaelo." She shook, tears streaming down. "Thank you."

CHAPTER TWO
THE THESIS

Eighteen Years Earlier

"Geezes, Niko! How many times are you going to keep coming to me with the same flooding idea? No, no, no, no, and today of all days? Did you see the news? Millions of mid-Western Americans are watching the solar flare destroy their homes and towns today. And you think taking another run at me with the nanobot idea's going to fly somehow?" asked Niko's thesis professor.

"The flare has nothing to do with me," countered Niko.

"Doesn't it? What if instead of wasting your time trying to breathe new life into that horrific nanobot technology, you actually found a way to help people? Let the idea go. Come up with something to help the regions constantly ravaged by storms or tsunamis. Come up with something that even hints at keeping Manhattan dry, and you'd make a mint." The bald professor bowed his head and took a breath, shuffling the books under his arm. "Please, listen to me this time. You're running out of time, and your thesis idea has to have real, redeemable, social value."

"But they do have redeemable value," said Niko, his fists clenched. "Can you just look at the proposal?"

The professor cursed under his breath. "I'll say it again: nanobots are dead. I will not be the one standing there with the blood of innocents on my hands. They were banned decades ago because of arrogance like yours, and where did that leave how many thousands? Hear me when I say this Mister Rafaelo, I will *never* approve this idea or one remotely related to it." He glared at Niko, who was glaring back at him. "You're running out of time. You have what, ten weeks left?"

"Eight."

Shaking his head, the professor said, "Eight weeks, geezes. We both know what happens if you don't have an approved thesis by that point— you're out of here, and no other college will pick you up. I know full well that you need this because of your home life, but that's not my problem. I have a standard to maintain, as well as the college's reputation to worry about."

Niko stood there fuming, watching the professor as he walked off towards his office. "What's with the allergy you have to anything revolutionary? About fixing the errors of the past so that we can make a brighter future? Why can't we *dare* to reclaim what we've lost?" he yelled, walking up to him.

"There's plenty that we don't have today that we had in years gone by and I'm fine with that. The early part of the twenty-first century was fraught with excess and ego. Why would we want to bring that back?"

"Because we believed in things, we dared to imagine," snapped Niko.

"And if I believed that was your goal, I'd read your proposal. But what I see is you ignoring all the work that hundreds of brilliant minds did that still ended up, because of weekend hackers, killing thousands upon thousands of people. I saw the news reports when they originally aired. Imagine being eight years old and hearing how innocent people were dying because little robots in their bloodstream were releasing weeks'-worth of medications in seconds. I was terrified each night that I'd find one of my parents dead in the morning."

"My nanobots wouldn't be in the body though."

"And that sounds safe, to you, right now, but is it? I'm not willing to take that risk," replied the professor.

Niko scratched his shaggy beard in frustration. "You've granted some of my peers the go-ahead for some absolutely stupid ideas."

The professor's face went red. He waved his door open, revealing a hoarder's dream of an academic office. He stared at the floor shaking his head. Then glancing about the empty hallways, said "How about some blunt truth, Mister Rafaelo? If you were as brilliant as you seem to think you are, you'd have tackled this idea by the time you were twenty, and the world would already be singing your praises. You're what, twenty-five? Granted, you're a smart guy, but neither you nor your grades match up to the reputation you had when we accepted you. You need to face reality. You aren't the guy you think you are." He took a steadying breath. "The guys who founded TalkItNow, they invented it while in their second year here. And then, they swallowed everything from the new online world and the remnants of the old Internet into their universe, with little exception."

"Go, watch the news, come up with something good or you're done." He stomped into his office and waved briskly at the door sensor, causing it to close abruptly in front of Niko.

Niko stood there, his chin trembling, his hands shaking. He leaned against a wall and slid down. Putting his head on his knees and he focused on keeping his emotional dam from breaking. With a huge sigh, he ran his fingers through his long hair, putting it back into a ponytail. He felt the grime from it and got up. It was time to head home.

The next morning, Niko stepped out of the steamy bathroom into the main room of the tiny, second-floor apartment. His mind was still wrestling with his argument with his professor.

Mechanically, he walked over his mattress to his blue-brown discolored dresser. Beside the dresser was an old, low resolution holographic video streaming box that occasionally worked.

Pulling out a shirt and giving it a quick sniff, he put it on along with some relaxed pants. As he reached for some socks, he caught a glimpse of the gold trimmed envelope containing the offer letter from TalkItNow. He'd received it nine months ago, and they'd confirmed by voice and message that it would remain open for a year. The salary they'd offered was generous, but he couldn't imagine himself working for anyone.

He'd stopped at a campus cafe on the way home and got caught up on world events. The raw power of the destruction had left him speechless and in a daze, the whole way home.

He glanced at the purple bedroom door and noted it was ajar.

Bracing himself, he bellowed, "Are you still home?"

"Yeah," replied a young, female voice amongst a sudden roar of rustling. "It's here somewhere… come on. There we go! Yeah. Only for a sec, though. I'm going over to Tatiana's. Is it okay if I stay for dinner?"

Niko was relieved he wouldn't have to face her. "Sure. I'll be at the office then. Send me a message when you're heading home."

"You're always home," came the snarky reply.

"Hey," he snapped. "Did you see what happened? They were showing images of the solar flare on the news."

"I did. Crazy stuff," she replied. "I'm happy no one was there to get hurt."

Niko nodded.

"Hey," she said, "don't start season four of The Wizard Killer without me, okay?"

"I won't. Though you know, you're not technically old enough to watch that," he replied, shaking his head.

"Intellect versus number of trips around the sun. It didn't stop us from watching the first three seasons!"

He shrugged, a chuckle escaping. "Maybe that's just bad judgment on my part. Anyway, I doubt the old holo-screen's up for it today," he said to it. "Even if it can form an image today, it probably won't even hover much over the screen. I wish we had the money for a new one."

There was the sound of drawers opening and closing. "You'd just get distracted by a new one. Anyway, I'm sure the old clunker's in a good mood," came the bouncy reply. "Oh, hey, weren't you going to see the prof today?"

He cringed.

"How did your pitch go? Did the idiot finally see the error of his ways?" she asked.

Niko hung his head and sat on his mattress in the middle of the living room. "My thesis advisor is not an idiot. He's just—"

"Stop defending *the idiot*. You've got a brilliant idea and he is being an idiot. I mean, does he even *know* the history of penicillin or oh, I don't know, flight? Did you *tell* him that you solved the search algorithm thing… for bacteria… thingy?"

"You mean the algorithm that allows my nanobots to identify the bacteria of the host and consume it as an energy source."

"Yes, that."

"I didn't even get that far," said Niko with a heavy sigh, his arms at his side. "It doesn't matter. I can't get passed his fear or need to conform or whatever it is. He won't listen. Maybe my ideas *aren't* that good."

"Don't!" she said, staunchly. "Firstly, he *is* an idiot. I even saw his idiot certificate on TalkItNow. He's an official idiot."

"Stop with the idiot stuff," said Niko.

After a moment of hesitation, she replied, "Okay. But don't doubt yourself. Remember that saying, 'The one can be right and the hundred wrong.' That's what you always say to me. You're right and the thousand are wrong."

Niko rubbed his face. "I didn't think you were ever listening."

"You need to remember that you're ten times smarter than any of these guys. You have to be because that's what I tell all my friends. You don't want *me* to look like an idiot, do you?" she asked.

A humble smirk forced its way onto his face. "You know, I'm sure none of your friends talk like this. Go back to being a kid."

"For the record, my friends talk like I do, but age has nothing on mental strength. LOOK AT THESE BRAIN

MUSCLES!" She jumped into the room, flexing her string-bean arms and pointing to her head, before dashing back into the bedroom.

Niko smiled and shook his head. "You're going to be late."

"See what happens when I reveal the kid inside? It's not pretty." There was more rustling in the bedroom. "You're going to do this nanobots stuff, I know it. You always say how we're born to explore this stuff, how you want to go beyond the limits of… of the human…"

"Limits of the human architecture," he replied.

"That. You're going to find a way to do this," she said. "I've got faith in you. This much!"

"You know I can't see your actual arms," he yelled. "Anyway, it's not that easy." He closed his eyes, his hands smoothing his long, wet hair, reinforcing the little puddle that had started on the mattress. He felt a kiss on the top of his head and a bounce on and off the mattress.

"Maybe it is. I'll be back before dinner."

He nodded, waiting for the door to slam. When it didn't, he looked up.

"Hey," she cooed, her voice easily dodging all of his defenses. She was hidden in the doorway's shadow, only a Cheshire cat smile and glinting eyes visible. "You've taken care of us this far. I know we're going to be okay and I know this is going to happen. Forward or nothing! I believe in you."

He waved her off. As the door closed, he lay back on the mattress and stared at the peeling ceiling. "I'm glad *you* do." Forcing himself up, he opened the dresser drawer and took out the offer letter. Biting his lip, he went into the kitchen and with hands shaking, burned it in the sink. "Forward or nothing."

CHAPTER THREE
SEMINAL MOMENT

The next three days crawled by, with only the erratic weather providing any distraction. Each night Niko slept less, and the knots in his stomach tightened. He fought hard to keep his worlds separate, offering smiles at home, and keeping his worry and fury for the campus battlefield.

"Hey Niko," said a red-head, making him suddenly aware that he was on campus, and that there were dozens of people milling about.

"Oh, hey Andrea," he replied with a quick nod, his hands resting on his father's old backpack's resewn straps. They'd met a few times at graduate student events.

"You okay?" she inquired.

"Yeah, you're all hunched over," said a woman with mocha colored skin, short curly black hair, and a beautiful square jaw. "You look like you're carrying quite the burden. I'm Phoebe Collins," she said, putting her forearm out.

Andrea stared at them in surprise. "You guys don't know each other? How's that possible?"

Niko completed the greeting and knocked forearms with her. "Niko Rafaelo." He scratched his face. "I think we've seen each other a few times at grad functions. Just... I don't know. I'm not great at the people stuff."

Phoebe smiled in response.

"Niko's a Ph.D. candidate in Informatics. Nano-tech, right?" asked Andrea.

He nodded.

"I'm a candidate in Sciences; Advanced immunology and analytics group," said Phoebe.

"Ah," replied Niko, somewhat interested. "Well, pleased to meet you."

He was about to leave when Andrea asked, "Are you going to the Edge of Humanity lecture by that visiting professor later? I think it might still be your kind of thing. Yoshi wanted me to mention it to you."

Niko glanced at the ground. "Doctor Martin Curie, right?"

"Yeah," replied Phoebe. "I've read quite a few of his books, and several of his papers. This talk is one where he summarizes the ways various sciences and eras have looked at a topic. In this case, it's the human body. He believes it's an open system, still adapting."

Niko scratched his head, "Hmm. I'll need to make arrangements first. He might have some interesting points on the microbial cloud. Maybe he could answer some of the questions no one wants to answer." He nodded. "Okay, I'll try to make it." He headed off.

"Odd cookie, but nice guy," said Andrea.

"Hmm," replied Phoebe, pulling on her brown string, three bead, necklace.

"Oh, oh, no. Not that type of hmm. He's guarded by Cerberus."

Phoebe laughed. "Is he in the Greek underworld or something?"

"I'll explain," said Andrea with a smile. "Come on. I've got a class to give. We'll talk on the way."

———————

Doctor Martin Curie took a sip of water and looked at the room. He didn't care that it was only a quarter filled, he got paid the same amount either way. Fewer people just meant less idiotic questions, in his mind. He'd been on a lecture tour for the past six months, presenting to most of the remaining colleges in the eastern states.

As if his autopilot had suddenly disengaged, he gazed out at the crowd in momentary confusion. He glanced over to see what the holo-screen was showing and quickly continued, with only a few beats missed. "So lastly, there's the microbial cloud. Discovered, and I use the term loosely, in the early days of the twenty-first century. This was seen as a potential source of all kinds of things, information in particular. There was a belief that it could be used to accurately determine whether or not someone had been in a room, provided they were in it for say an hour or so, and provided the room wasn't too large… or had any ventilation, et cetera."

He shook his head. "It boggles my mind sometimes at how readily grant money was given away once upon a time. Anyway, I digress. They were able to differentiate between the dust, clothing particles in the cloud, and the bacteria which did contain the DNA signature of the host individual. That was interesting, but despite the problem of needing ideal conditions to do anything with that information, there was a litany of other issues of significant concern: one of my favorites was being unable to differentiate between someone having been in the room and someone having used a spraying device to simulate it."

The visiting professor paused, shaking his head. "And that entire problem space would end up pretty much solved by the societal embrace of drones. We take for granted that they are our postal couriers, law enforcement eyes and ears, truant officers and more. I've even seen prototypes of them for enforcing corporate policies, nicknamed nanny-drones. Thus, the chances that something occurs without any eyes capturing it are very slim these days." He leaned on the hundred-year-old lectern and stared at the drowsy crowd. Oddly, there was one enthused gentleman with a scruffy beard who kept glancing at the top right corner of his presentation, where the time was. He looked like a frog in a pot hoping to get out before the official boiling time.

"So that brings us to the question," continued the

professor, "can we take the next step off the edge of humanity? We've tried many ways over the course of human history to extend ourselves and failed. Perhaps it is solely the domain of time, and whether you call it evolution or environmental adaptation doesn't matter."

He smiled expectantly at the crowd, but they looked back at him blankly. Furrowing his brow, he said, "Often at this point, I get some student who brings up cyborgs, and artificial intelligence, and other dreams of the by-gone era. We've all learned, the more prosthetics, the exponentially harder a system it is to manage on behalf of the individual or along with the individual. Thus, no killer cyborgs from the books I so enjoyed as a youth. And what about artificial intelligence? Well, other than reasonably good assistive technology, they get to keep those killer cyborgs company in fiction."

He paused, expecting more than the mild amount of chuckles. A hand went up. Professor Curie frowned. He'd informed them at the beginning that all questions were to be held until the end. It was the bearded man who didn't want to be boiled.

The professor shook his head and then was about to continue when the man stood up and blurted out, "Professor Curie, I have a question."

"I can see that, but now is *not* the time. Wait until the end of the lecture," he replied. He then seemed to recognize the young man.

"I'm running out of time. I need to get home for seven o'clock."

He grumbled. "Does it really need to be stated that in this situation, someone in my position does not have to abide by anyone else's timetable but their own? I don't care what your question is."

"That's Niko Rafaelo," said someone in the crowd.

"I figured," replied the professor. "I was actually warned about him." He made eye contact with Niko. "You have quite the reputation Mister Rafaelo, and I mean that in the strictly negative sense."

Niko hesitated, glancing over at Phoebe and Andrea a few seats away. Phoebe seemed curious what Niko would say, whereas Andrea was clearly embarrassed. While Niko had been disruptive before, and subsequently warned about doing so, he'd never been so explicit about it.

Professor Curie folded his arms and put on an expression of one ready to do academic battle. "Go on, Mister Rafaelo. Please, share with everyone. What is so *vital* —" he shook his fist in the air "that you feel the absolute need to derail my lecture and be so rude to everyone?"

Swallowing and then licking his lips, Niko replied, "Assuming that one could separate the dust and other particles in the microbial cloud from the human bacteria, do you believe there are enough bacteria that a nanobot could derive sufficient energy from a cluster of them within—"

"Stop," said the professor waving his hands. "Just stop.

You're embarrassing yourself, Mister Rafaelo."

Niko clenched his jaw. "I didn't even get to—"

"You're layering bad premise on top of bad premise. I feel sorry for you that no one has set you straight, at least I can do some social good here. The matter of separating the bacteria from the other particles, in real-time, for a particular nanobot would be so energy intense that should you even have a magical way of consuming bacteria in a highly efficient manner, they would spend all of their time hunting and eating. The entire structure of the nanobot would be solely devoted to that end."

"No but—"

"I am *not* finished. I've seen what you posted on TalkItNow, that they would then serve to provide all kinds of fantastical services, to have a communications network leveraging an individual's natural magnetic field, et cetera, et cetera. If you were a science fiction writer, I'd call you brilliant. But as a technologist and researcher? You're deluded to the point of damaging your college's reputation."

Niko's face flushed as everyone turned to him, many started to whisper. He caught sight of many watches and phones coming out, likely posting thoughts and snarky comments to TalkItNow. "But I already have the algorithm."

"Really? Is it tested?" snapped the professor. "Do you have actual, concrete evidence? Do you have a nanobot design that is so beyond what the world has ever seen, that it can be hyper-efficient at consuming bacteria *and* be able to do some other function? No? Is that what I'm understanding from your lack of reply? Thank you very much for the detour down imaginary lane, but the rest of us are going to get back to my lecture. If you'd be so kind, please leave." The professor stepped back behind the lectern. "Any time now, Mister Rafaelo."

Niko nodded. He glanced over at Andrea and Phoebe. Andrea had her back partially to him, whereas Phoebe was looking at him, her expression blank. Slowly he made his way out. He kept touching his forehead as he did so.

Once the lecture was over, Phoebe headed directly for Niko's office. She wasn't surprised he wasn't there. She couldn't imagine how mortifying it had been to be him in the seminar, and if she were him, she'd want to hide too.

After checking a couple other student-favorite hiding spots in the building, she decided to head back to her office. As she crossed the campus' underground courtyard, she spotted the lone apple tree, the centerpiece of the high ceiling, indoor garden. "You know, I wouldn't be surprised if he was hoping for an apple to the head for inspiration." She laughed as she saw Niko sitting on the other side of it, all of his papers, tablets and other stuff spread out.

"What are you doing here?" she asked. "Didn't you have to be home for seven?"

"Have you seen the wind storm outside? The city's on

lock-down. No transition, emergency vehicles only, you know the routine. I called my landlord to take care of… my obligation," he replied mechanically, continuing to work feverishly.

Phoebe glanced about the courtyard, "I hate being so cut off from the outside."

"It's just like the outside, but better."

"No, it's like… pretend outside."

"The outside gets soggy a lot," said Niko.

"Still, I'd rather be out there."

"I think the key is mindset," said Niko, looking up. "Life is an illusion, isn't it? All the elements here seem the same as the way things supposedly once were, from natural light to birds to even some insects. It's us that decides whether or not we want to accept the limits or push passed them."

"No, it's not. I appreciate all of this, but I'd rather be in the real world, than in a concrete pretend one."

Niko stared at her for a moment, absorbing her point, and then turned back to his work.

"Hey, Niko?"

He didn't react.

She snapped her fingers. "Hey, Niko."

He glanced up for a second, before returning to his work. "Yeah, Phoebe. I'm here."

"Are you okay? You took a pretty severe beating in

there." She gestured to the direction she'd come from.

"Yeah well… welcome to my life. But that's in the past. No need to worry about yesterday, today, right?"

"Yesterday? That was today." She put a hand on his forehead. "No fever."

He pulled away. "Please don't do that. I'm… I'm not comfortable with people doing that."

"Yeah, well, tough. You need to unplug from this and be a person. If anyone knows anything about hiding in their work, it's me."

Niko frowned and then relented. "I'm fine. Separate worlds. Everything's fine."

"No, it's not," she said, taking him by the hand. He gazed up at her, confused.

"I'm buying you a cup of coffee or a can of Ace or whatever. Get in your mental spacesuit because you need to leave your world. Consider this a trans-dimensional… dammit, I lost it there."

Niko laughed and collected his things. "That was pretty good, though. Really."

"It was, wasn't it?" she replied, pushing her hair back with a smile. "Oh, one question. Do you really have a guardian named Cerberus?"

"What?" he asked, all packed up and ready to go. "Sorry, didn't hear you."

"Never mind. Come on."

Phoebe laughed so hard she snorted. "Oh flood!" She covered her face as she went red. "Good thing the cafe is practically empty."

A relaxed smile spread across Niko's face.

"What is it?" she asked.

"I don't know. You're just… different," he said. "I usually only get listened to at home."

"Different how?" she inquired, playing with the two green and single, middle white bead on her necklace.

He shrugged. "I don't know. Everyone else just seems so… I don't know. I'm not good at explaining this stuff."

Phoebe laughed again.

"What?" asked Niko, a look of self-consciousness on his face.

"You spent twenty minutes explaining to me, in detail, how the nanobots would work. And yet, you cannot explain how I'm different?"

He toyed with his empty cup and lightly scratched his forehead. "They are different knowledge domains. Different reasoning systems, different vocabulary and grammars and…" he let out a sigh of defeat. "You're smart, and you laugh, and you don't give me the confused look whenever I open my mouth. Is that better?" He looked up at her, his eyes those of a vulnerable kid.

She smiled. "I'll accept that. My dad's like that, master of some domains, fumbler of others." She took a final sip of her coffee. "Anyway, you were talking about innovation."

In a blink, Niko's face lit up again. "So the problem is, how does one shift the societal mindset from being afraid of the unknown and new, towards real innovation once again? I mean, yes, there are startups that are creating things that haven't existed before, but they aren't solving big issues or taking risks. They are making whatever is there and then adding one to it, if you know what I mean. And their entire focus is on making more money for some people, or helping other people lose less money."

Niko glanced about. "There's no innovation there, there's only financial displacement. What about up-ending how we think about ourselves and our world? I get that we can't go to the moon anymore, but even if someone just focused on bringing back things we could do decades ago, like video calling, *that* would be something. But instead, everyone talks about how TalkItNow is the pinnacle of modern innovation. TalkItNow! You can't get more a literal example of what's old is new again than them. An online destination where people can post things and discuss whatever they want. Maybe the world had a tremendous need for posting pictures of cats after a fifty-year gap. Maybe I'm the one who doesn't get it." He rubbed his face vigorously.

Phoebe smiled and leaned back in her chair.

"Am I making any sense? Sometimes I feel like it only makes sense in here," he said, tapping his temple.

"It makes complete sense. I still can't get over you taking apart micro-factories and building nanobots at the age of seventeen."

Niko raised a finger. "You understand that the initial micro-factories were really for microbots, right? They were almost a thousand times bigger than what I have now. That point didn't help the inventor though, neither did Japan being liberal on the issue. No one would touch the product, no matter how harmless he said they were."

Phoebe nodded. "Niko, you treat that part of your story like everyone does stuff like that. It's amazing, and you don't think anything of it."

Niko shrugged.

"How many generations of micro-factories have you gone through since you started?"

"Forty-two. I call the latest one Douglas," he said with a wry smile.

She looked at him blankly.

"Don't worry about it."

"I've never even heard of a micro-factory before today," she confessed.

"Well, there *were* only ten. The inventor, Hiro Hamada, wanted to teach kids with them. He created ten of them, hoping to reignite his career in his twilight years, but passed away shortly after. He's one of my heroes. He dared to yell at the world that we shouldn't retreat from innovation, that we didn't have to just focus on the here and now."

"So how did you get them?" she asked.

"My mom ran across an article he'd posted, trying to find something that would intrigue me. She was a lead industrial robotics engineer, so she liked the idea of us having a connection, like my dad and brother did. So, she bought me one of the kits from his widow… It arrived a few days after they had… ah… they'd all… it came after the funeral by courier-drone."

Niko fought off the emotion that wanted to invade the moment. With a sigh, he continued. "I used part of my inheritance to buy the other nine. I spent almost every waking moment for months understanding exactly how they worked, learning Japanese along the way. I wrote to the inventor's widow, and she sent me all of his notebooks. It was like oxygen to my soul. It filled half of my life with purpose. Then the other half was filled in by—"

"How are we doing on time?" interrupted Phoebe, a look of guilt on her face.

Niko grabbed his old cellphone and motioned it to wake up. "Ah, terribly. I have to get home."

Phoebe stood up and collected her things. "This was fun. We should do it again."

Niko nodded and then caught the look in her eye. "Oh."

"Is there a problem?" she asked.

He looked at his phone. "No. No, just… I have some complexity in my life," his expression twisted to one of discomfort.

"Oh," she replied, disappointed.

Niko glanced up. "No, it's not a girlfriend. It's... She's very protective of me. She's... kind of ended a few relationships I've attempted in the past."

Phoebe raised her eyebrows. "So we're in the preliminaries of a relationship, then?" She smiled as Niko's face went red, his expression flustered.

"No... it's. I better go," he said collecting his things. A well-dressed woman with long braided hair immediately stopped him.

"Mister Rafaelo. I'm thankful you're not a hard man for the sweepers to find. Did you know it was another grad student, one who was having trouble finding a thesis like you, who invented them? Miniature drones, limited abilities and not of commercial interest, but helpful here on campus for things like finding people." She glanced up at the high ceiling as one of them whizzed by. "I'm sure you could have done something like that." There was a finality to her statement that sent a chill through Niko.

Phoebe and Niko both recognized the Dean of Informatics.

"Dean, why are you here?" asked Phoebe, worried.

Niko stared at the Dean, his mouth suddenly dry and his hands sweaty.

"I bumped into Doctor Curie. Martin was furious."

Niko was about to reply when the Dean raised her hand to silence him, and was stunned to see him ignore it. "At every turn, I'm trying to do exactly what you and this college committed to when you accepted me into the program. I'm trying to innovate. I'm trying to bring the best of who I am to the table. Yet at every turn—"

"That's enough, Mister Rafaelo," she said firmly.

"No, it's not," said Niko, sensing he was passing a point of no return. "The idea for my thesis is as good if not better than any—"

"That's it, you're done," said the Dean softly. "I was conflicted with what to do, but you certainly made the decision easy. You have until the end of the week to clean out your desk and make room for the next candidate."

"What?" said Phoebe, as she watched Niko's expression collapse. "No. No, you—"

"He's done, Ms. Collins. Please don't get involved. As Mr. Rafaelo is famous for saying, he likes to keep his worlds separate, so let this be separate, shall we?" She turned and left.

"Oh my god. I'm so sorry, Niko," said Phoebe, rubbing his arm.

He was white as a sheet, sweat beading on his forehead. He stared at her with the eyes of a terrified, cornered animal.

"Niko? Niko, listen to me," she said, taking his hand. "Sit, okay? Sit and let's talk. Okay?"

Niko's chin quivering, he shook his head. "I need to go. I need to get home. This world's a mess."

"Can I check on you later?" she asked.

He turned and dragged himself off.

"Niko?"

CHAPTER FOUR

INFLUENCE OF PEERS

The office door slid open. A tattoo-headed man of slim build and big eyes looked up from his desk and holo-screen. "Oh, hey Niko. You look like extra crispy crap this morning."

"I'm finished, Yoshi," replied Niko, stepping into their closet of an office. He slumped into his chair. His desk and Yoshi's were side by side.

Yoshi bit his lip and nodded. "I heard a rumor."

Niko rubbed his face. "Yeah, rumor. I didn't sleep last night, not like I was getting much anyway. I'm sure that your thesis advisor is going to be ecstatic when he gets back.

"I kept going over and over things. I don't know what we're going to do. I think I'm going to have to accept the offer. I don't know what else to do."

Yoshi whistled his surprise. "You? Working at TalkItNow as a senior developer?" He put a finger to his head. "Bang, done. No way. Maybe if you're drugged-out or something, but you'd never survive. You'd eat your brain."

Niko's hands failed to gesture and instead, dropped to his side. "What am I going to do? All the inheritance from my parents is long gone. I can't just think about myself."

"I know. You're a noble soul," said Yoshi, his eyes sympathetic. They'd joined the Ph.D. program at the same time, and were the closest thing to what either of them thought of as a friend. "You're doing the right thing"

"Well then why does life just seem to keep beating me up for it?" asked Niko, shaking his head.

"Nah, man. My dad would say that you are to suffer so that you can appreciate the gifts to come," said Yoshi, doing his bad Japanese accent, and making Niko smirk.

"How can you be half-Japanese and not nail that?"

"I have many talents," replied Yoshi.

Niko leaned forward and bumped elbows with him.

Yoshi swiveled his chair and looked at the painted wall. "Maybe the red is all wrong, you know? Maybe it needs not to give into the white to become pink, but become the yellow."

"Are you just screwing around looking for some philosophy?" asked Niko.

"Was worth a try," he replied with a grin.

"It was," said Niko with a grin, standing back up. "Well, I have until Friday to clear out my half of this garbage dump." He shook his head at their mess. He then noticed how Yoshi was dressed. "That a new skirt? Hey wait, did I see—"

"Yeah, we're matching."

"Did she pick the outfits or did you?" asked Niko.

"She did," replied Yoshi with a smile.

"That's great. So it's working okay between you guys?"

"Hey man, if I have my way. I get this stupid gesture pad algorithm improvement done, marry her, and move to nowhere and live a good life."

"That sounds nice," replied Niko tapping the door frame.

"Not for you. You, you need to be bigger than life. If you aren't, I'm going to hunt you down in ten years and kick your butt. You got me?"

Niko nodded, tired. He tapped the door frame again, and left.

"Hey Niko," yelled Phoebe to the man blazing a trail across the soggy campus.

He stopped dead and glanced up, wondering if one of the police-drones or sweepers had called him out. After a moment, he realized there was the dark, curly haired woman coming towards him. "Oh. Hey, Phoebe."

"You're looking a bit better. Everything okay?" she asked.

"No," he answered drily.

"Oh," replied Phoebe. "Listen, I was thinking. Your idea

on the microbial cloud elements. It sounded pretty well thought through. Is it? Is it core to your whole idea?"

Niko frowned. "Well, I don't know. What are you getting at?"

Phoebe glared at him. "Just… just answer the question. Did you build something or have anything that would show it's more than just a random thing you said to me?"

"I built a prototype of about a half-dozen nanobots that demonstrate how my algorithm for finding bacteria and consuming it works. Does that count?"

A smile crept across Phoebe's face. "Great. Now, does that have to be in the Informatics faculty, or is there enough organic elements to this that it could fit in Sciences? Because the Dean of Science *famously* hates the Dean of Informatics."

Niko's eyes came alive. "Oh geezes, you're right." He bolted, yelling back, "Thanks Phoebe!"

———

The office door slid open and Dean of Informatics peered in. She detested how small the offices were, and was even more bothered by how the grad students treated them.

"Hello Yoshi," said the Dean. "It's been a while."

"Dean," he replied, glancing up from his holo-screen.

"How's the new gesture pad enhancement coming along? I'm having lunch with the donations VP from the company today. I was wondering if I could share anything with him."

"I think I'll have it ready for work by the next

checkpoint date. Just doing the simulation work before I get hands on," he replied, pointing at a mess on the shelf above his desk. "I've got better power efficiency and sharper recognition. I think it'll make it able to work as a general use device. Heck, I think I could even use it for developing software. Odd to think this thing's not really changed in twenty years."

"What a weird era we live in, sometimes. But I'm glad to hear the news." She frowned and pointed at Niko's desk. "He hasn't cleared out yet?"

"No," replied Yoshi. "Why would he?"

The Dean sighed. "Yoshi, you are bad at pretending to be out of the loop. I'm sure you heard that Mister Rafaelo will not be continuing with our graduate program." She pulled back her sleeve and looked at her watch. "Given that it's already four o'clock on Friday, I would have expected he'd have had the courtesy to clean out by now. But then again, I understand how hard this is for him. The new candidate is coming in on Monday, however. I'd like to have it cleaned before then."

Yoshi smiled quizzically. "Well, um, there would seem to be a complication then."

"And that is?" she asked, amused at the prospect.

"Niko was accepted into the Science Ph.D. program yesterday evening."

The Dean frowned and then laughed. "Hilarious. Based on what?"

Yoshi's face lit up. "Oh, I'm quite serious. When he broke down the constituent elements of his thesis, and its integration with the microbial cloud, the Dean of Science felt that there was significant innovation there, never mind on the nanobots side. It met the criteria the college sets out for such rare cases, so it was granted."

Folding her arms, the Dean thought, stroking the side of her face. "Sounds like a bunch of hand-waving. All just so she can try to show me up? Huh."

"Well, either way, he was granted funding this morning."

"Going to her was a dangerous move, but gutsy, I'll give him that. I don't think it'll save him, or the tarnish he'll bring to this college, but it'll be on her. I respect his tenacity."

"If I may say, Dean, I think we missed out on an opportunity that's going to change the world. But at least the college will get some credit."

"Are you saying that because you're his friend, or because you've seen something?"

Yoshi hesitated, unsure if he was stepping into the realm of politics. "I think this is the part where we all become witnesses to history."

———————

Eighteen Months Later

Niko stepped into the seminar room ready to defend his

doctoral thesis. He was out of breath and his pants were soaking below the knees. He'd barely made it into the building before the automatic flood lock-down kicked in.

Exhaling hard to calm his nerves, he looked about. Everything was officially laid out. Having been in the audience of doctoral defenses before, it seemed weirdly different now that it was his turn.

There were two large holo-screens set up, one on either side of the vintage lectern. He glanced about and smiled as he realized it was the very room Doctor Curie had presented in. Spotting Yoshi and Phoebe among those in the audience chairs, he gave them a wave. He then turned his attention to the long table for the panelists. To his bewilderment, he saw Doctor Curie.

He scratched his trimmed beard, and then smoothed his neat, short hair. Shaking off the disaster scenarios that started to build up in his head, he walked over to the professor and put his hand out.

The professor stared at it, and finished putting down his leather satchel. Straightening up and sporting a smile, he shook Niko's hand firmly. "Mister Rafaelo, I wouldn't have taken you for a shaker. Mind you, I didn't take you for a brilliant man at first, either."

Niko's response failed him, as he took in the final statement. After a moment, he found a reply, "My mom was the one who taught me about handshaking, and its place in the world. Forearm bumps are fine for avoiding germs, but there's history in hands."

"There is. I also see that you were rather determined in getting here," said the doctor, pointing at Niko's pant-legs.

Niko glanced down, alarm spreading across his face. "I had to make sure everything was good at home and—"

"You look fine. Those wet pants are a mark of pride and determination these days, if you ask me. Don't let it distract you." He leaned in. "When I had to defend my thesis, I had the most horrible itch on my face. It was maddening, but I still got through it. You'll be fine."

Niko smiled and nodded. "I can't believe this is actually happening."

"Well, I'm looking forward to your presentation, and how you manage to defend some of your claims. Compared to most, your paper was particularly well-written. And for the record, I did appreciate the thoroughness of the data you included with your analysis. It's rare for anyone to do that anymore."

"Thanks," replied Niko. He noticed two people in business suits walk in and take up seats at the far end of the panel table.

"Who are they?" he asked Doctor Curie.

Looking over his shoulder, he replied, "They are from the college's investment fund."

Niko squinted and looked at the doctor, uncertain. "Why would they be here?"

"I called them," he said, uncomfortably. "With the

support of both the Deans of Informatics and Sciences, I might add." He put his hands in his pockets and bowed his head. "I have a confession to make, Mister Rafaelo. My... issues with you didn't end the day of my seminar, or with my tirade in front of the Dean of Informatics. When I learned you'd switched faculties, I sent a letter of... anti-recommendation. I've known the Dean of Science for decades. She's been perfect for the college, and I urged her to reconsider. I was certain she was making a mistake, but in her defense, she wouldn't listen to a word of it."

Doctor Curie put his hand up defensively. "I am not proud of it. My marriage was falling apart. I was angry at the world. Shortly afterwards, I had a divorce and heart attack. I was a man adrift.

"When the Dean of Science asked me to read one of the early drafts of your completed thesis, Mister Rafaelo, I reluctantly accepted. To cut the rest short, the presence of the investment fund representatives is my way of saying I believe your ideas have real merit."

"Wow. Thank you," said Niko, rubbing his forehead in disbelief.

"Show me you can change the world. I think we could all use some excitement to distract us from Nature's vengeance."

A young girl stepped into the room, clearly out of place. Niko smiled and pointed to the audience seating. She nodded and followed his direction, glaring at Phoebe as she walked by.

Niko took his place at the front of the room.

CHAPTER FIVE
FUNDING

One Year Later

Niko stuck his hand out and smiled. "Thanks for coming, Sandra."

The woman standing on the other side of the office threshold was in her mid-twenties. She was dressed like him, in casual pants and a long t-shirt with a forgettable saying. Her striking face gave hints of her Columbian roots, and her shoulder length hair showed a passing interest in style on some level.

Glancing at his hand, and then up at his face, she cautiously shook his hand. "I wouldn't have expected that. A bit old world, isn't it?"

"Why does everyone have that reaction? It's not like I'm trying to put fingers in your ears... Also, I don't offer it to everyone," said Niko, his nostrils flaring.

Sandra stared at him. "Do you explain everything like that or only when you're nervous?"

Niko's cheeks reddened.

"Nervous it is," she said with a smile.

He motioned for her to step into the single room office.

The room was a hallmark of the old downtown. The walls and ceiling were cracked plaster, water stains on the ceiling. The window had weather-beaten bulletproof glass with a set of thick black cables coming down through it. Occupying most of the room was a large butcher block table and a misfit collection of five chairs.

Two developers were standing between the table and the window, back to back. Their wall-mounted holo-screens were dirty, with exposed wires, clearly on their last legs. Sandra caught a glimpse of them glitching. The developers were oblivious to her presence; their gargantuan headsets kept them immersed in their own worlds.

She felt like she was standing in a weird mix of the past fifty years, instead of the office of a high-tech startup company. "What are the cables for?" she asked, sitting on a well-worn, plastic chair.

Niko glanced around, before relaxing and taking a seat. "Supplementary power. The community electrical grid around here is nonexistent, so we're tied into the main. And the main isn't very reliable as you might guess."

"It's like a kid playing with a light switch in my neighborhood," said Sandra. "What did you put on the roof?"

"Armored solar charging batteries. We use a pessimistic protection scheme, so at the slightest sign of problematic weather, they clam up."

Sandra sat back and gazed out the window. "That costs a pretty penny."

"We… ah, spent about half our initial seed money on it."

She squinted at him. "Okay, I just need to ask. Are you insane?"

"No, but given the micro-factories we're powering, we need constant, clean power, and it's worth it. Well, I hope it will have been worth it."

"At least you're an honest nut."

Sandra noticed a few books piled on the corner of the table, along with an open sketch book and a worn, little tub of lip balm. "You don't strike me as the type to be reading Breadcrumb Trail."

"Great book, but that's not mine."

"Another member of the team? Because I'm guessing it's not theirs either," she said gesturing at the two developers.

Niko's expression hardened. "No."

"Then who?" she asked, leaning forward.

He grimaced and stared at the floor. "I've been experimenting with that world overlap with the one for here. Moving on."

"Hang on a second, worlds?" asked Sandra, staring at him.

Niko continued to stare downwards, his fingers twitching as he searched for the words.

One of the developers pulled his headset off an ear, but kept his eyes focused on the holographic images hovering above the screen. "It's what he calls the different parts of his life. Important project? That's a world. Office life? World. Personal life? That's a world too. He's a master at it."

The other developer piped up. "We think there's eight or so. It's freaky sometimes. He'll flip from angry to calm and back, depending on its context. You get used to it."

"It's emotionally and intellectually efficient. Nothing different than having different notebooks or files or boards," said Niko, his lips tight, glaring at them. The developers got back to work.

"Emotionally expensive, isn't it?" asked Sandra.

Niko stared at her.

"We can move on," she said.

He pulled back his sleeve and woke up the contraption on his forearm. "It's three o'clock, so she'll probably drop by sooner rather than later... We better get the interview moving."

"She who? The one the books belong to?"

"I'm letting my worlds touch, not cross."

Sandra shrugged. "Okay, whatever."

"Do you have any questions about the job?"

Sandra scanned about the small office. "Aren't you supposed to ask me a lot of questions first and then ask that at the end of the interview?"

He scratched his head. "Oh, am I? I've never had a job

interview before."

"What about them?"

Niko looked back at the two developers. "They're contractors. I showed them code, and asked if they could explain it to me. They failed horribly, but better than the others, so I hired them as contractors. You, you wouldn't be a contractor."

"Oh," replied Sandra, sitting back.

Niko's face lit up. "Ah, I do have a question. What are we trying to do here? I sent you the five pager. You tell me."

"Ah... by the way, that technical briefing was very dense, and you really should have people sign a non-disclosure before getting it."

Niko shrugged. "One of the angel investors is having someone draw that up, but I don't have time to waste. And granted, if most people could make sense of what it said, that would be a concern. Most people get lost part way through page one, jump to the middle of page two, then to the end to see if it makes any more sense to them. None of that helps. So what did it say?"

Sandra clasped her hands and leaned on the table. "Basically, you want everyone to be able to interact with the world around them as if it was magical. You want taxis to come with a thought, messages to get written and sent with a few gestures, and... I don't know."

His expression was stoic, he leaned back and waited.

She noticed a hand-drawn sign stuck to the back wall.

"KnowMe. That's going to be the company name, isn't it?"

Niko leaned forward. "Why would you think that?"

"Because really, you're after having the world know the person the NanoCloud's on. And for them to be able to know the world around them more."

"Huh," replied Niko, nodding gently. "Anything else?"

"I do have a question," said Sandra.

"Go ahead."

Tilting her head and thinking through the question first, she asked, "Why was the time on your forearm thing set to an hour ahead?"

"Hire her," said one of the developers, glancing over to Niko and then putting his headset back on.

Niko smirked. "I think we just might."

One Month Later

Sandra glanced across the table at Niko, and then over at the two developers standing at their workstations. She thought it was funny that she and Niko both liked their old-school worlds of gesture-enhanced keyboards and portable holo-screens, even if they were bought from an old college lab.

A gentle alarm sounded. Niko pulled the sleeve back and checked the message.

"I still can't believe that you lug that thing around. You

could just use a cellphone you know."

"Like I keep saying, I need to force myself out of the paradigm that we're used to. If I use a cellphone all the time, it's going to shape all my thinking. With this, and I fully recognize that I've incorporated a phone into it, but it makes me think differently. At home I have one setup like the old goggle interfaces."

Sandra grinned and shook her head. "You think it up, I'll build it. Well, me and these clowns."

The two guys raised their hands and waved.

Niko read the message and leaned back, his tongue running around his teeth.

"That's an expression I'm not used to," said Sandra.

He looked at her, and scratched his beard. "I've been asked by Simon, the rep for our angel investors, to come to a funding meeting."

Sandra's face lit up. "That's great, when?"

"Now. I don't like it. Every other meeting we've had, they've given me at least several days' notice, usually a week or so."

"But you said that no one's stepped into the ring for the next round of investment yet."

He glanced at his armband. "No, they haven't." He flipped his arm over and unstrapped his device.

"Why are you doing that?" she asked.

Niko carefully put it on the table. "This gets more questions in meetings than it's worth. *Is that one of your devices? When are you releasing it? Are the nanobots inside it?* And so on. Not worth the hassle." He turned his piercing gaze on her. "I want you to come to the meeting."

"Now?"

"Yes," replied Niko.

She laughed. "Seriously? I've only been here a month."

"You're my number one. You got those guys to change their ways. You even got me following your coding standards."

"Sometimes," she added.

He smiled. "Are you up for it?"

"Lead on, MacDuff," she said, noticing the Shakespeare plays in the stack of books on the edge of the table.

The elevator door opened and Sandra and Niko stepped out, chatting away.

"You seriously think that in another hundred years, elevators are really still going to be the same?" asked Sandra.

"Some problems are considered solved. There's no innovation to be had. Efficiencies yes, but innovation? No. They've become an embedded part of the human psyche and it will take a serious change to dislodge that notion. It's just like with— oh, hey, Simon. What are you doing here?" Niko stopped and stared at the excited young man with the slicked-back, shoulder-length blond hair.

"Double collar *and* a y-split tie? Suit? What's going on?"

asked Niko, frowning and taking a step back.

Simon's grin couldn't get any bigger. "I didn't want to spoil the news, but I wanted to give you a heads up just before we start. They're all here."

"Who?" asked Sandra, glancing back and forth between Niko and Simon. Their expressions were dueling.

"We haven't met, I'm Simon Malo. I work for the angel investors of KnowMe. They call themselves the Trio, because, as you might expect, there are three of them. Niko only gets to see them once a quarter or so?"

"If I'm lucky," replied Niko.

"Otherwise, he gets to see me on a monthly or sometimes semi-monthly basis. And for these types of meetings, I'm usually the Trio's representative. That is, except for today. This was big enough that they felt it only right that they be here in person."

Sandra smiled. "I'm—"

With a patronizing smile, Simon waved her off. "Oh, I know who you are, Sandra. Anyway, everyone's waiting for you in the conference room just over there. With the new money this should bring in, we won't have to be renting random conference rooms in parts of a building, we'll be owning a building."

Niko raised an eyebrow and glanced at the shiny metal conference room door and then back at the slick investment rep. "All three?"

"All three," replied Simon, teeth showing in his grin.

Niko shook his head and folded his arms. "But you didn't think to tell me to dress up today? And you didn't even give me an hour's notice. You *intentionally* gave me absolutely no notice, why? What's going on, Simon? Something's not fitting. If all three are in there, then there's no way this was set up at the last minute. You've known about this for at least a few weeks."

Simon's professional grin shifted to a smug one. "He's a sharp man, your boss," he said to Sandra.

Sandra noticed Niko's shifting posture. "Why are we having funding meetings already? I thought we were good for at least six, maybe more months."

Rolling his eyes, Simon glanced at Niko who nodded towards Sandra. "Deals take time, the more time you have, the less desperate you come across, and so the better terms you can negotiate. Also, you might be able to find competing parties who will fight to be part of the deal, or both come in and give you a stronger position. Six months of cash is almost out of money in startup terms."

"Now come on. They've been talking for an hour already and—"

Niko closed his eyes and scratched his forehead. "Wait, they started without me? That's not the deal. They've never done that before."

"Ah…" Guilt was all over Simon's face.

As Simon and Niko continued talking, the sudden sliding of a door caught Sandra's eye. She looked over at the conference room, and saw a finely dressed woman her age standing there. The woman turned and stared at Sandra, and then at Niko. Her predatory gaze chilled Sandra to the bone. "Who is that?" she whispered.

Niko glanced over and froze, as his face went flush. He stopped himself from grabbing Simon by the collar.

Simon took a peek over his shoulder. He waved and smiled, the metallic door slid closed. "That's Harriet—"

"I know *exactly* who the flare that is," said Niko in a hushed voice. "You've got to be out of your flooding mind if you think we're having anything to do with her or that company." He ran a hand through his hair. "I can't believe you guys."

"Eversio Investments," said Simon, gritting his teeth, "is *the* biggest name in funding, period. How many companies do you think want to run the risk of being shut down by the government? Until you get all the certifications needed, what we are doing here is quasi-legal at best. Even then, it might not be enough. You should count your lucky stars we landed anyone, never mind them. You got struck by lightning to get seed money from the Trio, but to get the whale of whales? Eversio? That's like being struck twice more."

"Getting electrocuted would be preferable to having them anywhere near our company," said Niko, his hands shaking. "No."

"You don't get to choose who—"

"Simon!" snapped Niko. "I'm only going to say this once. Never in a million years will I work with Eversio. Never in a million years will I be anywhere *near* Harriet Binger. Never will I allow her step-mother, Lucinda Feer, within a million miles of our technology. And for the record, do you have any idea what Eversio does? Because I've been keeping tabs on them for years."

Standing up straighter, Simon replied, "They make companies into superstars. They create *massive* shareholder value. Never mind the weight they have with key politicians. I can't believe how ungrateful you are. You should be jumping for joy."

Niko stepped right up to Simon's face. "They are toxic. They have no morals. They are like playing with fire when you're wearing a gasoline suit. They rip companies apart with no care or consequence. They use lawsuits like siege weapons to do what they want, when they want, and laugh at the fines for crossing legal lines. And don't try for an *instant* to tell me that that's just bad press, because I've seen it first-hand." He waved his hand angrily over their elevator's summoning sensor. "I can't believe you let them know we exist. It's like alerting the minotaur that you're in the labyrinth." He stepped into the elevator.

"Wait, where are you going?" asked Simon.

"I'm going to push my worlds apart and get back to work."

Simon put a hand over the elevator sensor. "Worlds?

What? Anyway, you are not going anywhere." His face was red, sweat was beading on his brow. "Look, you've made your point that I shouldn't have ambushed you with this, fine. However, you have a duty—"

Niko motioned for Sandra to join him.

She smiled at Simon. "I get the feeling we're going. It was nice meeting you." She gave him a small wave.

"Niko! This is about the future of your company."

"I know," he replied, staring at the ground. "I know that those people have no lines they won't cross to drive their ambition. We're done."

"If you don't go in there, you know they'll fire me." Simon curved his lips in.

Niko sighed and glared at the investor representative. He'd always found Simon overconfident. He regularly lauded his role over Niko, yet still Niko felt bad for him. "Simon, if you'd come to me when this was an idea, I could have explained why I don't want to be within a lightyear of those people. Goodbye." He carefully pushed Simon back and allowed the elevator to close. "I shouldn't have let her come to the office. That world... that was too close," he muttered to himself.

Sandra stood there, glancing at Niko and then the doors. Finally, she broke the eerie silence. "Is that woman really that bad? What was she, a high school bully?"

Niko stopped, his eyes revealing a rage that his voice had only hinted at. "Some people you can talk to, some people you can manage, and some people are a destructive force of nature. Now that she knows I'm behind KnowMe, she's going to do everything she can to take us down."

"Why?" asked Sandra.

His eyes darted about as he debated his answer. "Just know when she comes for us, we cannot underestimate her."

Sandra nodded.

They walked to the office door in silence. Sandra stopped Niko from opening it. He frowned at her, "What?"

"The guys are going to pick up the mood you're in. Then they are going to realize that we're back without having had a funding meeting discussion. Then they are going to think we're out of money, which we pretty much are. And then—"

"Productivity is going to go in the toilet." Niko stroked his beard. "Suggestion?"

"Maybe we should go grab some burgers or something? We could talk some of this stuff out, before we tell the team. You and I both know that we really only have about two months of money left."

Niko stared at the floor, massaging the back of his neck. He turned his attention back to her and nodded. "Okay, let's go. Have you ever been to Fillion's?"

"Never heard of it."

"It's up on Castle Avenue. Come on, it's a bit of a hike but worth it," said Niko, heading back to the elevator.

"Any ideas about getting new funding?"

"Well, given the social climate these days, we need a real investor to step up." Niko stared at the ceiling of the elevator as they stepped in.

Sandra nodded. "So how do we get one?"

He turned to her and said with a smirk, "We put a vid of us on TalkItNow."

"A vid of what?"

"Us giving the pitch of our lives and doing a NanoCloud demo with our final batch of nanobots. Hopefully it makes the rounds enough that it lands in front of our future investor."

"That's insane," replied Sandra with a laugh.

"Absolutely."

"I'm in," said Sandra.

CHAPTER SIX

THE STAGE

Ten Years Later

The lights dimmed in the opera hall and the crowd's roar eased to a rumble. All eyes were drawn to the in-air holographic projections throughout the theatre as they cycled between KnowMe's corporate logo, and images and videos from previous launch events.

The uplifting and powerful music fueled the sense of electric anticipation. Rumors of what NanoCloud Four would be capable of had been circling for months, and every fan had their secret feature hopes. The world was holding its breath as the reveal was only minutes away.

Hundreds of millions of people were watching from around the world. Only the most devout five thousand had managed to beg, borrow, steal or afford the scalped tickets in order to be physically present. They would be legends on TalkItNow for weeks. Some would go on to resell their gold trimmed tickets, giving others a false moment in the sun.

Then the music abruptly stopped and the holographic projections disappeared. Everyone whispered in the darkness, wondering if a power outage had happened, or if it was time for the event to start. Then came the distinctive sound of sneakers on tiled floor, three smacks as they climbed a few stairs, and then silence.

"Everything's nearly in place…" boomed a deep voice from overheard. The crowd vibrated with excitement, savoring the end of their wait. Whistles and isolated screams filled the cavernous room.

A burst of triumphant instrumental music took over the room and then gave way to the overhead voice, which boomed once again, "Welcome everyone, to KnowMe's second annual reveal. We've been waiting to tell you about NanoCloud Four for some time, and in a few minutes, that wait will finally be over."

Rocking music started and holographic images of Niko at university appeared. "Doctor Niko Rafaelo's first prototype, NanoCloud Zero, did little more than show that his impossible idea wasn't." The images reappeared, this time of Niko surrounded by four scruffy looking developers and a tablet saying KnowMe. "NanoCloud One got the attention of the gods of industry, as they sensed a change was coming. Then NanoCloud Two came out, and KnowMe eliminated the need for almost every other personal device except the content lens display. The old gods came at us, and the old gods fell. Their era was over." The crowd screamed and clapped.

"KnowMe shocked Wall Street just before going public, when we released NanoCloud Three, announced the single biggest military contract with the federal government ever, and created the world's biggest charity endowment fund. When KnowMe went public, we hit the trillion-dollar mark in *six hours*."

"Niko Rafaelo has already brought us a new way to communicate, a new way to work, and a new way to play. He has inspired a revolution in startups and innovative thinking. What else could there be? Is he done, as some wonder on TalkItNow?"

The crowd roared back, "No!"

An electric blue outline appeared on stage, and the sneakers man walked into it. He was barely visible, but there was enough to confirm to the crowd that it was indeed the man they'd come to see. He offered a short bow, and like a drip becoming a waterfall, one person in the crowd stood and clapped and then the rest rushed in. The sound was deafening to even the most prepared.

The voice spoke again, with even more energy, "Now, the man you have all been waiting for, the inventor of the NanoCloud, the founder of KnowMe, a man of history, the one and only, Doctor Niko Rafaelo!"

The silhouette disappeared and the stage lit up. Camera-drones were visible high up, capturing the spectacle for the worldwide audience.

Niko had short, dark hair and a neat beard. He had his trademark white shirt with red sleeves, which he wore with its curvilinear collar turned up. The archaic jeans were navy blue, a nod to one of his heroes from technology's history.

Before walking the stage, waving and smiling, Niko pointed and winked at a young woman in the audience. She smiled and waved back.

Niko motioned for the crowd to settle, and along with it the music quieted down. He stopped his pacing and stared at the crowd. He let several seconds tick by and then used his trademark opener, "Hi everybody. How's the day treating you?"

The crowd, and millions around the world, replied at once. Niko laughed and waved. "I'm glad. Funny meeting you all here."

Laughter broke out in pockets.

"At KnowMe, we have learned a lot in the past few years. *I've* learned a lot in the past few years. This reveal today, this is easily the biggest we've had. We have a whole new architecture that apps can now take advantage of, we have a whole new way of thinking about where the future is going, and you're going to be able to be a part of that."

"I wanted to say thank you," he pointed at parts of the audience at random. "Thank you for your amazing support. Thank you for the feedback. Thank you for helping show the world that one idea can change everything. We've shown that innovation matters, and we've all seen amazing technologies show up since then. At KnowMe, every day my team and I work our hardest to come up with the best that we can give you."

"You're welcome!" screamed a few in the first row.

Niko laughed. "One of those lessons we've learned is if you admire what another company does: don't copy it, team up with them. Better to bring your two heads together and see what brilliance you can make happen, instead of using all that energy fighting it out. Not everyone thinks that way, but the folks at ContactFirst did. That's why we made them our first acquisition. Evan, Sarah and the team over there were so far ahead of the competition, but they were having trouble getting in front of customers."

"I guess it's no secret that we solved that problem for them," he continued. "It's been amazing to watch glasses disappear, and the lens-display take over so ubiquitously. It doesn't hurt that there's just nothing like them. I'm sure that our team will one day give us personal holographic projection but... I'm getting ahead of myself."

Cheers and hoots erupted from the crowd.

Niko smiled and brought his hands in, palms together in front of his chest, hushing the crowd. He watched as the camera-drones swiftly and quietly changed positions, and one flew out of service. "The human body is a limited architecture. We can't help that or change it. For a while, humanity had lost the ability for everyone to have a bit of the digital world that was theirs. We'd lost our daring, our desire to dream. Our generation grew up hearing about some amazing things that had been possible in the past, but the closest we could get were our limited phones and watches. To me, they were little more than a sign of stunted times."

He paused, and a somber moment took over the room. "But then," he exploded with newfound energy. "Then the NanoCloud came along and reignited our imagination. We've recaptured so many features lost long ago, from video calling to being able to look up our favorite restaurant with a gesture. With each generation of NanoCloud, we get closer to true integration. I expect within the next couple of years, we'll have it able to pick up directly from our thoughts." The crowd hushed.

"And a lot of this, is because of you guys. People like each and every one of you are creating amazing new apps and add-ons to the NanoCloud every day. My job is to provide the platform and spark the imagination, but you guys are the roaring fires of the impossible." The crowd roared. "That's what I'm talking about."

Niko leaned forward, with a devilish grin. The crowd's excitement grew. They braced themselves for his other trademark phrase, and he made them wait for it. He paced about, letting the tension build. "I'm sure everyone loved the gestures we introduced in Three. Personally, I felt like I was conducting an orchestra, they were so big. It'd be nice if they were more… modest, wouldn't you agree?"

He tapped his chin, playing to the crowd. "What about needing only two spray cans of NanoCloud to upgrade, and only one every other week for regular maintenance? That'd be nice, and save everyone some money, too. Oh well." He threw up his hands and started to walk off stage.

"Oh." He stopped and turned to the crowd. "Did I mention I have something to show you?"

"Four! Four! Four!" cheered the crowd.

An hour and a half later, the woman on stage waved at everyone and said, "Thank you so much for coming."

"Thank you, Sandra!" yelled back the crowd to their favorite lead developer.

The lights turned up and the music started pumping. Everyone waited for a minute before getting up, having seen or heard of Niko having returned to the stage at past events. But as the seconds ticked by, doubt spread like a wildfire, and everyone started packing up to leave.

Suddenly the music was replaced once again with the distinctive sound of sneakers on tiled floor, three smacks as they climbed the stairs, and then silence.

Everyone froze.

"Oh, if you aren't too busy, I had *one more thing* to show you," said Niko walking back on stage.

The crowd went insane.

Niko breathed a sigh of relief as the vintage curtains closed behind him. The muffled applause gave way to the familiar sounds of people getting up to leave the opera hall.

"Here you go, Doctor Rafaelo," said an assistant handing him a fresh shirt and can of Ace. He was likely a junior in college, all fresh faced and giving Niko the celebrity-awe stare.

"It's just Niko back here," he said, mechanically replacing his sweaty shirt. "And I'll pass on the Ace, no need for rocketeer caffeine at this point in the evening."

"Are you going to the big party?"

Niko smiled, his exhaustion showing. "No. These types of events, they take everything out of me. Now I just want to go home, and pretend this world doesn't exist. Just read or code or whatever."

"Oh."

He gave the assistant a sideways glance. "The real world's a bit different than you expected?"

He nodded.

"Go and enjoy the party. I'm good," said Niko. He watched the assistant hesitate, and then excitedly take off.

"Your messaging must still be off," said Sandra, coming up from behind him.

He frowned at her. "Can't I—"

"Trust me, turn it on," she said with a smirk. She'd changed into her usual developer garb and removed her makeup.

Niko paused. "Why don't you just tell me? You're practically vibrating."

"Cloudest just issued a press release. Big announcement."

His back stiffened, the exhaustion on his face brushed

aside. For years they had been battling it out with Eversio via its proxies. Every few years they'd buy the number two and three competitors to KnowMe, merge them, and bring a flaring fight to KnowMe's door. Each time, KnowMe had prevailed, sending the company into bankruptcy, often picking up the patents and key people in the process. Niko had felt each time like they had dodged a bullet, despite his executive team's assurance that they were simply better. "When did they send it?"

"Right after you walked off stage." The edge of Sandra's mouth curved up.

His hands on his hips, he stared at the ground and braced himself. "Okay, let me have it."

"They threw in the towel! Eversio's going to dismantle the company, sell off the patents and factories!"

Niko punched the air. "Yes! That's what, three attempts now?"

Sandra had the names at the ready. "AllKnowledge, NanoMate and now, Cloudest."

"Oh, I needed to hear that. Honestly, I was starting to think they might actually have something with Cloudest." He caught the shock on Sandra's face. "We aren't invincible, Sandra. At some point, someone's going to figure out a way to compete with us, really compete. The only way we can stop them is by innovating like our lives depend on it."

Sandra raised a finger and glanced around. "Phoebe didn't come, again? I thought she said she was this time."

Niko rolled his shoulders and looked away, squirming. "Moving on."

"Niko. Why do you keep—"

He scratched his brow. "I don't know. Every few months we chat, and she talks like she did when we dated, and we seem to get closer and then she pulls back. I don't know, I'm terrible at this stuff. Anyway, separate world, and I'd prefer we kept it that way."

"I noticed Tasslana before making my way over here. It took me a minute to recognize her. She's changed," she said with a knowing smile. "Is wearing her hair in a ponytail on the top of her head a thing?"

"She calls it her topknot," he replied, chuckling and looking away. "Well, you know, college changes people. One semester to go and she graduates with her bachelor and master's combo degree in literature and business."

"That was fast."

"Time flies. I am ever thankful that I can just use the scramjet to go, have dinner, hang out and then come back in the same evening. I can't imagine what she'll do when she finishes."

"Coding, literature and business… that's a heck of a package," said Sandra.

"Are you going to the party?"

"No, heading home."

"Ever feel a bit old for a startup?" he asked.

"Sometimes."

CHAPTER SEVEN

THE BIG SIT

Niko tapped nervously on the overstuffed arm of the beige leather chair as he waited to be called to an identical chair on the set. If one more person came up to him to adjust his hair or trim another hair of his beard, he was sure he was going to snap.

He hadn't planned to do any more interviews, instead wanting to focus on having some research time, but then the call had come for him to be on The Big Sit with Eleanor DeBoeuf. Saying no would have been a public relations disaster. Her following made his immense fan base seem quaint. She was a legend, and her show was an institution.

People bustled about the studio with near panicked senses of importance. He watched the drone-camera technicians check and recheck their armada. The KnowMe public relations team were acting like worried parents before a big recital. Everyone glanced his way at some point, making him feel like the mark in some grand plot.

He closed his eyes and relaxed into the chair. There was something bugging him, something taunting him from the back of his mind, something important. He wondered how many people were trying to send him messages, either video, audio or text. Silence was truly golden.

Opening his eyes, unable to shake whatever it was loose from the back of his mind, Niko gazed up at the holographic title projected above the set, *The Big Sit with Eleanor DeBoeuf*. The words moved about in a circular arc around the set. He wondered about how holo-screens, in-air holograms, and lens-displays each had a different use case, and a different effect on people.

Ignoring the nervousness in the pit of his stomach, he was enjoying the quiet time. A message punched through, bringing a smile to his face. It read: *Good luck! I've got the room packed. We're waiting to watch you on Sit! - T.*

Suddenly, Niko popped out of his chair and ran to the exit doors. Almost everyone suddenly skidded to a stop, their jaws open, and then in unison everyone glanced at the huge hologram of a countdown clock. There was only fourteen minutes left until they were live.

"What the hell just happened?" yelled the producer, rubbing her bald head. "Did he just…? Flaring son of a—! Hey, KnowMe idiots!" she yelled, marching over to the cluster of public relationships reps. "Where did your guy just take off to?"

White panic spread over all their faces.

Several minutes later, Niko returned, wondering why a half dozen people were glaring at him. He tucked the white envelope into his suit jacket and waved at the studio audience. "Wow, you've let them in. We must be getting close to air time."

The producer shook her head and glared at the KnowMe PR team.

"Is everything okay?" Niko asked the group.

"Yeah, great. Nothing to worry about," said the producer, before shouting, "Someone tell Eleanor—"

"No one needs to tell Eleanor anything," she replied, seeming to appear out of nowhere. She was petite, which surprised Niko. Her hair was a classic bob, and her brown eyes seemed like they could grab people and hold them hostage. "Everything okay?" she asked, frowning.

"We're good to go," said the producer.

"Good." She turned and gave a professional smile to her guest. "Niko, I'm Eleanor DeBoeuf. Welcome to my show."

"Thank you for the invitation," he replied with a boyish smile. "I'm—"

"Time to take your seat," said the producer, taking Niko by the elbow.

The music for the show started and immediately the petite woman who seemed half interested in what was going on transformed into the huge personality she was known for. "Welcome to the Big Sit! I'm your host, as always, Eleanor DeBoeuf. Today we have a man some call a legend in the making, a changer of the world, Doctor Niko Rafaelo.

"A few months ago, he released NanoCloud Four. Sales have gone through the roof, critics have fallen over themselves to claim how amazing it is, but is the trust and faith well earned? Where's he taking us? And what do we know about the man himself?

"Welcome to the show, Niko."

"Thank you for having me," he replied, lightly grabbing the arms of the chair.

"We hear all about the amazing success you've had. We've all seen you deliver some interesting pieces of technology with a showman's flare over the past two years, but I'm sure there's one thing that *my* fans would love to know. What's the last thing that you failed at?" she asked, a smirk across her face.

He stared at her and then at the drone-cameras floating about. Trying to hide his hard swallow, he chewed on his lip and leaned forward. He'd been warned what it would be like being on the show, and that he had about a minute or two before she'd make up her mind which way the rest of the interview would go. He'd watched her absolutely tear presidents and captains of industry apart, live. Several had even walked off the set. He rubbed his beard and looked up.

"I've made tons of errors and mistakes, but I don't regret them," he said. "I try to learn from them. Either I find a way to fix them or I find a way to make up for them. Take NanoCloud Four, for example. There were several key things that I insisted it be able to do. In isolated testing, they all worked fine, but in the real world they fell apart. I'd ripped out too much redundancy from our communication protocol, pushed the modest bandwidth it had so far that things were unreliable."

Niko looked around and sighed. "It was one of many humbling experiences. I pulled my direct team and they each brought ten members of their teams. We gathered in a college auditorium and had one of our jazz meetings."

"I've heard of that, what is it?" she asked, intrigued.

"After I explain the problem, no idea is declared stupid. Instead, other ideas that are offered need to weave what was said before into it. If someone says something like 'use pickle juice' it can be either funny or frustrating, but we always end up at the same place, a good place. We figure out how to make the truly essential features work, and push the rest for another day. We then look at what was missing to make the release really something we could be proud of, and make it happen. Every mistake taught me something, and sometimes what seemed like a terrible mistake turned into my greatest creation."

"Interesting," said Eleanor, taking a sip from her mug. "Everyone likes to say that they learned from their mistakes, everyone pulled themselves up from their own bootstraps as—"

"I didn't," interrupted Niko, catching a glimpse of one of his PR people freaking out at for him doing so. "I had support along the way. Support from those who picked me up when I lost faith in myself, and people who finally listened to what I wanted to do and took a chance on me. I didn't do any of this all by myself."

Eleanor rubbed her hands together. "And what about your parents? Your mother was an industrial roboticist, a quiet leader in her field, and your father was an exceptional —"

"What's your point?" asked Niko, his cheeks red.

Tapping her fingers together, Niko could see her forming battle plans. "Their death, along with that of your brother, was tragic. One of the last, if not the last, times an auto-taxi was hacked."

His face twitched, his hands gripped the arms of the chair. "You can understand why security is extremely important to me. The nanobot disaster more than sixty years ago resulted in the death of thousands of people as several weeks' worth of medication was released in seconds, all because of a hacker. Is that what you wanted?"

Eleanor stared at him, rubbing the side of her face as she considered the answer. "You never talk about your personal life."

"No," Niko replied, staring at one of the chair's arms.

"Why?"

He took a deep breath and pulled his gaze up to match hers. "Because I like to keep my worlds separate. It allows me to be the me that I need to be, without carrying personal baggage across those borders, without requiring myself to always be the same version of myself."

Eleanor looked into the distance, shifting her position, glancing at him as she tapped her lips with a finger.

"Is everything okay?" asked Niko, realizing he'd been told several times in preparation for the interview not to seize those moments. He was supposed to let her eventually come back to him.

"I'm just..." she said, pausing again. "I'm just surprised by the amount of sincerity you radiate. I didn't expect it. For those of you watching," she turned and looked at the cameras, "there's a real sense of groundedness that Niko gives off, something that you have to feel to believe, but believe me, it's there." She smiled at him. "Is there anyone who was there in the early days, who played maybe a small but important role, that you've lost contact with? One person more than anyone else?"

Niko sighed and brought his hands back to his lap. "Ah... well, more than anyone would be my friend, Yoshi. I hope he's doing well. He helped me get to the starting line for what became KnowMe."

"Huh," said Eleanor, smiling and leaning back. "Now, I understand that you lost your family at a young age, but you also—"

Niko quickly slid forward in his seat, and leaned forward, his hand out, nearly touching Eleanor. "No," he said sharply.

"Excuse me?" Eleanor's face went steely.

He noticed his PR people and the producer already getting into an argument over his actions. "I make a point of keeping my private life, private. If you have issue with something in it, I'm happy to discuss it, but I've worked hard at keeping my worlds separate." He leaned back into the chair. "Sorry to startle you, but I am fiercely protective of those that I care most about."

"Is that why you ran off the set with only a few minutes to spare to get the white envelope?" she asked, pointing to his jacket.

Niko tapped his fingers on the arms of the chair, before reaching in and handing it over to her.

"What are you doing?"

"Open it and read it, to yourself," he said.

Eleanor touched the envelope and stared at Niko. "I make no promises that I won't tell the world what I read."

Niko let the envelope go.

Eleanor sat back and opened it, revealing to the world that it was a classic, hard paper, birthday card. She read the card and then looked at him, bewildered. "Was this a trick or stunt? A prop to get me to… it wasn't, was it?"

Niko shook his head.

She carefully put the card back into the envelope and handed it to him. "She's a lucky girl."

He smiled and put the card back in his jacket.

Eleanor poked the arm of her chair with a finger. "I

wasn't expecting you to be sentimental. I expected the hard core type. It's hard to imagine you sending something by courier-drone but after reading it... You know, there are very few, if any, great men of history who would do that. You know that, right?"

"I do now," replied Niko. They laughed.

"Let me ask you, do you think you're making the world a better place?"

Niko stared at the floor. They'd prepped him mercilessly for variations on the question. He could imagine the entire KnowMe board of directors tuning in with nervous anticipation.

"I don't know. I hope so," he replied. Quickly he flicked the air.

"What was that?" asked Eleanor, annoyed.

"I'm making sure that no one can send me messages right now."

"Was someone trying to tell you what to say?" She leaned in.

Niko smiled. "I'm doing my best to improve the world, the best that I know how. If I ran across something that revealed I was doing any harm, I'd share that." He noted her skeptical look. "I would. What would be the point, just to have money? I have money. Legacy is earned."

He glanced at the producer who seemed eager for Eleanor to tear into him. He turned back to her, and saw the internal debate going on behind her eyes. "I'm not like some of my idols of history. The most important things in my life are the people who would still be with me even if everything was gone tomorrow. Their birthdays, the special moments in their lives, I do my best to be there for all of them. I will fly from the other side of the planet by scramjet to make it, and then fly back to make that important meeting."

Eleanor nodded. "We started with a question on failure. What are you most proud of?"

Niko looked up. "Our new architecture of the NanoCloud. I know that means next to nothing to ninety-nine percent of the people out there, but it was extremely hard to make the huge leap it required. In NanoCloud Two, we had audio calls and then in Three, we introduced small video windows. But as everyone knew, the video calls had to be short because they weren't robust. There's so much interference in the world around us, so few high bandwidth resources available, that we'd pushed the architecture as far as it would go. We needed something new."

"But video calling is something that my grandmother had, back in the day," said Eleanor.

"True. There are a lot of features that they had back then, but it was a very different world. Bit by bit, I feel that we're reclaiming the best of what they had, but in ways that they could have never imagined." He paused, clasping his hands together. "We started to see the return of video calls on cellphones about ten years ago, but the carriers couldn't manage it, so that went away."

"As a society, we've patched and bolted on to the infrastructure of the past, but there's been so much environmental damage, that it seems every time there's been the will and money to do something new, it's been wiped out."

Eleanor nodded. "We don't have to think back too far to come up with examples."

"No, we don't," continued Niko. "I really want to bring people to a new way of doing things, and that's why I keep pushing the idea of nanobots and what we can do. I appreciate the huge leap of faith the public took when we introduced NanoCloud, and I am very much aware of the amount of social trust that has been placed in me and KnowMe. Nanobots was once a dirty word, but now?"

"Well, I'd argue that nanobots *is* still a dirty word, but you've made NanoCloud a whole different thing. As if whatever the magic of NanoCloud is, it keeps those dirty little things in check," said Eleanor.

Niko stopped and sat back, a youthful grin on his face.

"What is it?"

"I've never thought of it like that before, but you're right. Huh," said Niko.

Eleanor couldn't help herself, she grinned from ear to ear. She saw out the corner of her eye her producer cheering as he checked the online statistics of how the show was going. "Should I assume that having bigger video windows and multiple video calls are in our future? What about streaming video like we have on our holo-screens?"

Niko raised an eyebrow. "I should leave *some* secrets for NanoCloud Five, shouldn't I?"

"You should indeed," she replied with a smile.

The rest of the interview flew by.

Standing up, Eleanor brought the show to a close. "This has been one for the history books. I'd like to thank our guest, Doctor Niko Rafaelo. We all have his technology, and now… we know a piece of the man behind it all. Stay tuned on TalkItNow where, as always, we'll be revealing our guest for next week and my after-show thoughts."

"We're clear," yelled the producer, confirming what Eleanor's lens-display was telling her.

Niko stood up and she stared at him, making him stop.

"You aren't anything like what I expected," she said. "I'm going to remember this. Don't let the fame and money go to your head. Stay true to those values you have, and keep those people in your life close."

"I will," he said smiling.

"So many people get lost along the way. The riches and power, it corrupts who they are."

The producer came and ushered Niko off the set as Eleanor prepared to do the after-show.

With great hesitation, Niko turned his messages back on. Immediately he deleted all the ones from KnowMe except for the last one from the chairman of the board: *Ignore everything else I said, great job, stock's up two points!* He couldn't care less. Then another one came, *Awesome job! - T, PS: Here's a photo of me and my gang.* He chuckled.

One of the KnowMe public relationships people came over to him. "We have to get going, we have you—"

"No," interrupted Niko. "I've got to go see someone. I have a birthday card to deliver."

CHAPTER EIGHT

DELEGATED PROBLEMS

Two Years Later

"Not now," said Sandra, shooing away one of her direct reports as she saw Niko storm past her office. She leapt up and began walking with him. "I know that look. I think we need to change direction and go grab some burgers, right now."

"I'm going to find him and ring his neck," muttered Niko, sharply turning a corner and then poking his head into an empty office. "Doesn't look like he's been in at all today." He then headed for the conference rooms.

Niko rarely flew off the handle, but she had seen it from time to time, and it wasn't pretty. In the early days, he fired the entire software team for 'not trying', fired the entire communications department over a serious blunder, but he'd softened over the years. Sandra gestured carefully as she tried to keep pace with him, finally landing on the likely issue.

"Security glitch?"

Niko slid the door of a conference room open, scanned about at the stunned people, and then closed it. "It's only a *glitch* if it's a little thing that was unforeseen. I *told* our illustrious VP of Technology that this would happen if he didn't implement the process improvements I mentioned, and run the automated tests that I'd mentioned. I should never have hired him; I should have given you the job."

"I was on maternity leave on and off for a year and a half," she said.

"Doesn't matter, you would have still been better overseeing things five minutes a day, than the mess he's been creating." He stopped and stared at her. "Geezes, where are my manners? You've only been back a week. I didn't come by and say hi."

She smiled. "You did."

"I did?"

She nodded.

"Oh." He glanced about. "Good." He ran his hand through his hair.

"You look like you've been running yourself ragged."

"The NanoCloud Five launch was nearly a complete disaster. The feature set was adequate but not impressive in the least, never mind it looks like we have a new competitor showing up. Some of our folks went over to it, which gives them a stronger starting point."

She took his hand. "Okay, breathe."

He squinted at her, withdrawing his hand. "I don't have
—"

"Just breathe, and think. You are on an old school war
path. I know when I get like that around the kids, I'm no
use to anyone. I hand everything over to my husband, and I
go have a coffee or whatever at the cafe down the street.
Then I come home, sane."

"I used to do that."

"Why don't we head on over to Fillion's, grab a burger,
get caught up, and then address this."

"I've already coded up the fix, it'll be releasing in
seventeen minutes," he said with an inward look at his
lens-display countdown.

"Then there's nothing we can do," she said.

"Except fire him."

She nodded. "Has he been that bad?" She waved and
smiled at onlookers as they passed in the corridor.

He glared at her.

"Wow, so the rumors weren't exaggerations."

He shook his head.

"What are you going to do?"

Niko quickly gestured and issued a message to the head
of Team Management and Development. His hands were
shaking from the adrenaline. "He's fired. I override his—"

"This *isn't* an FBI case or missing child or anything that
gives us moral cause to use that. You know that. We've had

to fire developers who found a way to hunt an ex with our tracking." She frowned at him. "Let's just go, get some burgers, and chat."

Niko lead the way to the elevator and waved over its sensor.

As they entered the elevator, he broke the silence. "I've got too much on my plate lately."

Sandra smiled and looked at him. "From the sound of things, they've only gotten worse in my absence. Mind you, before I left, you were already on the edge of going crazy."

He scowled at her. "I don't like to accept that I have limits."

"I know," replied Sandra. "Still, you're only human."

Niko stared at the floor, rocking back and forth on his shoes. "Don't you ever feel like that's a copout? Deep down, I'd like nothing more than to change that."

She nodded. "I hate to bring this up, but you do realize you've created another problem. You need a new VP of Technology."

"I've always hated that title. I like VP of Development better. Technology is so general... I mean, we're a technology company. I don't know why he wanted it to be technology. I should have known right from the beginning he wasn't a good fit," said Niko, smoothing his beard.

Sandra shrugged. "Call it the spinner of widgets, whatever it is, you now have more on your plate, not less."

He sighed. "I need to delegate all the extra marketing

stuff as well as the development stuff. I really need to get back to research, to exploring, to thinking about where we're going long term. What ground can we break three versions from now? That's where I should be."

"I completely agree," said Sandra. "I think that would go a long way to giving us back the Niko I know is still in there."

As the elevator door opened, Niko stepped out and turned to her. "Come on, Ms. Vice-President of Development."

"What?" replied Sandra.

Niko motioned for her to come along. "You're my new VP of Development. Not director of a piece of it anymore. You run the show. You're back, and even if you have more kids, we'll work around it. I should have made you the VP in the first place."

"Why? Why me?"

"Because Sandra, you're one of the very few people I completely trust. You've been part of every major and significant minor technical decision. You've been part of every launch except for Five, and you'll be up to speed on what happened with that in the blink of an eye. With you running development, and getting someone to properly run marketing, I can focus on other stuff. Will you do it?"

Sandra sighed and shook her head. "The things I do for you."

"Burgers?" he asked.

"Damn straight we're going for burgers."

———————

Six Months Later

Niko stomped around his second floor home laboratory, glaring at the three tables of electronics and the holo-screens that continued to defy his will.

Grabbing an old-style swivel chair by the back, he wanted to throw it out the floor-to-ceiling window, but he couldn't. Despite the appeal of the drama that might show on the outside, he always had something inside him holding him back, something to lose. Occasionally he wondered if it prevented him from achieving true greatness.

A video message popped up on the holo-screen. He swiped for it to play. The beautiful heart-shaped face of a twenty-three-year-old appeared. Her hair was blue and in playful pig-tails. "Hey, just wanted to let you know that I got a promotion today. Won't be able to make dinner tonight, going out with office mates. We're still on for your birthday, Friday. Love ya." The image finished with her heart-warming smile and wink.

Niko laughed, "You're always awesome, Tass."

A text message appeared from Phoebe, hoping that he was well and wishing him a happy early birthday. He wondered if she was still going to call him as she did every year, or if the distance he'd allowed to grow between them would claim the contact as a victim. He'd decided to take a step beyond just keeping his worlds separate, but to also keep them simple. Right now, he had to focus.

Turning back to his nemeses in the microscopic world, he sat back down and slid over to one of the developer workstations devoted to the embedded programming of the Captains. They were the nanobots who managed all the others in the NanoCloud. They provided a basic hierarchy, and whenever one was damaged or destroyed, a regular nanobot would be randomly selected by the other Captains and change role.

He felt like he kept trying to attack the same problem the same way, again and again. He'd made the communication protocols more efficient, he'd improved the performance so that the nanobots would have more computational time to dedicate to things other than finding bacteria to feed off of, and he'd doubled how long they could last before needing to feed. But ultimately, it was peanuts compared to what he was after.

He ran his hands through his overgrown, greasy hair and wondered how long it had been since he'd showered. He glanced about, before realizing he'd once again banished any signs of the time or date, other than when he explicitly called it up on a screen. He didn't want to feel the pressure of time, just the knowledge of the sun as it rose and set in the background. He stared out at the forest and mountains in the background, rubbing his tired eyes. "What am I missing? Or is this it? End of the line?"

He gazed about the room, from the pile of Ace cans in one corner, to all the tossed cartons of food from the past several days in another. Life was not providing any hints. He closed his eyes, put his hands over them, and tried to rummage through his mental dumpsters of discarded ideas. "Think, Niko. Think. There's got to be something here."

After a while, he opened his eyes and stood up. He walked over to the window and leaned his forehead against it. Scratching his stubbly chin, he laughed as he remembered Tass' reaction to him musing about shaving his head once. He'd never heard her put her foot down so fast in all his life.

"Maybe there's something from the office that can help me shake an idea loose. I haven't checked in a while." He walked over to a state-of-the-art holo-screen setup that was separate from the rest, and stepped on its gesture pad. He picked up a silver token, activated it with his thumb, and waited for the alert that the secure connection to the KnowMe office had been made. He brought up his messages and riffled through them. "Let's dump all of those, because I don't care. And these because I don't care… and—" A video call image appeared. It was Sandra calling from the main office. Reluctantly he waved his acceptance.

"Hey Niko—" she stopped and chuckled. "That's an… interesting new look. Going for mad scientist? It's very… bad."

He glanced down at himself. "It's not that bad."

She nodded with a smirk. "Whatever gets us progress. Listen, we have a team meeting in a few hours. Are you coming to this one?" she inquired.

"I wasn't planning on it," he replied. "Your forehead's showing some real concern, what's up?"

Sandra glanced about, before focusing back on the screen. "Niko, I know you need time to concentrate, but we can't keep working this way. You're paralyzing a lot of decision making. The board's not happy either. The chairperson came down to see me this morning. They're getting concerned."

"They shouldn't be, it's my company. If there's anything really important, I'll be there."

"But you haven't been," threw back Sandra. "Listen, there was a not-so-subtle hint dropped about how you don't have majority ownership of this company, and you haven't for a long, long time. If the board had some additional support, they could take matters into their own hands."

"They're just trying to rattle you." Niko paused. "You still got a hold of me, granted it was at the last minute."

"Twice. Twice, and I covered for you both times," said Sandra. "I don't need the extra stress. We're trying to get NanoCloud Six features done, and we're tripping over each other. Never mind the new VP of Marketing you hired, Andre; he's got a real strong personality and I'm the only one able or willing to try and put him in his place."

Niko paced about, stroking his chin. "I just... I just need more time. You guys just need to hold it together for a while longer. I keep running into walls and I can't keep being distracted with this stuff."

"Look, I understand. However, as a member of your executive team, I'm telling you, you can't have that concentration time unless you free people up to make decisions without you needing to always give your okay. If that's what you want, you need to put that in writing so that we're all clear on it."

"I hate that idea," replied Niko, his hands on his hips, glaring at the holo-screen image of Sandra.

"I know," she replied with a sigh. "But you've put us all in an awkward spot."

They looked at each other.

"They asked you to bring this to me, didn't they?" asked Niko, staring at the floor.

Hesitantly, she replied, "Yeah."

"I'm sorry for putting you in that position."

She shrugged. "It's part of the job. Overall, the job is interesting. I miss being in the trenches some days, but knowing that I'm clearing the way for the men and women trying to create wonder and amazement is pretty close, most of the time."

"I'm guessing everyone's been trying to tell me this but I haven't been listening?" He looked up at her.

She nodded. "I'm guessing you're back to that old habit

of deleting whatever messages you don't want to read."

A flash of guilt crossed his face. "I *never* do that."

"Yes, you do," she answered with a knowing smile. "I've *seen* you do it."

"Okay, so I do it. But it's because I get so much—"

"Don't even go there. Don't. It's your responsibility. And consider this a kick. You need to be here leading, or you need to delegate things more, or something. I don't know what the right answer is, but you can't just keep us in limbo."

Niko nodded. "Okay, I hear you, thanks."

"Happy early fortieth birthday, in case I don't see you," said Sandra.

"Thanks," he replied, ending the call and glancing about at his lab.

For the past six months, he'd grown more and more distant from the company. He knew it was unfair to lean on Sandra so heavily. "She has a point about delegation. I need to change up the leadership model, because otherwise it's…" he stopped, his eyes going wide and his body shaking with excitement. "That's it! I need to change the delegation model! The Captains… they've gone as far as they can, I need something more… I need… I need a Meta-Captain."

He rushed over to his drawing workstation and brought the holo-screen to life. "If I introduce a new role… no, it needs to be more than a new role. Let all the Captains serve as optimizing repeaters, but have a bulkier new nanobot as the Meta-Captain to handle the bigger job, that would free up a lot of the Captains' responsibilities, and simplify the tasks for the nanobots." He immediately started playing with models in the air. "Yes. Yes, that's it. They'll need..." and he stopped, dropping his arms to his side. "They'd need to be two to three times the size. Creating a specialized nanobot's going to introduce all the problems I've avoided by making them all the same." He yelled and kicked at the air, slipping and smacking his head on the hardwood floor.

Sitting up, he rubbed his head, relieved there was no blood. "It's not like I could make them..." He noticed the last micro-factory that he'd built, sitting on a shelf under a glass dome. He walked over and took it down, looking it over.

"What if the Meta-Captains could be built by other nanobots? I mean, the principles are all here," he said to the micro-factory. "Just, scaled up for people, so if I can scale them down, I can give the nanobots limited construction ability. Maybe cannibalize two or three nanobots to form a Meta-Captain, make the Metas and the regular Captains responsible for determining the Meta-Captain count needed... this *might* work."

He spent the next hour modifying and re-modifying the model, annotating everything so as not to lose a single idea. "I'll have to simplify this a dozen times over, but this could work."

He stood back and smiled, his arms folded. "Happy early birthday, indeed."

CHAPTER NINE
CHALLENGED

One Year Later

Niko arrived in the conference room, surprised to see someone there already. His white shirt was rumpled, and his jeans frayed at the ends. His hair was shoulder length, his beard a mess. He had bags under his eyes and his cheek bones showed a bit more than usual.

He glanced at the time on his lens-display and confirmed he was twenty minutes early. "Hey Sandra, everything okay?"

She waved away her work, lowered her fingers to the table, and acknowledged him. "It's good to see you, but really… next time, dress code."

"Dress code? Since when do we have a dress code?" asked Niko, looking back into the hallway and realizing that people were not casually dressed.

"A few months," she replied. "Do I need to mention this was announced in a message and—"

Niko waved his surrender. "That's fine, just… feels weird."

"Well, we grew up a bit, I guess. We're not a tiny startup anymore."

"It wasn't your idea, was it?"

She shook her head. "Still, I don't mind looking good, and my husband approves."

Niko sat at the head of the table and slowly looked around the glass-walled conference room. He wasn't a fan of the design and its starkness, but he accepted it. If he'd continued scrutinizing over every detail, he'd have lost his mind or soul. "I walked by Fillion's on my way in this morning, and it hit me. It was a little over a year ago that you took over as VP of Development."

"Year and a half ago, actually," she corrected.

"What, really?"

She nodded.

Niko scratched his head. "Doesn't feel that long."

"We're about to release NanoCloud Six, after taking a hit for delaying it a few months. Anyway, now you're *finally* going to show us all why you've abandoned us for your one true love."

He smiled, leaning forward on his elbows. "I'm really excited."

"Me too."

Niko noted her reply was missing something, some element of energy or conviction. He leaned back, tugging on his beard.

"Honestly, I've been surprised you've been able to keep

it a secret from me. You used to tell me everything."

"Those were different times. I don't feel like I had that much to share, and when I did, I did share with you."

"True. I just… I don't know, I miss the old days," she said, staring at the table.

"Me too," he replied, looking out the open door.

"Well, my husband thinks that you might just be faking. He hopes you've secretly been racing yachts or building an underwater lab," she said with a laugh.

"Your husband is a funny man."

Sandra tapped her fingers on the table. "We haven't had you over in a long time. You should come for dinner. The girls would like to see you."

Niko acknowledged the idea. "How's your work-life balance these days, speaking of the family?"

"Not what I'd like it to be, but the family's not rioting," she replied, scratching her cheek. "I'm hoping after we're done getting NanoCloud Six launched, that I can take some time off."

Niko slammed his hand on the table. "Do it! Seize the day. Carpet that diem!"

Sandra laughed. "Well, sadly, it's not entirely up to you anymore, now is it?" she retorted, gesturing to the other empty chairs. "You delegated key decisions to the executive committee, and a VP going on vacation *is* a key decision. Have you ever read any of the minutes from our meetings?"

"Um."

"You didn't know that there were minutes, did you?"

He squinted at her. "I think I knew."

She shook her head. "Do you really even work here anymore?"

"Sometimes, I'm not sure," he mused. "The team will support your vacation, I'm sure of it. Everyone knows how hard you work."

She moved her head from side to side, before cracking a smile. "I know; I'm just giving you a hard time."

"I keep thinking of this story that I read as a kid, written by some guy… Zouak or something? About a king who brought democracy only to regret how little got done. He watched his realm fall apart and led a revolution to take it back, only to have to hand it back. Sometimes I wonder if we'll be able to go back. The changes we've made still don't sit well with me."

"Hey guys," said Andre, the silver-haired head of marketing, as he walked in. He had a paper notebook in hand.

Niko pointed at it and said, "Nice piece."

He offered a polite smile. "You like it? My wife found it in a bazaar and had it etched for me. I love the feel of classic notebooks. Limited storage capacity, but there's nothing like the feel to get the ideas flowing. Never mind the sound of ripping a piece of paper and crumpling it up."

"Huh, look at you, an old softy," said Sandra

awkwardly. Her dynamic with Andre was still a work in progress.

Andre gave her a half-smile.

A few minutes later, the other three members of the executive leadership team filed in.

Niko leaped out of the chair. "Okay, let's get started."

"No holo-screen?" asked Sandra.

"Sorry, this is really overwhelming. Can we back up a bit," said the head of finance, her wry humor getting a chuckle out of everyone.

Niko grimaced. "I thought and over-thought how I could present what I've been up to, where we've been going, and I realized, probably the best thing to do is to just talk first, then show you. I don't need slides or models."

"Dangerous," quipped Sandra.

"I don't know. Sounds simple *and* tangible, though a bit hand-wavy for me," said Andre rubbing his meaty hands together. "Come on, Niko, impress me."

Niko began pacing about, his head slightly bowed. "As you know, I've been spending a lot of time over the past while asking the question: where are we going? I've given it a name now, NanoCloud Nine."

For the next twenty minutes, Niko talked about his inspiration and how Nine would be the biggest change they'd ever seen. "So are you all with me so far?" he asked. "Do we need a break?"

The head of finance looked at her colleagues, her

expression had been one of confusion from the outset. "Sandra?"

"You threw a lot of ideas and possibilities at us, but I think it was a bit too... off the cuff, maybe?" said Sandra.

Andre weighed in. "Personally, I don't want a break until I actually get to see something that makes me think this isn't just you making stuff up on the spot. Seriously, in marketing, I live and breathe all this vision and hand waving stuff, but so far, I've not seen anything real. You said this would be simple and tangible, and so far, that stuff wasn't simple. Hopefully there's still something tangible to this. Come on, show me something, genius. I need a wow moment, just one. Give me one." He had a finger in the air. He glanced at his colleagues. "Am I wrong here?"

The room went silent.

Niko scanned the faces, scratching his beard. Apart from Sandra, everyone was clearly needing more than he'd offered. He'd never had to convince people, let alone people who weren't very technical, of what he had in mind before. For the first time in a long time, he wasn't having any fun whatsoever. On top of it, he wasn't sure if he was being challenged for his leadership or simply asked to make the best use of their time. He scratched the top of his head.

"Okay," said Niko. "I'm going to commandeer all of your NanoClouds and send my video to your lens-displays."

"What's that supposed to mean?" asked Sandra.

"I was hoping you'd know," said Andre. "Is this a new feature thing? We're going to let people just take over other people's clouds? Sounds dangerous."

"No," replied Niko firmly, standing up straight. "It's just—" he shook his head— "It's just a new part of *my* experimental cloud. It's one of the developer tools I've created. I need it for testing things out, advanced diagnostics and the like. We've had a basic version of this from day one, but it doesn't work on commercially released editions of the NanoCloud, only on mine.

"Okay, now one of the greatest limitations of the human body's architecture is its inability to be extended. There's no way to communicate with cells, there's no way to access our memories other than by actively triggering them. There's no way to make something become a natural part of us. Similarly, our current NanoCloud architecture has limits. It's a lot better than the one we started with, but still, it has serious limits. We've been scraping every last ounce of bandwidth and computing capacity we can to come up with new versions of NanoCloud, but really, we're hitting a wall. No matter what we do, we're just dancing on the head of a pin, shifting the focus without really increasing the real estate."

"You lost me," said the head of finance.

"Me too," said another.

Niko stared at the table, shaking his head in frustration.

"Well, I've finally cracked it, found a way to breathe new life into the NanoCloud. It's essentially the first step towards real, robust, distributed micro-intelligence. Every little piece, able to work together towards a high order problem, but without the pressure of expecting it to be cognizant or falling into any of the classic traps of old world artificial intelligence. This is beyond that old world thinking. I was inspired by cells as well as nature."

"So, working together like bees?"

"Oh for flood's sake..." Niko scratched his head. "Sure, like bees. Moving on. I believe I've take the first step towards something well beyond what I ever thought possible. Let me show you the first, small step I've taken," he said, performing a new, two handed gesture.

Everyone's lens-displays flashed blue, momentarily blinding each of them. When the lens-display restored their vision, they realized they were seeing some aspect of the world from Niko's position.

"I think I'm upside down. Is this from behind you? I'm going to be sick," said the head of finance, closing her eyes.

"Sorry, I forgot some of you might initially connect to nanobots that aren't facing forward or right-side-up." He brought his hands together, correcting everyone's point of view. "This is in perfect quality and resolution, and in true real time. No little windows of video, no secondary devices needed."

Andre stumbled to his feet, knocking his notebook over.

"Andre, what are you doing?" scolded Niko.

"Geezes! Make it flaring stop!" yelled Andre, stumbling backwards into the window.

Niko waved the feature off, cursing under his breath. "Everyone, calm down. I *said* you were seeing things from my perspective." He ran his hands through his hair, giving him a wild appearance.

Andre peeked out at the world and then sat down in a huff.

Sandra stared at Niko in complete disbelief. "How did you do that? We've discussed the theoretical links of the architecture many times, but that's impossible. And I don't mean by a little, I don't mean improbable, that was supposed to be impossible."

Niko looked at her, his mood sliding over to a child's grin.

She shook her head, annoyed that he wasn't saying anything. "Come on, Niko. I know the specs. That's more than an order of magnitude more bandwidth and computing capacity of the nanobots than we have now." She pointed a finger at him. "And I know for a *fact* you were yelling and cursing last week about not being able to do more than twenty percent more. Was this all smoke—"

"No," he said definitively, turning his gaze to the floor. He hated being there. He glanced around the room. He hadn't missed being in the office much. "This was real."

"Then—"

"Not here, Sandra," he said politely. "Not now, and not until I have it completely solved. What you all saw were my nanobots not only able to take in my environment as full body video, but then render it and broadcast it for your NanoClouds. Granted it was only for ten seconds, but still."

Sandra just sat there shaking her head, her colleagues were whispering.

"Was that enough of a wow for you, Andre?" Niko asked him.

Andre rubbed his sweaty his face. "That was flared up, that's what it was. A wow? I'm not sure."

Niko frowned and twitched disapprovingly. "There are at least a dozen practical applications that *I* can think of. I expect you to find more, when the time comes," he said. "For the second and last part of the demo... I'd like you to all look at the formerly empty corner of the room. I'm sure everyone recognizes a friendly face from the cafe downstairs. Hello." He waved.

The team followed Niko's gaze to a full sized, grainy, black and white apparition of a man. The man waved back.

"Farouk?" asked the head of finance. "Is that you? From downstairs?"

The man nodded and laughed.

Sandra leaned back in her chair, her eyebrows up, shaking her head.

"Is this live?" asked Andre.

"It is," replied Niko with a grin.

Sandra got up and walked over to the image, Andre right behind her. "This is in full three dimensions," said Sandra, with a hint of being impressed.

The apparition laughed. "Hello to you too. This holo-screen makes you look very close. Is everything okay on your side?"

"Oh, everything's... amazing," said Sandra, making her way back to her seat. "The sound's direction is perfect. How are you doing that?"

"Thanks for the help," said Niko, dismissing the apparition. He folded his arms, leaned against the wall and tilted his head down. He stroked his chin pensively for a moment, before replying to Sandra's question. "When I have it all perfected, I'll share. I just wanted to show what I'd been playing with. Why we've made the changes that we have, and to give you guys an idea of what we're going to be capable of."

The room was quiet.

Niko saw a flash on his contact lens-display and quickly pulled up a diagnostic window. "Well, it went better than the last time I tried this. I've still got a NanoCloud density of twelve percent left this time. As for yours," he said staring at the group. "I'm not getting any signal back. They're probably entirely fried. You'll all need to completely respray after the meeting. Sorry."

"That's a heck of a nanobot death toll," said Sandra, shaking her head.

Andre threw his hands up. "We can't sell that."

"It's an *early* prototype," snapped Niko. "They lasted for the demo, that's huge." He scratched his head furiously for a moment. "What I'm trying to get you to understand is this is *normal*. Sandra, you've seen our research cycles before."

"I was *part* of the research cycles before." She shifted her gaze away from him.

He frowned, annoyed. Looking around the room, he shook his head. "What am I not getting?"

Sandra gazed up at him with an expression he didn't expect. She leaned forward and rubbed the back of her neck. "I hate to ask this, but I have to. Have you been holding out on us?"

"What?" asked Niko. "For real? Did you just ask me that?"

Sandra opened her mouth and paused. After a second, she said, in a very measured tone, "You didn't just bump up the bandwidth by a bit, Niko. You had a fundamental leap across a chasm. It's like going from the telegraph to cellphones in a few weeks? Months? And this all happened since the last status update from you a week ago? Or whenever it was, it doesn't matter. A year and a half, nothing, then *bam*, this?"

"The ideas I've had, but it took time to get it even working at this level." Niko scowled at the team.

"This is just, I don't know, too huge of a change," said

Andre.

"That's what *genius* does, it makes huge leaps," yelled Niko, massaging the back of his aching hands.

"Where's the humble celebrity now?" sniped the head of finance.

Niko glared at her. "This isn't about *ego*. I've been working an endless stream of days and nights to find a way to give KnowMe that leap to the future. True invention isn't found an inch at a time, it's found from failing and failing and failing and then BANG, you're a thousand miles away. You have no idea how many times I've ripped this down to the bones and built it back up. And finally, I think I've figured something out. Enough such that I could show you."

"I don't see what the big deal is," said a member of the team.

Niko climbed out of the chair and barked at the group, "Why are you reacting like I've just shown laser guns to monkeys?"

The room immediately went icy.

After several seconds of silence with everyone glaring at Niko, and him glaring back, Sandra said, "That crossed a line."

Niko shook his head and looked at the floor, his hands on his hips. "You're right. I'm sorry. I'm just… I'm tired. My muscles ache, I have a headache that keeps coming and going… We're the leaders of the top tech company, how can we be reacting this way to what comes next? KnowMe is either out in front, or it's nothing."

Andre stood up and looked Niko in the eye. "Are you done? Or does the genius need some more tantrum time?"

Niko sat down and politely gestured for Andre to retake his seat. He covered his nose and mouth with his hands for a moment and took a calming breath. Then with a sigh, he put his hands face down on the table. "Let's see if we can put this back on track, shall we? I've shown you two things that we're going to be capable of. This isn't everything. There's more to come, it's just what I had in any shape to be able to share. Now, can I have your thoughts on what I presented in terms of them as features? Andre, would you like to go first?"

Andre sat back down and clasped his hands. After a darting glance around the table, he nodded. "I see the value on the apparition stuff. It's a bit low res, but I think we could sell it, particularly if we do some free upgrades every few months. But we can't offer that and the weirdo full video thing you did. What did you call it? Full body video? I'm not even sure what the value is there."

"The value is—" said Niko jumping in and then stopping himself. He motioned politely for Andre to continue, and proceeded to stroke his beard.

Andre continued, "I think we either show new capability or better capability. Either we go apparition or full body video thing, but providing both to the market at the same time is going to be a confusing message. Look we have super high res, and look we have super low res."

Niko calmly nodded, mulling over what he'd heard. "That's a fair point," he replied.

"If we could hold off releasing NanoCloud Six and get that in there… I don't know. The press and stockholders would revolt, but I think we could handle it, and I think we'd be forgiven for doing so. What do you need, two or three months to get this ready to go?"

"What? No…" said Niko, dropping his head. "You been listening?" He glared at Andre. "This is where we're *going*. It's not going to be ready in three months. Maybe I'll be able to hand it over to Sandra's team in a year."

Andre laughed. "Yeah, well, that's not going to work." He turned to Sandra. "So, can we get it done?"

"Excuse me?" said Niko. "*I* said no. I'm calling this NanoCloud Nine for a reason. This is still a few years away from being released on the market."

Giving Niko a dirty look, Andre said to Sandra, "You need to talk to him."

Sandra massaged the bridge of her nose. "Yeah, okay."

"Sandra?" inquired Niko.

She shook her head, her expression steely and tired. "Andre didn't feel that we had enough strong features for NanoCloud Six to really stand on its own for a year. And he's right, I wouldn't say that it's junk, but honestly? We polished every knob and icon in that damn thing, pulled everything we didn't include in Five and put it there so that we had *something*."

Niko was mystified. "Why didn't you—"

"Ask you? We tried, you weren't around," snapped Andre.

Sandra continued. "Because of that, and a few other things, we met as an executive team. I invited you, for the record. *We* decided that we'd put Seven out as a quick, free, release six months later. It'd let us recover a bit by nailing one or two cool new features, and quickly addressing as much of the feedback we'll get after Six is released."

"That's… never mind, go on," said Niko, leaning back and trying to keep his expressions in check. He tugged hard on his beard.

"What we came up with is good, but not great. It *might* get us by. So we're putting out Six, then quickly going to announce and put out Seven, and hopefully earn us a pass until Eight a year after. But here's the thing, we have no flaring ideas for Eight. We're tapped out, and I'm exhausted."

"Well, genius, any thoughts?" asked Andre.

"Honestly? That's an idiotic plan. Best to hit the brakes now, fix it, and make every release count." Niko rested his hand on his chin.

Andre's face tensed. "Actually, it's a damn fine plan. One that's going to buy the company some time, a company that you've all but abandoned!" he yelled. He spun his notebook. "Anyway, I'm done with you. Sandra, I'll go get the next meeting kicked off, but I'll hold off anything interesting until you're there. Come on guys." He motioned to the others, who immediately stood.

"Where are you going?" asked Niko. "You work for me."

Andre scoffed. "These days it feels more like we work for the board. Do you even know what the next meeting is about?"

Niko was silent, shifting his gaze between different members of the team. Clearly everyone knew the next meeting was extremely important, everyone except him.

Shaking his head, Andre continued, "We have to submit a formal response to the senate committee on Public Technologies and Homeland Affairs. Remember that little deal we have with the military? You know, the one that's been vital to our bottom line for years? Well, they aren't happy. They want a roadmap of where we're going. They can't complete their planning without our plans."

Andre rubbed his hands together and chuckled. "And then there's the matter of that new whack-job senator on the committee making a lot of noise. She's the one that founded that new party, what are they called? The New Founders or something. She's coming at big contract companies like us, with guns blazing."

He turned and pointed to the other members of the team, who were ready to leave. "We have to reply ASAP and if we don't, things are going to get nasty. Luckily for us, Sandra's quarterbacking all the tech stuff. You know, KnowMe being a tech company and everything. So if you don't mind, we have actual important things to do for this company." Andre then brushed passed Niko.

Niko watched as everyone except for Sandra left the room. With a sigh, he closed the door. "What the hell was that?"

Tapping her fingers on the table, she shook her head gently back and forth. "That's you not being here, Niko," she replied matter-of-factly. "I don't know what to tell you."

"Since when can they take decisions like that?" asked Niko.

"That *they* you just used, that includes me. You had a choice, you chose to delegate in the extreme, and this is what happens. We don't have a president or CEO to guide us, we have you off playing in your lab, losing track of time. What you brought back is cool, but it's not going to help us *today* or even soon. Our executive committee is running the show, and I can tell you, the board's not happy about it," said Sandra.

"Delegation was your idea," grumbled Niko.

"No, no, you don't get to drop that on me," said Sandra. "I *told* you that you needed to do something. You had to be here or delegate or *something*. You delegated, you delegated like you were bailing water out of a sinking ship. You wanted to run away and play inventor or explorer or whatever you feel like calling it? Fine, but there's a price to everything. Maybe you should just be the Chief Technical Officer and hand the CEO reins over to someone who will actually run the business."

She stopped and saw the pain of her words hit Niko. Her shoulders slumped and she shook her head. "I hate that you put me in this position Niko, but please, listen to me." She stopped and looked at Niko. He'd slid down in his chair, pulled his knees in and was staring off into space. He looked like the weight of the world had been dumped on him.

"Burgers?" he proposed.

Sandra stood, wincing at the suggestion. "I can't. We're going to be in that proposal meeting all afternoon." She tapped the table and looked at him. "You're losing control, Niko, but it's not too late. There are provisions in the delegation agreement you signed that says if the current CEO is present for thirty consecutive business days, then the agreement is voided. So make today count. Be here from now on."

She paused, hoping he would say something, but he didn't. "Niko, we're seeing sharks in the water, new competitors who *aren't* backed by Eversio. NanoCloud Five was *not* a home run. The features for Six will only add fuel to their fire. Fingers crossed we can make people feel some renewed faith with Seven, and that could bridge us to talking about the amazing, fantastic, unbelievable Nine you're planning."

Niko shook his head. "But the ideas for releasing Six and Seven, they're terrible."

"Then be here and make a difference. We don't know what else to do," she pleaded.

"You can't use focus group marketing like I'm sure Andre has been doing. People don't know what they want until you show them what you've done and only then do they say, 'oh that's what I wanted from the beginning!'"

Sandra closed her eyes and licked her lips. "And whose fault is that, Niko? You weren't here for *a single* planning meeting. Do you know how many video and text messages I sent you? Hundreds. How many—"

"I get it," he said, waving for her to stop. "Anyway, I know you're going to be fine with that committee document of yours."

"Actually, no, I'm not. I don't know what to write. You need to step up and be a part of that. I'm a builder, not a visionary. You envision, I build, that's been the partnership since day one. This document we need to put together, it needs vision. You need to be in that meeting and all the others until we are clear of this."

"They aren't going to listen to me," he said, pointing at the closed door. "I can't start there."

"But I'll listen to you."

Niko stared at the table, thinking. Biting his lip, he said, "I can't be here, Sandra. We need a home run, and I need to give us one. After I've done that, after I've got it stable, I'll be here. You have to hold the fort until then."

He stood up and glanced about the empty room which still felt hostile and icy. "I'll send you some ideas about the document. I'll reply to as many of your messages and voice calls as I can, but none of this matters if I can't make Nine solid."

"Niko—"

"That's the best I can offer right now, Sandra," he replied. "After I've nailed it, I'll be back."

Sandra looked at him for a long time before collecting her things. "Ready or not, we're going to need you here leading in weeks, not months. The board of directors isn't going to support this for much longer."

CHAPTER TEN

THE RETURN

Niko climbed aboard his scramjet, the door quickly sealing him in. Popping his ears, he gazed about the pristine, elongated cabin.

One of Tass' early paintings was on the front wall, another on the back. The table had a secured, transparent fruit bowl, restocked with some of his rare favorites, including a lone banana. The cushions on the couch were properly aligned, his oversized comfy chair where he always spent most of his time had been fluffed up, and he caught the faint whiff of cinnamon-scented cleaner.

Letting himself fall into the oversized chair, he stared out the window. He woke up his NanoCloud up, and waved to connect it to the plane's systems. "There we— wait, what? Connection dropped?" Niko grumbled and tried it again, then again. He tapped the holographic projector on, the entire cabin coming to life as his workspace. Opening several development windows, he pushed them from his lens-display into the holographic space around him. "Let's find out what I broke and why."

Several minutes went by before he found the culprit. He

pulled out a silver token from a pocket, activated it with his thumb, and motioned to connect to one of his vaults. He scowled at the error message that came back. "Connection not available? What the flood is happening today? Okay, give me a direct satellite connection." He rubbed his face in anger. "Seriously? Are there *no* satellites talking?" He closed his eyes and thought. "If I try to compile this with my NanoCloud, it'll take up to three hours, I'll go crazy by then." He got up grumbling, and glared at the holographic shapes and windows floating around.

Pulling a can of Ace out of the mini-fridge, he leaned against the cabin wall, thinking. Snapping his fingers, he brought up one of his diagnostic screens. "Please don't tell me I didn't fix that bug... Where is it? There's the comments about the over-saturation and hyper-density problem. Ah, good! Okay, and my current NanoCloud density is ninety-one percent."

Opening a cabinet, he ran his finger back and forth along the security pad of the mini-vault inside. He removed two dark-grey, translucent cans and checked the dates he'd scrawled on them. "New enough. My cloud will have reprogrammed them quickly enough. Okay, let's see if hyper-density can be a feature."

Grabbing two nozzles from a drawer and screwing them atop the cans, he then stood up straight and sprayed himself. Putting the spray cans away, he slapped his hands together, and dropped himself back into his seat. "NanoCloud density of two hundred and eighty... three hundred... three hundred and six percent. Okay. This should get the compilation done in fifteen to twenty minutes. No time like the present."

After instructing the NanoCloud to compile his code, he removed his shoes and massaged his aching feet. Some days he was feeling much older than a forty-year-old.

He went to pull up his virtual notebook when he stopped and laughed. "No point in stealing any computing power from the nanobots for that." He got up and grabbed a pen and paper he kept in a drawer for just such emergencies. Shaking out his sore hand, he jotted down his idea in barely legible scrawl, along with question marks about its potential value versus danger.

Sitting himself back down in the seat, he twisted it back and forth as he waited for the NanoCloud to finish its work. His thoughts went to KnowMe and how long it had been since he'd effectively told Sandra he needed just another minute before he'd return to the helm. Progress on NanoCloud Nine had been a lot slower than he'd hoped.

Over the past week as he'd been contemplating returning before things went from bad to worse, he'd been documenting all the areas of curiosity still remaining. His latest changes to the nanobots and management code had yielded interesting results, some of which seemed like errors at first but which he'd come to realize were incredible opportunities. He knew he couldn't trust that if brought to the company, they would be used responsibly, and so he'd have to make a decision shortly about what paths he'd seal off forever, removing any trace of their existence from his designs and documentation. Yet this vexed his curiosity, while appeasing his conscience.

"Done!" he yelled with a clap. "Okay, let's connect. Alright, hello AFS. How's my Automated Flight System today?"

"Good morning and welcome to the automated flight system," boomed an automated voice from the cabin speakers.

Niko winced and waved down the volume. "Let's just get in the air."

"Attempting to connect to local tower."

"And let's have no more talking," said Niko, switching the system to messages only. "Huh. I guess you can't connect to anything either. Twelve hours out of date? Whatever, we have a reserved flight path home regardless... Actually," he tapped the arms of his chair. "Change to the secondary reserved path, take me to the KnowMe office. No more procrastinating. I might as well start today. Nothing like some pressure to force me to figure out when I'm going to hand over parts of Nine..."

The cabin voice returned. "There are too many errors and concerns to allow for take-off."

Niko glared at the ceiling. "I told you to be quiet." With several swipes, he authorized a bypass and the engines boomed.

"Vertical take-off commencing."

"FINALLY!" he yelled.

The scramjet rumbled into the air, pushing Niko into his chair. As it leveled off and adopted the prescribed path, Niko lost himself in his work.

Ten minutes later, Niko was crouching down, playing with a holographic model with one hand and typing into a screen in the other when a message popped up. "Oh good, finally some ground center communication. Let's find out what— What the heck is that?" he said staring out the window. There was a column of brilliant red, yellow and white slicing through the sky.

"Emergency correction, invalid flight path," said the plane. The cabin's emergency red lighting came on, the holographic projector shut off, and a dull warning bell started repeatedly sounding.

"What the?" Niko tried to stand just as the scramjet banked hard and did a rapid ascent, sending him crashing into the wall and then into the table. The plane shook violently as it then dove hundreds of feet at a time.

Niko made a break for his chair and belted himself in. Sweating profusely, his heart pounding, he kept trying to pull up a screen, but his hands weren't steady enough.

"Primary systems offline. Secondary on… secondary…" said the AFS, its voice cutting out. The cabin went dark and the engines went silent. Niko felt his body being lifted gently. Fighting off the urge to panic, he took advantage of the still moment and brought up a utility screen. "AFS manual reboot… What the flood's the code? No, try this one. No… YES!" He cheered as he heard the engines kick back in. "AFS, emergency vertical landing! Anywhere!"

"Voice command accepted."

———————⟋———————

"Hey, anyone alive in there?" asked a gruff male voice from the open plane door. "I'm unarmed. I'm coming inside."

Niko slowly turned his chair around and stared blankly at the huge man making his way over. Niko swallowed and glanced about, his eyes not wanting to stay in one place. He couldn't feel his body.

The man came and squatted down beside him. "Can you understand me?" he asked, adjusting his thick-framed glasses. He had a stubbly face, and a mane of bushy, brown hair. His face had rough, red cheeks, likely from too much sun and wind.

Niko tried and failed to say anything. His head jerked as he nodded. He glanced down at his body, surprised to see it twitching and trembling.

"You're in shock. I'm going to unbuckle your seat-belt, now. Is that okay?"

Niko looked at his kind eyes and nodded. He swallowed again and stared about the cabin. The fruit had gone missing, but everything else seemed unchanged.

"Okay. Next we're going to get you out of here. Now, don't worry. Your plane landed intact. It burned a number of tents, but no one got injured." He took Niko's arm, put it around his neck, and helped get him to his feet. "You're cold and sweaty, that's a symptom of the shock."

As they stepped out of the plane, he put Niko down on the ground, and crouched down beside him. Niko gazed at the dozens upon dozens of people staring at them from a safe distance away. They looked like a misfit group assembled from history, some in dirty tatters and some looking like they'd left an office job days ago. Most of them stared at him with narrow eyes and scrunched up faces, the younger ones in particular.

"These are my people," said the man, pointing at them. "You scared them, well, all of us. And you burnt some of their tents to the ground."

"S...so... sorry," he mumbled, his face twitching.

"No one got hurt. Just some stuff got burnt." He patted Niko on the shoulder and walked off. "I'll be back."

Feeling the rough, charred ground, Niko searched the top of the tree line for signs of how the scramjet had come down. It didn't take long before he found the burnt path the secondary engines had left. He shook his head in disbelief.

The crowd had mostly dispersed by the time a girl with short, dark hair came over to him with a wooly blanket. As she left, he noticed she only had one arm. Frowning, he watched how they worked and organized. He couldn't believe at the number of tents which went on as far as he could see.

As the stranger headed back over to Niko, a woman called out to him. "Ray, I'll bring the soup over when it's ready."

"Thanks, love," he replied, making his way over to Niko and sitting back down beside him. "You probably heard, Gret. She's making something fresh." He squinted and pointed. "Over there, we've got three communal pots, big ones. We have them going pretty much around the clock these days."

Niko looked at him, his brow furrowed. "Thank you… Ray."

"I'm sure if I crashed in the middle of your living room, you'd have helped me too," he replied, making them both crack a smile. "How are you feeling?"

Niko blinked slowly and rubbed his face with a hand. In a delicate, whisper of a voice, he said, "My body feels numb and hurts at the same time. My mind feels like it's just barely working." He gazed at his shaking hands.

"It sounds like you're gradually getting back to normal."

Niko put his hands in his lap. His face contorted as he tried to resist the need to ask the question burning in his mind. Finally, it broke through and he turned to Ray, who was waving at the one armed girl as she ran by, playing. "Have you ever had a near death experience?"

Ray gave Niko a cold stare, and nodded. "Did you see something?"

After a moment of hesitation, Niko answered. "My friend, Yoshi. We went our separate ways after I created my company. I finally tried to find him two years ago, only to find out that he'd died in a tornado saving a pregnant lady or something."

Ray crossed his legs. "Did he say or do anything when you imagined seeing him?"

"Just him saving a lady, how I imagined it I guess."

"You know," said Ray, rolling up his stained, green sleeves and revealing his tattooed arms. "When I had mine, I saw my brother before he slipped through the ice. We were kids, I couldn't save him then, I couldn't save him when he flashed in front of me. I thought he was trying to torture me…" He grabbed some of the burnt dirt and crumbled it in his hands. "But a few days later, I had this feeling that he wanted me to let go. Not just of that bit of guilt, but everything. Just live without compromise. Not to apologize for who I was. Yeah, it causes some friction every now and then, but I've done things I never thought I could." He gestured to the tent city, "so I started this."

"Huh," said Niko, scanning about, a hint of a grin on his face. "You said no one got hurt, right?"

Ray nodded. "Some people were scared senseless. We don't usually have hi-tech planes come burning out of the sky. By the way, I've never seen those type of thrusters on a scramjet."

Niko raised an eyebrow at him.

"I used to be a science teacher, planes were a hobby of mine. I checked them out before coming in. After-market, but brilliantly made. Strictly emergency use, I take it?"

"Yeah. An idea I had years ago. Also made sure they were as mechanical as possible, and heavily shielded. In case of an electro-magnetic pulse."

"Wow, that was thinking ahead," said Ray.

"You want to know the irony? They were scheduled to be removed months ago. I kept delaying it. I don't know why." Niko clasped his hands and ran his index fingers along the middle of his forehead.

"Any other decisions you've been delaying in life?"

Niko narrowed his eyes. "What do you mean?"

"Sometimes in life, we're putting things on a table randomly. Then one day, a picture begins to form, and we realize we've been working on a puzzle the whole time."

"Huh," said Niko, staring at the greenery. "You seem to see life pretty clearly."

"It's the glasses," he replied tapping them.

Niko stoically shook his head.

Ray took them off and stared at them. "Without these, life's pretty blurry. I used to have contact lens technology, but they broke. If you're not in the system, you can't get more. A pair of glasses, though? At worst, it's a couple of days ride to find some."

Gazing about at the tall trees surrounding them, Niko asked, "Where am I?"

"A few miles outside of the Hershey ruins, in South Pennsylvania."

The one-armed girl carefully came up to them, holding a ceramic pot by its handle. She had a stained, homemade shirt with string in place of buttons at the top. With a smile, she handed over the pot, and pulled a spoon out of her pocket.

"Thanks, Mouni," said Ray.

She ran off.

Niko turned and looked at the scorched earth. "I'd like to pay for all the damage I caused."

"I appreciate the thought," said Ray, stroking his chin, "and I mean no offense, but money doesn't mean a lot to us. South Penny's pretty much ungoverned. We defend ourselves, feed ourselves, and we make our own clothes. We do pretty much everything ourselves. And what we don't have, we trade for."

"You're Foremans, aren't you?"

Ray rubbed his hands together and looked at Niko. "You've heard about us?"

"I read a lot," Niko replied, pulling on his beard. "I know you started up after the Flare..." he stopped and looked at the sky. "A flare, is that what I saw? I remember seeing something out the window."

"Yeah," said Ray. "I meant to ask you what the flood you were doing flying during a solar storm. I'd heard on the radio— yes, we have a radio. It's what keeps all of us connected. Anyway, they were talking about the beginning of the solar storm season and that there was a freak flare that was going to reach Earth. It hit somewhere in the Atlantic Ocean, thankfully. Didn't you hear about it?"

Niko stared at the ground and shrugged. "Maybe? I don't know. I've been so ruthlessly focused on trying to finish working on this project of mine before I have to take the helm back at my company, that it's possible. I went to visit my friend Yoshi's grave in hopes that I could find the answer I needed, but I didn't."

"Did you like doing the inventing stuff?" asked Ray.

Niko raised an eyebrow at him.

"I'm not a luddite, I know who you are. Took me a while to believe it, but the logo on the plane didn't hurt."

"Honestly? I live for it. I love how the world melts away, and nothing exists other than me, my tools and the data, and we're all just one and the same thing."

"You're in your zone and you don't want to leave, I get that. So why are you going back? Give someone else the reins. Go into your zone and stay there until you discover whatever it is you need to discover. Embrace it whole-heartedly."

Niko sighed and shook his head. "I can't do that."

"Because of your ego, or because of something else?"

"I made a commitment to someone. She's been taking the brunt of everything for me for a long time. I promised I would come back. The company's a mess right now."

"So go back, fix it up, hand it all off, and then return to what you love. You said you were being ruthless before, but it doesn't sound like you were. You had too much going on and trying to do too much. You're only human."

Niko twitched.

"It's true, even you. We all have limits," said Ray.

He looked away.

Sighing, Ray put the small pot of soup in front of Niko. "Eat up, I'll be back in a bit. We'll have you on your way once you're ready."

Niko watched Ray leave and then cautiously sampled the chicken noodle soup. With a kid's smile, he dug into it. He observed how everyone moved with purpose, occasionally giving him a curious glance. For every task, an extra pair of hands appeared. Children helped parents and neighbors fold clothes, grandparents drew children to them when adults needed to do other tasks. Watching everyone cooperate made him realize how unnecessarily complex his nanobot cooperation algorithms were, and how complex he'd made his life.

When Ray returned, he picked up the pot and smiled. "Wow, I wasn't sure you'd get to the bottom of it. How do you feel?"

Niko looked up at him and sighed. "I feel okay."

"Care to stand?" he said, offering his hand and helping get Niko to his feet.

"It was good, thanks. Listen, I remember reading that

Foremans are always short on sugar or salt, or something along those lines. Can I offer that as my thanks?"

Ray hesitated and looked away. "We shoot drones and like our privacy. Can you get it here by person?"

"Yeah. It wouldn't be a ton, but enough to make a difference. I'd include some replacement tents and blankets for the ones I destroyed," said Niko.

Scratching his chin, Ray nodded. "Okay, then some sugar would be greatly appreciated. We regularly trade for salt, but sugar's been a bit harder to come by lately for some reason."

"Great," said Niko.

"You look like something's still weighing on you."

Niko nodded. "I realized when I go back, I have to stop all my research. Moreover, I have to hide any signs of the avenues I haven't completely explored yet. I watched what they did in my absence, and I don't trust them."

Ray folded his arms. "Hmm. Well, what about the *screw them* strategy?"

"Screw them?"

"Yeah. You're the boss, so screw them. We always tell the kids: *you get what you get and you don't get upset*."

Niko laughed. "I don't think that'll work at KnowMe."

"Well, what about telling them about two or three paths you've explored, and giving them crumbs about a few others that you've *also* explored. You'd have time then to explore the other stuff, right? You'd still be doing a crazy amount of work, and I'm sure the frustration level would mount quickly, but you might buy yourself enough time to get everything under control so that you can then hand it over to someone."

"Huh," replied Niko, tugging on his beard. "Is that something you do with your kids?"

"Actually, it's what my mom used to do with me. I picked up a few things."

Niko offered his hand. "Thanks. I think I can head home... well, to the office now."

Ray smiled and shook his hand.

"Come in," yelled Sandra without looking at the door. She was standing with her back to the door, manipulating models and objects. "I've only got five minutes, so you better make it quick."

"Hi."

Lowering her arms and spinning around, Sandra stared in disbelief. "Niko?"

"Hey."

Brushing her long brown hair back over her shoulders, she shook her head. "Now's not really a good time to drop by. We've got a strategy meeting in five minutes."

"Great, I'll come," said Niko.

Sandra straightened her suit jacket and looked him up and down. "Niko, we don't dress like that anymore, and you know that. Plus, I don't think that's a good idea to just randomly drop in."

He stepped forward, his head bowed. Looking at her in the eyes, he said, "I'm not dropping in. I'm coming back, as of right now. You've held down the fort for me long enough. I'm back. I want to come."

She leaned back and rubbed her forehead. "Wow, really? Now? That's… great." She smiled at him. "Does that mean that you finished Nine?"

"No, but it's advancing. I'll start sharing some of the base design, plans and features in the next few weeks. Does that work for you?"

"Ah… yeah," she replied standing straight.

"Oh, one sec," said Niko. Sandra stared at him confused as he gestured. "Sorry, I had to send a shipment of sugar to someone."

"What?"

"Never mind. Shall we go to the meeting?"

She straightened her jacket. "Sure… and I guess, welcome back."

CHAPTER ELEVEN

INSTITUTIONS

Two Months Later

Niko stepped out of the auto-taxi at the end of the cemetery, and watched as it drove off. He gestured to shut off all alerts and messages, wanting to be present and alone for Phoebe's father's funeral.

The past two months had taxed him to his limit, as he fought his way back into the minds of his executives at KnowMe. Being present full-time was a painful distraction, but a seemingly necessary one. While his days were spent running the company, his nights were devoted to Nine. He felt like he'd set fire to his inner candle at both ends, and then thrown it in the oven.

He wrapped the red scarf Phoebe sent him as a birthday gift around his neck, and dug his gloved hands into the deep pockets of his brown trench coat. The clouds were moody, and were drizzling cold Seattle October over him.

Ahead was a sizable crowd of mourners, everyone dressed in their traditional best. He was happy for Phoebe that her father had warranted a good turnout. Niko had only met Eric a few times, but he liked him. Eric's sharp mind and sharper sense of humor were difficult to forget.

While Niko had forgotten to reply to Phoebe's invitation to attend the funeral, he'd made absolutely sure he was going to be there. He'd booked his calendar with all day private meetings, three deep immediately upon getting the invite. Only when he'd boarded the scramjet did he begin getting insistent requests to join meetings that he didn't really need to attend. Some were keeners hoping to impress the big boss, while others were plots by members of his executive team trying to overwhelm him and force him out. He'd promised himself not to do anything drastic for ninety days, but each day was proving to be a real challenge.

Standing at the back of the crowd, he listened to Phoebe's speech and the soft music in the background. Somehow the light rain fit right in.

While Niko knew that Phoebe wouldn't be surprised to see him, he knew she'd still have that electric smile that always made him lose his train of thought.

Niko glared at the video call request that appeared before him. He walked away from the crowd, swiped the air, and braced himself for what Sandra needed him for.

"Niko, you need to be in the exec meeting this afternoon. We need details on Nine, beyond the rough outline you gave."

He massaged his aching hands. "Not going to happen.

I'm in Seattle."

Sandra's face twisted in confusion. "What are you doing in Seattle?"

"What's so important about the exec meeting? We meet twice a week; I think I can miss one."

"Not this one," she said.

"Why?"

She rubbed her forehead and glanced down at him. "Look, you're on a roll. Missing this one will just set things back."

He played with his neat, short hair. "Sorry to disappoint you, Sandra."

"We need to know what's happening with Nine, in detail. The written overview you gave, and the models, they're nice and everything but it's not going to help us get moving on it."

He rubbed his temples. "They aren't *for* that. There are still some glitches I need to work out. Important ones."

"There will always be bugs," threw back Sandra. "We need to get moving on things, and soon."

He stared at the peaceful surrounding. "Finish getting ready for the quick NanoCloud Seven release and then we'll talk. You need to give me a bit more time."

"You keep saying that."

"Well that's because it's true! I'm *not* going to put something out there that—" he stopped himself. "I know that look on your face, you don't believe me that this is really coming together, do you?"

She shrugged. "You've not given me or anyone anything new in a long time. Feature ideas, yes. Enough to buy you some more time with the board, yes—"

"Me? Don't you mean us?" asked Niko, stopping Sandra in her tracks.

"Us, of course."

"Sandra, what's going on?"

"Nothing. You did like you promised and returned and while you did do the Six launch, Andre thinks you did more damage than good without doing a *one more thing* moment."

"There wasn't anything else," said Niko gesturing wildly. "There was barely anything to celebrate, but we did, and that's it."

She sighed and leaned towards the camera on her holo-screen. "I'm stuck. My developers are finishing up with Seven already, and there's not that much on the menu for Eight right now. They'll be done before we know it, and then what? I need something to give me some faith, Niko."

He grimaced at her plea. He'd never heard her like that before, and it bothered him. "Fine."

"By the way, we just got the response back from the committee. In brief, the military contract issue is on the agenda for the next board meeting."

"Great…" replied Niko. He moved his fingers and stared at the swollen knuckles. "The weather here in

Seattle's something else. Makes me feel old."

Silence.

"Niko, are you going to give me something? Can you at least tell me if you solved the robustness issue? Last time you said you had them lasting two minutes, that sounded great, but that was weeks ago."

Niko was silent.

"I know you solved the robustness issue. You wouldn't —"

He ended the call.

She immediately called back.

He mulled over what to do. He'd come to attend the funeral, not get sucked away from it, back into KnowMe business. With a heavy sigh, he answered it.

"What the hell, Niko?" snapped Sandra.

"Just look at where I am," he said, turning all of his nanobots to capture the surroundings.

"What are you doing at... wait, this is full body video. Oh... oh wow, Niko. This is amazing. The fidelity, the..." Sandra reached out to touch the image. "This is even better than old world video. How did you... wait, is that a funeral?"

"It is, and I'm missing it talking to you. Now you know where I am, why I don't want to be bothered, and I'll take that wow as confirmation of faith restored. For the record, my NanoCloud density didn't drop at all. Bye." He vigorously swiped the call away. "Why do I feel like you're going to run off and tell everyone about this, Sandra?"

All of a sudden he felt a sharp shock throughout his body and lost his balance. "Geezes! What was that?" he mumbled, glancing around, catching himself on all fours. There was nothing close to him.

An error message popped up on his lens-display: *Connection to Host lost - Niko coding note - No one should ever see this error message in real life because the only possible way for this to happen is for them to be dead. Just putting it in here for defensive coding purposes. I mean really, dead people don't see messages!*

Niko felt cold with sweat and fought off a coughing fit as he got back to his feet. A second later, the lens-display reset and showed everything as normal. Niko pulled up the logs, and found nothing. He slapped his chest a few times and felt better.

Wiping his forehead, he stared longingly at the crowd gathered; he felt like he was on a different planet entirely. Fishing a silver token out of his pocket, he removed a glove and activated it. He watched as his NanoCloud made a secure connection to his personal data and computing vault sitting at the bottom of the Mediterranean Sea.

Waving off a call from Sandra, he searched through gigabytes of programming code for where the error message appeared. Angrily, he dismissed another call from Sandra and pushed on. Finally, he found it. Meticulously and methodically, he went through every path in the code and checked every condition to see what could make the error message actually appear.

"There's nothing. This shouldn't have happened," he said to himself, his hands behind his head as he paced about. He squinted up at the drizzling sky, searching for inspiration. "Maybe the new nanobots aren't strong enough? Or I'm losing connection from them? But then there would have been an error listed in the NanoCloud diagnostics log. Protocol error? Interference?" He glanced around. "Not likely interference here." He caught a glimpse of the crowd and remembered why he was there.

He walked back up and listened to the end of Phoebe's speech. She had such a way with words. His head bowed, he listened to her share memories of her father and their vacations in Vermont, just outside Burlington. He shifted from foot to foot, fighting off memories of the last funeral he'd attended, the one for his parents and brother.

His mind quieted and his heart lightened as Phoebe ended her speech, noticed him, and smiled.

———————

As storm clouds began rolling in, Phoebe finished thanking the last of the funeral attendees and made her way up to Niko. Her long, dark blonde hair was down, framing her square jaw and letting her brown eyes capture his attention. Her black three-quarter length coat was cinched at the waist.

"That was a great speech," he said with a boyish smile.

"Thanks for coming," she said, giving him a hug,

wiping her eyes. "I was starting to wonder if you were going to make it. He liked you, you know."

"I know. But even if he didn't, I'd have come."

She tugged on her beaded, brown string necklace.

Niko chuckled, eyebrows up. "I'm surprised you still have that thing."

"This?" She pulled on the necklace. "I've got a mile of replacement string and about hundred replacement beads."

"Huh," said Niko tilting his head.

"Huh, what, smart guy?"

"I didn't realize you believed in reincarnation."

She stared at him stunned. "You got that, from this?"

He nodded. "Am I right?"

She frowned. "I just bring it back, a bit different each time. It reminds me of my mother. You know, there are times where you can even weird me out, Niko." She took his hand and they walked. "On a different topic, thank you for the birthday card. Every year I'm surprised to find that the *master of technology* is sending me a piece of shredded tree with dirty black markings on it, by courier-drone, from somewhere on the planet."

"You really know how to kill the sentimental element," he replied, fake scowl. "I hated that master of technology nonsense article… can we finally let it go? It was years ago."

She poked him. "Never! It's one of the few things that make your cheeks go red that's not—"

"Listen..." he turned to her, taking her hands. "I'm... I wanted to..." he stopped and bit his lip. "I think we need to go to the reception area."

She nodded, shrugging away her confusion.

"Why did you break up with me back in College?" asked Niko, breaking past his anxiety.

"Ah..." She glanced at him and then at the building they were approaching. Immediately she was taken back to the conversation with her father, where he'd advised her to end the relationship with Niko. He'd talked at length about how Niko was going to be a man of history, and if he was going to become who he needed to be, she had to leave him be. She'd never mentioned to him how challenging Tasslana had made things, and so it was easy to accept his reasons as her own, whether or not she believed them. "I don't really remember. I'm glad you're here now though."

They entered the reception hall to discover it empty, except for two trays of food. "Crapster," said Phoebe, bowing her head. "I don't think I mentioned this on the invite."

Niko motioned in the air, bringing up the invite, and regrettably confirmed her suspicion.

"I guess it's a good thing that I only paid for the most modest catering package," said Phoebe. "The speech did run a little long. If ever I do that again, I'll make sure to watch the time."

Niko smiled and shook his head. "You spoke from the

heart. Just do that, don't think about the time. Anyhow, given that there's no one here, how about we go for coffee?"

She let his arm go and checked the time on her lens-display. Scratching the top of her head, she raised her shoulders and said, "I'm not sure, Niko. I think—"

"I'm just asking to have coffee," he said with a certainty she'd not heard before. "Really?" He quickly waved off yet another call from Sandra.

A curious expression crept across her face. "Coffee where?" she asked.

"In Burlington," he replied, with a wry smile. "I have the scramjet ready. And in case you're wondering, I double checked to make sure that there are no solar storms or anything today."

Phoebe raised an eyebrow at him.

Niko and Phoebe silently stepped out of the auto-taxi. Before them was a six story, glass office building surrounded by lush, leafy forest. The hum of the auto-taxi was quickly over-taken by the chirping of birds.

"You've been pretty quiet since we took off," said Niko. "I was hoping the fresh, clean air here would revitalize you."

Phoebe shrugged. "I don't know. I guess I just hadn't had a quiet moment to myself. You looked kind of busy and distracted, so… I just enjoyed the quiet."

Niko smiled. "I get it."

"Do you travel like that all the time? My brain's feeling all... I don't know. We were at the cemetery in Seattle an hour ago, and now we're here."

"Yeah," replied Niko. "It's highly efficient and... it changes your perception of time, among other things. It makes me wonder what teleportation would be like."

Phoebe stared at the shiny new building, and its wonderful gardens. There were the four standard parking spots, all empty. "What is this place? It doesn't exactly look like a cafe."

"Oh, there's coffee inside. I know because I swept through it with a drone before releasing the contractors."

She furrowed her brow. "You own this building? Why did—"

He raised a finger and then lead her gaze to the name on the building.

"The Eric Collins Research Institute of Advanced Immunology? What?" She stared at him. "What is this?"

Niko massaged his hands as he paced about. "I felt that we keep drifting towards each other and then apart, and I realized that that might never change, but your work... your work is important. When I heard that your father got sick, it gave me an idea, so I found this building, had it renovated and well..." He snapped his fingers. Suddenly, the deed, legal contracts, a five-year budget, a full bank account, and other materials appeared on her lens-display.

"Woo..." She took a step back. "Woo, Niko. I—"

"I'd hoped that it would be ready before he died... but honestly, I lost track of time. I know how much he meant to you, and how he inspired you. You've been doing great work at the federal labs but I know whenever you mention work, there's frustration in your voice. Now, you call the shots, as you want."

Phoebe's eyebrows slowly raised.

"You own the building, the research institute, and you have an endowment fund which will give you enough money every year without having to chase donations, provided the investment portfolio stays balanced."

Phoebe wiped her mouth in disbelief. "And what about... you?" she asked, squinting.

"No interference. All the money is secured and severed from me, and I have no representation on the board of directors if you choose to have one. This is yours, and honestly, I don't want anyone knowing about it."

She touched his arm as she took it all in. "Why here? Why not in Seattle?"

"Apart from the frequent riots and the constant threat of being washed away in the torrential rains? You've told me many times about your trips here with your dad. You even mentioned it in your speech today. And I thought, maybe you'd be happier here. Is that goofy?" He cringed.

She raised an eyebrow. "It's sweet actually. But you didn't just stop there, did you?"

He chuckled. "Ah. I might have done some research

into the area."

"Some?" she asked, raising an eyebrow.

He grinned. "For me, some. Others might have considered it a touch on the obsessive side. Turns out, the state government has worked hard to recover from the floods and fires over ten years ago, but are chronically under-funded and under-skilled. The two universities are solid, potentially world class, but likewise, under-funded. I made an offer to the governor, and yesterday presented to the legislature. I've taken several billion out of my pocket and am putting it towards a number of projects, including creating what I've nicknamed Startup Strip. I've even leased space here. I'm figuring maybe I'll use it for a KnowMe research center or something, I haven't decided yet."

Phoebe smiled at him uncomfortably. "So you're going to be working out of that office all the time?"

Niko didn't follow. "No, I work out of my home in Connecticut... Oh, OH, you figured this was a ploy. Ah, no. I just figured if an institute like yours is going to have a sufficient skill pool, you're going to need complementary high education and high skill—"

"It wouldn't have been a bad thing," she said, taking his hand. "And I get it, you were thinking bigger picture. Huge picture, actually. So now what?"

"We go in. Oh, one thing," said Niko. "No NanoClouds beyond version three allowed until I tell you otherwise."

Phoebe raised an eyebrow. "Why?"

"Personal paranoia. I'll write whatever additional software you need, but not beyond three, okay? Just trust me, please?"

"Okay. So what do we do with people who have a newer one?"

"Zero them, respray with the version Three that I'll make sure you have plenty of."

"Is that even in production anymore?"

"Not really."

"You made a factory somewhere?" she asked, glancing around.

"Something like that," he said, wincing and rubbing his hands together.

"Everything okay? You look in pain."

"I'm fine. Just a bit stiff and sore, that's all."

Phoebe studied Niko's face. Finally, she sighed, and turned back to stare at the building's sign bearing her father's name. "I can't believe you did this. Does it actually have a working coffee machine?"

"Working? Oh, I didn't test it. Never thought of that," he replied with a wink.

CHAPTER TWELVE
THE HEARING

Two Months Later

Niko stared out the limo window at the steps up to the new senate building. His lawyer was seated beside him, talking away with his colleagues back at the firm, trying to get any last minute information about what to expect from the committee hearing they were about to step into.

The camera-drones were hovering just outside, waiting to capture every glimpse of Niko as he walked into the building. Every moment would be torn apart by commentators looking to elevate themselves, none of them likely concerned with the real matters at hand. He was thankful that the question and answer session, as it was officially being labeled, wouldn't be open to the media.

He brushed his forearms, wincing at the sensitivity of his skin below the layers of his coat, sweater and shirt. Pulling out a sleek little pillbox, he expertly removed another painkiller and took it, washing it down with a swig of Ace.

His lawyer's expression concerned him. Beads of sweat

were forming on the man's forehead, and they hadn't even set foot in the building. Niko's stomach tightened.

With a few quick gestures, he brought up the video message of support he'd received from Phoebe that morning. It was a warm reminder of how things had changed in recent weeks. He then pulled up Tass' photo stream. Every half hour for the past day she'd been sending him silly old photos, making him chuckle or laugh outright.

Waving it all away, he turned to his lawyer. "Are you ready?"

The lawyer motioned for another minute, ended the call and nodded.

"You look nearly panicked," said Niko.

"I think we're going to be okay. Just, stick to the simplest answers you can give," replied his lawyer.

Niko took a good look at his lawyer. Despite only being in his thirties, he had streaks of silver around the temples. His very short haircut and clean shaven face, his perfectly set y-split tie and sharp collar, all spoke to a need to control everything. "Are you sure?" asked Niko.

"Yeah, we're good." The lawyer opened the door and headed quickly for the entrance of the senate building.

Niko issued a few sharp gestures, bringing up a menu of experimental features. He selected Image Privacy and stepped out of the limousine. Immediately the camera-drones swarmed him, and errors erupted on his diagnostics screen.

"Crapster," he muttered, swiping away his display. He glared at the camera-drones as he made his way to the peaceful sanctuary of the building's vestibule.

Entering the inner set of doors, he took a moment to appreciate the lobby. The marble and opulence were over the top for him and his views on government spending, but it had a sense of grandness that he appreciated. The walls were covered in paintings capturing the burning of the National Mall in the riots of thirty years ago and in the process of being rebuilt. Along the walls stood soldiers at the ready, with security-drones hovering along the high ceiling.

Niko stared at the blue carpet that led to the inner-chamber. He glanced about, curious if they'd made any changes to the scanners and security measures he'd helped improve as part of the contract KnowMe had with the government. Grudgingly, he shut down his NanoCloud and walked the gauntlet.

Entering the hearing chamber, Niko noted several people sitting in the audience area. He put a hand up, stopping his lawyer and nodded at them. "No one's supposed to be here."

His lawyer shrugged. "I… I don't know. I'll call—"

Niko shook his head. "You can't. Your NanoCloud's blocked in here."

"Oh," replied the lawyer, glancing about. "I… I didn't realize that."

Niko frowned, wondering why he'd been sent with a rookie. He'd have to make a point of talking with their new general counsel.

Walking up to the unexpected attendees, Niko kept trying to figure out who the woman in the middle was. It was clear she was surrounded by a small contingent of lawyers and two corporate types, but she had a presence that he could sense even from behind. She had short auburn hair, dangling earrings, and was dressed in a power suit.

As he stepped past, she turned to him and said, "Hello Niko."

He nearly tripped. "Harry," he said continuing passed. Arriving at the witness table, he turned his furious gaze on his lawyer. "Listen very carefully," he growled. "I need to understand why Harriet Binger from Eversio is here, and how the hell she's allowed to be here."

There was something in his lawyer's eyes that betrayed surprise.

"I—"

"Save it," said Niko, turning to look at the committee behind their grand bench, as if they needed greater height and a safe distance from which to hurl judgement onto those they'd called before them.

At the center of the panel committee was the familiar face of their chair. Founder of the New Founders party, it was like she'd taken the best pages out of the disruptive political movements of the past hundred years, and followed them to a tee. Senator Liza Franklin had gone from activist, to senator, to junior member of the committee on Public Technologies and Homeland Affairs, to its chair in remarkable time. Recently she'd been on a quest to break the backs of the large government contracts. Most famously, she'd led the charge to seize the patents and designs from a weapons manufacturer who refused to lower their prices. He could see she was ready and eager to take on world famous KnowMe next.

Fumbling his hands to grab the back of his chair, Niko took his seat. He kept stopping himself from turning around to see if Harriet was really sitting there, watching. He wondered if she was enjoying the irony of him having been called before the committee that he'd helped put in place. At first the committee he'd advocated for had been used to make sure that all deals were in the public interest, but more and more, it had become a cudgel for political grandstanding.

He gazed up at Senator Franklin, sitting at the center of the panel. Her grey hair had streaks of white, and appeared more sculpted than styled. She kept glancing down at him between laughs and comments she made to her colleagues. Her laughs were precise, her gestures sharp.

She jangled her silver bracelets in front of the razor thin microphone in front of her. "Are we on? Everyone ready to go?" Her colleagues nodded.

Niko wrinkled his nose at the completely unnecessary

actions. He glanced around the room, wondering how many artifacts of bygone eras should be part of the day.

The senator looked to her left, then turned and smiled to her right. She quickly went through introducing members of the panel. "Alright, let's commence. First, I'd like to put forward a motion to use our informal process. This has been working well for us recently. Do I have a second?"

"Seconded," said a senator on the far end.

"It is now put to a vote. All in favor?" she asked. It was unanimously supported. "Excellent, so noted. Now, let's get down to business." She turned her attention to Niko. Her expression melted from cordial to that of an eagle spotting prey.

"I'd like to welcome Doctor Niko Rafaelo and thank him for *finally* coming to answer for why his company has been so negligent in providing the United States government with essential information pertaining to the safety of its citizens."

Niko glanced at his lawyer, who was silent. He whispered to him. "Isn't that prejudicial or something?"

"Do you want me to say something?" he whispered back.

The senator cleared her throat. "I'll remind everyone in the room that these proceedings, given the informal process, are not subject to recording or transcription. We're after a defined set of next steps, not capturing who said what along the way. That being said, we're going to speak freely here, Doctor Rafaelo. This avoids the need to have your lawyer popping up every three seconds like a sales coupon on Black Friday."

Niko grimaced and slowly stood.

She scowled at Niko. "I thought I just—"

"Sorry, Senator Franklin, there's one thing that's troubling me. I was led to believe that this meeting was going to be private." Niko glanced back at Harriet and her team. "Why are they here?"

The senator scoffed. "Doctor Rafaelo, I have a notification here from your company requesting them to be here." She waved a tablet.

Niko frowned. "May I see that?"

The senator sighed and steepled her fingers. "Doctor Rafaelo, it is not the purpose of this committee to help you identify communication problems within your organization."

"But I'd like at least to validate its authenticity," he pressed.

"*Doctor* Rafaelo. Please sit down. Your internal matters are your own," she replied, the corner of her mouth turning up.

Niko was tempted to turn his NanoCloud on and get to the bottom of it. Glancing up at the heavy-duty security-drones, he wasn't willing to chance them instantly reacting.

He couldn't imagine anyone at KnowMe requesting or

authorizing the presence of Binger and her team. Niko turned to his lawyer. "Did you know about this?"

The lawyer shook his head.

"Are you here to help or hinder me?" he asked, glaring.

"I'm sorry, I wasn't supposed to be here. I got called in to substitute this morning. I'm here to help."

Niko bit his lip and shook his head. He was definitely going to need to have words with his general counsel, as well as others. "Either do the job I'm paying you for, or leave."

The senator cleared her throat. "Doctor Rafaelo, can we get things moving? We do have a schedule to keep." She folded her arms and leaned on the judicial bench.

Niko held his gaze on the lawyer. "We're ready, Madame Chair."

"Excellent, counsellor. Now, Doctor Rafaelo, you were granted the immense privilege of providing this country with state of the art nano-technology several years ago. Recently, it seems that this privilege isn't taken with the seriousness that it should be."

"I take it very seriously," replied Niko.

The senator smiled at him and then her colleagues. "That's great to hear, because the response sent back from the KnowMe team was grossly inadequate. Though I was not here at the time, I went back and read the proposal you originally authored, and it was very extensive. If that was a master's thesis, then this was kindergarten scribbling. It wasn't lost on any of us that though your name was in the list of authors, there wasn't a hint of your usual style or insight. The information we received about your recent NanoCloud Seven release was even worse."

Niko was about to say something when she continued. "The objective here is not to give platitudes or get apologies. The objective here is to get down to the needs of our country. If you cannot provide us with a clear and meaningful understanding of where your NanoCloud technology is going, here, today, then we will need to take the necessary steps to protect our people. Do you understand?"

Niko hung his head, his tongue running along his top teeth. He thought of the number of times he'd asked Sandra and Andre to send him the final document before it went out the door, and how they'd told him to wait for someone else's comments first and then came the apologies that it had already been submitted.

He rubbed his temples and nodded at the senator.

"Now, we have a litany of questions we'd like to ask."

"Please," replied Niko, gesturing for them to go ahead.

The next two hours were filled with questions that required him to meticulously manage his wording so as not to give anything away. Some questions were well beyond the technical ability of the committee, while others were clearly about committee members trying to seem engaged or relevant.

Each time Niko glanced over at his lawyer, he shook his head. Every point he tried to raise, every question he tried to deflect, it failed. Niko rubbed his eyes and leaned back.

"Are we boring you Doctor Rafaelo?" asked the panel chair.

"Actually, no. I'm tired, and this feels more like you're trying to get me to reveal trade secrets to a woman who has tried to go head to head with me several times," he snapped before realizing his exhaustion had tricked him into speaking his mind. He rubbed his mouth and shook his head, wondering what to expect.

"What my client is trying to say—"

"Save it, counsellor," said Senator Franklin. "Your issues with Ms. Binger has nothing to do with this meeting."

"Actually, it has everything to do with it," said Niko. "I should have realized what this was about." He stood up and paced about, shifting his gaze back and forth between the senators and the floor.

Senator Franklin straightened up and pointed at Niko's chair. "Would you please—"

He stopped and raised his hand requesting a moment. "You want proof that this isn't all hand-waving."

"Yes," said the senator.

He gently rubbed the skin on the back of his hand. "Okay, I'll show you something, but they leave." He nodded at Harriet and her contingent.

"Need I remind you that—"

"That's my offer, Senator Franklin. I don't care who put whatever you've got there together, I'm not sharing this in front of them. I will forfeit the contract first."

The senator leaned back, an impressed grin creeping on to her face. "I'll need to confer with my colleagues for a moment."

Niko shot a glare at Harriet, who was surrounded by her team as they attempted to counter him. He turned to his lawyer. "Pack up your things."

"Why? I thought you said you were going to—"

"I am, but you're not going to be here for it. You can head back."

"But—"

Niko looked at the ornate ceiling and sighed. "But nothing. You're going, or your fired. Either way, you're not going to be here for this."

The lawyer slowly picked up his tablets and put them in his leather case, and left.

"Doctor Rafaelo, everything okay with your counsel?" asked Senator Franklin returning to her seat.

"Did you come to a decision?" he asked.

"Yes, and we came to the conclusion that it is in the national interest to see if there's *anything* of potential interest in what you have to offer. If there isn't, then we'll be able to take more immediate action to attempt to address the issue. You realize, this is an all or nothing moment."

"I do," said Niko, leaning against the table. While the

room was cleared out, he popped another painkiller and took a slouch in his seat.

"Doctor Rafaelo? Doctor Rafaelo?" repeated Senator Franklin, annoyed.

"Sorry?"

"You seemed to have drifted off. We're ready for the demonstration."

He stood up and bit his lip. He squeezed both of his hands, and transfixed on the heavy duty security-drones, he brought his NanoCloud to life.

The committee watched as he moved his hands and arms as if he was conducting an orchestra, until he finally stopped and dropped them at his sides.

"And are you now warmed up?" asked Senator Franklin with a chuckle. "That was—"

He closed his eyes and pushed the air with a finger. All of a sudden each of the senators jumped backwards.

Niko opened his eyes. "That message that you're all seeing? You're seeing that because I've just taken over all of your NanoClouds." He licked his lips and stared at the ground. "And they," he pointed at the drones overhead, "haven't even detected that I have a NanoCloud. Is this sufficient proof that what I'm working on is of national interest?"

The senators nodded.

Hesitating for a moment, he then went through a series of quick gestures and finished it as if he was waving dust away. A sigh of relief spread through the committee as the message disappeared.

"That seemed a bit elaborate," said Senator Franklin.

"That wasn't for returning control, that was for frying my NanoCloud."

"Excuse me, Doctor Rafaelo?" Senator Franklin leaned forward. "You did what?"

He tapped on the table and glanced around. "I'm familiar with your policies and protocols. It was the only thing to do to ensure that you don't try to confiscate my property, and to put you at ease that I don't have anything related to any of your clouds. I'm just... me, now. You can scan me if you like."

The senator stared at him, thinking. The edges of her mouth pointed downward. She glanced at her colleagues and then turned back to him. "No, I think the standard exit protocols will suffice. We appreciate your... thoroughness. Have a good rest of the day, Doctor Rafaelo."

"Thank you," said Niko.

As he got to the end of the blue carpet, an alert popped up on his lens-display.

"Are you okay sir?" asked one of the soldiers stepping forward as Niko nearly fell over.

Niko glanced at him and stabilized his balance. "Thanks. Just... I guess I misstepped or something." There, in front of his eyes, was the message: *NanoCloud Density at 15%.*

"Sir, you're not looking well. Do you need medical attention?" The soldier put his hand on Niko's shoulder and looked him in the eye. He must have been half Niko's age.

Niko moved his body out from under the man's hand, and shivered as his body went slick with icy cold sweat. "I'm okay." He moved as if in slow motion, his mind going in a million different directions. His NanoCloud had been instructed to self-destruct.

"Can I call you a vehicle sir? There aren't any waiting outside, and there are several riots going on in the area."

Niko was about to answer when another alert popped up: *NanoCloud Density at 16%*.

"Sir?"

Niko nodded and stared at the floor.

CHAPTER THIRTEEN

REACHING OUT

Phoebe stepped out of her old truck and reached over to grabbed her homemade coffee, smiling at the dog blanket in the passenger seat. Carefully heaving her leather bag with her tablet and set of papers on her shoulder, she nudged the door closed with her hip and headed along the path to the doors. As always, she gave a wink to the sign with her father's name on it.

Driving to work every day in her great grandfather's truck reminded her of all the great times she'd spent working on it growing up; at first, playing inside while her father and grandmother worked on it, and then just with her dad when she got old enough. Bit by bit, everything had been replaced and replaced again. It only had a few pieces of electronics in it, everything else was truly archaic, but she could print the parts she needed at home and loved the independence of it.

She walked through the three other, eternally empty, parking spots, wondering why Niko had made four of them. Few people in the entire state were rich enough to own personal vehicles, and there were only maybe a dozen who, like her, had inherited ones.

A gust of wind tried to steal some of the papers out of her bag, but she expertly maneuvered her body, shielding them. Another rain storm was probably coming, but she didn't mind. It kept everything green and fresh, probably much like the lost state of California had been once upon a time.

Her mind turned to the million and one things that she needed to get on top of. It helped that she came in at six sharp every morning, giving her a few hours to tackle issues in peace before her team started showing up.

She caught a glimpse of a shadowy figure and jumped back, nearly spilling her coffee. "Niko? You scared the living daylights out of me."

"Sorry." His shoulders drawn up, his face looked pale and pained. "I... ah... I need your... Can we talk?"

Phoebe stared at him. His expression immediately took her back to their college days. "Sure, come on," she said with a soothing lilt to her voice. "Have you seen a doctor? You don't look good." She continued heading for the entrance.

Niko followed. "I've seen one that I trust, but this is already beyond him. I need to keep this very quiet."

She glanced over at him, trying to decipher what he meant. "Does Tass know you're here?"

He shook his head.

"If she finds out, she's going to blame me."

"No, she won't," replied Niko.

"Yes, she will. Just stand up for me when she does, okay?" she asked with a smile.

Niko nodded.

As they entered the lobby of the building, only the trickle of the entrance waterfall and their footsteps kept them company. With a well-practiced rhythm, Phoebe made short work of the translucent stairs as she headed up to her third floor office. She allowed herself to steal a glance at Niko as he moved slowly. "What have you done to yourself, Niko?" she muttered to herself.

Stepping into her office, she awoke her holo-screen. She sat down and noted that the little box she kept her lens-display contact lenses in was dusty, a reminder of how much she disliked them. Pulling up her calendar for the day, she sighed with relief that there was nothing critical planned. She cleared everything else, blocked her entire day, and instructed the glass walls of her office to darken.

She moved over to the small conference table at the edge of her office and looked up, expecting to see Niko at the doorway. Her heart sank as she saw him half-way down the hall, struggling with each step.

Resisting the urge to shepherd him to the chair, she pretended to be preoccupied until he sat down. "Oh, that was quick," she said.

"That's a bit much, even for you, Phoebe," he replied. "Though, I appreciate the sentiment."

"I saw you on the news two days ago, going into a big senate hearing. I don't usually pay attention to the news, but it sounded important. How did it go?"

Niko closed his eyes and slowly stroked the side of his face. "I don't know."

"That bad?"

He gingerly put his hands on the table and opened his eyes. "I think KnowMe is a mess, but I have a bigger problem to deal with. I think…" he paused, biting his lip and staring at Phoebe. "I think what's happening to me might be related to my new NanoCloud."

Phoebe squinted and shook her head. "What are you talking about?"

Niko scratched his chin and stared at the floor. "I can't explain it, that's why I need some help. Can we run some tests, see what's happening? Maybe it's nothing to do with it, maybe it is."

"There's more to it," she said, crossing her arms. "What is it?"

He nodded. "There's no way I can allow KnowMe to start working on any parts of Nine as long as I think there might be a threat to the public. Remember, thousands of people died from medicinal overdosing because a zealous company put nanobots into trial with an easily hackable protocol. Overnight, people died. Imagine if I missed something. It could affect tens of millions of people. And I'm not sure who I can truly trust at KnowMe these days."

She sighed. "Hey, I get it. Okay, so how would you describe how you feel?"

"Like I have a horrible flu."

"I love that you decided to come and see me once you thought that you might have a horrible flu. Really, I appreciate it," said Phoebe with a grin.

"You know what I mean." Niko put his hands between his knees.

She'd never seen him like this. "When did this start?"

"I noticed something a few months ago. It's slowly built up, but yesterday it really changed for the worse. The day before, I went home from the hearing, and resprayed to bring my NanoCloud density back up to one hundred percent. But within a few hours, I felt really off. Then this morning, I didn't know what to do... so I came here."

Phoebe shook her head. "Wait, when did you have that doctor run some tests?"

Niko stared at the ground. "Okay, I lied. I didn't. I just..." he looked at her with one eye open. "I knew you'd be mad at me for having let this drag on."

"You're damn right, I am." Phoebe tapped her pen on the table. "And Tass has no idea?"

He shook his head. "She's got her life in Manhattan."

Phoebe rolled her eyes. "Of course she's living in tsunami central. Can't get more her than that."

"It's not that bad," replied Niko.

"That's you replaying what she said to you, isn't it?"

He cracked a smile. "Maybe."

They laughed.

Niko bowed his head and pulled his shoulders in. He quickly went quiet.

"Niko? Are you in pain?"

"Yeah," he whispered. "It'll pass. These keep hitting every now and then." He deftly pulled out his pillbox, swallowed one and was about to put it away when she snatched it from his hand.

Frowning, she opened it to see there was only a single pill left. "Geezes, Niko. This is—"

"I know."

"That's a serious painkiller. How many have you taken?"

Niko relaxed his shoulders and slumped in the seat. "Today? That's the third one."

She shook her head and jotted down some notes. "And still…?"

"It just takes the edge off."

"Flaring suns, Niko." Several times, Phoebe started and stopped saying something before it could make any sense. "Look, Niko, you know I never practiced medicine, so…?"

"I just need some tests done, to see if NanoCloud Nine has anything to do with this."

"How are we going to be able to tell that?"

Niko looked up at the ceiling. "I'm thinking, process of

elimination."

"That works great in movies," said Phoebe, "but here in the real world, tests are done to look for specific things." She reached out her hand on the table. Niko gently met her half-way.

"Then let's look for the obvious things, check my blood, my skin, whatever else. Who knows, maybe this goes away."

Phoebe patted his hand and then let go, leaning back in her chair and scribbling down some more notes. "Have you tried zeroing your nanobots? That would get rid of them all and then you should start feeling better."

Niko scratched his head and looked away. "Let's do the tests first, I have some things to figure out on that front."

She got up and went to her desk, and then stopped, grabbed by a bothersome notion. She turned to him. "You've suspected something a lot longer. It's why you set all of this up?" She gestured to the building.

Niko ran his tongue along his top teeth and swallowed, and then offered a gentle nod. "I had an inkling. Part of me also wanted to be one of those storybook billionaires that has a secret lab."

"You should have told me. And while I love the location, what kind of billionaire would build a secret lab in Vermont?"

"It'd be hidden in plain sight."

They laughed.

Niko carefully went through his pockets, finally pulling out a silver token, and placing it carefully on the table.

Phoebe looked at it and then at him. "What's on there?"

"Actually, I'd like you to put copies of all of the test results on there. I can't have any copies anywhere, and I need them in a safe place."

"You've got that paranoid look on your face," said Phoebe. "That says to me you've already run some tests over the past few months."

Niko straightened up.

"What's really going on, Niko?"

He sighed heavily. "I don't know. When can we get started?"

"Right now."

———————

Phoebe walked back into her office, quickly waving for the door to close. "How did your calls go?"

"No one's calling me back, or sending me messages. I don't know what's going on back at KnowMe. I hope that you've had a more productive few hours."

"Well, I have my right hand guy, Jay, working on it. He accepted that he couldn't know why or for whom the tests were being run. He's a good guy. Now, as for the blood tests, the preliminaries show that you've got elevated leukocytes… white blood cells—"

"I know what leukocytes are," replied Niko with a chuckle.

"Just checking," she smirked and joined him at her conference table. "But that could very well be you fighting a virus. There are so many these days, it's hard to keep track of them all, never mind test for them. We have an actual doctor on staff who will be in later. She could prescribe some anti-virals for you if nothing else shows up.

"I think it's best to assume that unless something else shows up. And if anything pops up on the genetic integrity test in a few days, I'll let you know."

Niko wiped his mouth back and forth, nodding. "Okay, at least it's something. At least it's a checkpoint." He pointed to a picture in the bookcase behind her desk. "I noticed you have one from when we were dating back in college."

She glanced around, finally finding it. "It's my favorite."

"It's a good one," he replied.

"Did you know that was the day that Tass hacked into my phone and wouldn't allow it to call you?"

Niko laughed, holding his sides. "No. Really?"

"That girl. Sweet smile, but wow, that techno-temper," said Phoebe.

"She was just trying to protect me."

"From what? I mean, I know that I look vicious and everything."

Niko leaned back. "It's complicated."

"And that's why we didn't last," said Phoebe, her

expression folding apologetically. "I shouldn't have said that."

"No, it's fine."

There was a knock at Phoebe's office door, before it slid open and in walked a tall man with long dark-blond hair and a beard. "Hey Phoebe, I got the test results for you, but who—"

Niko and Phoebe both looked up.

"Woo… are you really Niko Rafaelo?" said the man.

"Niko, this is Jay Norry. Brilliant immunologist, gripping novelist, and master of the obvious."

"Hi," said Niko.

Jay stared at Phoebe. "This is all for him, isn't it?"

Phoebe raised her eyebrows.

"Right, yeah. Of course," said Jay. "Um, hi. I'm a big fan of yours." He offered his hand to Niko.

Carefully Niko shook with him.

"Woo, you feel icy," blurted Jay.

Phoebe shook her head. "Did you have something for me Jay?"

"Yeah, I didn't want to send a message, you know, no traces like you said. But, never mind. There's a couple more tests that I'd like to run."

"Okay," said Phoebe.

"What do you write," asked Niko.

Jay glanced at Phoebe who smiled back.

"Ah, among other things, there's my Walking Between Worlds trilogy."

"I'll look it up," said Niko. "I need something new to read."

"Can... Can I tell my wife about this?" Jay asked Phoebe. "Gah, I know that expression. This is going to be torture. Alright, I'll go run those tests." He then left.

"Seems like a good balance for you."

"He is. He's great. Imaginative, focused, driven and the type of right hand who will kick my butt to take time off. Speaking of which, I'm surprised that Sandra's not returning your messages."

"Speak of the devil," said Niko as a message appeared on his lens-display. He tapped the air. "She says there was some problem with the systems, and there's an important meeting tomorrow morning. She asked if I could come in early to prepare for it."

"What's that look for?"

He stared at her. "In all the years of KnowMe, we've never had a systems problem. I'll see that doctor you've got, if she can be trusted, and then I need to get back to the office."

"Hey," said Phoebe as he started to get up. Her eyes darted about and her face tightened. "You still have that scramjet thing, right?"

Niko nodded.

"Why don't we do dinner? You know, before you head off to war."

"I'd like that," he replied.

CHAPTER FOURTEEN

BOARDED

Niko stepped off the elevator, tucking in his shirt, his hair was still wet from the shower thirty minutes ago. He'd dashed home after flying home this morning, and hurried back to the office, wanting to get a jump on what had been happening over the past few days.

He was pulled out of his own little world of random thoughts when he caught a glimpse of the main conference room's glass walls being dark. The door then opened and a young man hurried out and a minute later, rushed back in. Niko recognized him, but wasn't sure who he worked for. "Must be working on a proposal or pitch." He glanced at the time on his lens-display. "Seven thirty's a bit early. Must be important." He continued on to his office.

With his jacket hung on the wall, he slid into his office chair. He smiled as it sculpted itself to his body shape and raised him up and into proper position. His desk then came alive, bringing the panoramic holo-screens and gesture sensors into perfect position. With a wave, he brought up the supplementary computing panel, bringing it up to one hundred percent. "I'm going to keep my promise, and leave my NanoCloud on low power, Phoebe. See, I'm listening," he said to himself. "And I really should get this set up at home. Some billionaire I am, not having this at home," he said with a smile. "Hmm, mind you, I won't come in to the office if I do."

He pulled up the messages center and was surprised to see nothing had come in since the hearing, except for the one message from Sandra. He looked up the booking schedule for the main conference room and found that it had been booked since seven that morning, but the meeting description didn't make any sense. "No attendees or owner? I'm going to have to speak with tech about that. That's not supposed to be allowed."

"Tass," he said, snapping his fingers. He shook his hand, quickly regretting the self-inflicted pain. *How about I come out Friday for lunch?* he wrote and sent it. A few seconds later, a message came back, *How about the Friday after?* He accepted her counterproposal.

He sat back and wondered, staring in the direction of the conference room. Suddenly, a sharp pain ran through his back and his entire display showed the haunting message he was starting to get used to seeing: *Host lost.*

Slowly, he got out of his chair and carefully made his way over to his jacket pocket. The swagger of earlier was gone. Taking the pillbox from his jacket pocket, he took out one pill of the newly prescribed medication and logged the time, as he'd been asked. He wasn't sure what good it would do, but at least he was doing something.

Fishing a silver token out of his pants pocket, he went back to his desk and connected to his secure data vault. For the next hour, Niko flipped through the latest set of test results and notes from Phoebe. He leaned back and lightly tapped his lips with his fist as he processed what it said. There were a number of things that were irritatingly normal, and one test whose results he just didn't believe.

Sandra knocked on the doorframe and stepped into the room. "How are you this morning?" she asked.

Niko looked up. She was dressed in a suit, with a forced smile. "I'm doing okay. Still having trouble with my message center," he said subtly shutting his vault connection and slipping the silver token back into his pocket. His hands were already slick with sweat; something felt off.

"Oh?"

He shrugged. "By the way, what were folks working on in the conference room? I couldn't find anything on it."

Sandra frowned, "What are you talking about?" She straightened up, arms crossed.

"When I came in earlier, the conference room walls were already dark. I saw... I can't remember, but I think he works for Andre, going in and out. The guy who used to have the mustache."

"Saul?"

"That's him," said Niko. "Why don't I have anything on what you guys are working on?"

Sandra looked away. "Well, I'm here to ask you to join us in the main conference room now, so I guess it doesn't matter."

Niko stood up, his eyes focused on Sandra. "Sandra, what's up?" His stomach was in knots already.

She turned and started walking, her head leaned forward.

"Sandra?" He stopped by touching her arm. She looked at him, her cheeks red and her eyes glossy, and then entered the conference room.

Niko wiped his face with his hands, while his stomach was doing flips. Part of him wanted to bring his NanoCloud up to full power. He scratched the back of his neck as he remembered he had a can of spray from an early prototype of Nine in a cabinet in his office. He knew it would be futile, as he wouldn't be able to glean any helpful information with it.

With a sigh, he took a painkiller from his pillbox and slipped it away. Steadying himself, he followed Sandra.

"Come in, Niko," said the chair of the board of directors. He was seated at the head of the conference table and had the members of the board on either side of him. After came the KnowMe executive team, and then people he didn't recognize, with a woman at the end that made his blood run cold.

"What's Harriet Binger doing here?" he asked the board

chair, staring at her.

She blinked slowly at him, but said nothing, a wry smile on her lips.

"Niko, we've come to a decision," he replied. "You need to understand that your actions over the past few years brought this upon yourself."

"What are you talking about?"

"You're out, Niko," said Andre, a satisfied smile on his face. He leaned back in his chair and folded his arms.

Niko stared at the board chair. Though his expression was blank, his eyes were piercing.

"Niko, at a special session earlier this morning, the board, supported by your executive team, voted to remove you as CEO. We then moved on accepting a merger proposal from Eversio Technologies, including accepting Harriet Binger as the new CEO. They've amassed quite a set of patents and technologies. Our initial technical review confirmed that we should be able to bring these into our NanoCloud product line, and help us regain mind-share, never mind actual market-share."

"This makes no sense to me. I've not seen—"

"No, Niko, you wouldn't have," continued the board chair. "I explicitly asked that this be done quietly, without you. The reason is quite simple. We wanted to see what you had to offer, and I'll say this for Sandra, she tried her best to get any and all information from you to help build a case for you. But you were your own worst enemy. We're quickly approaching the red line after which we won't make an acceptable launch date for NanoCloud Nine, and so we had to make a decision.

"The hearing was the very last straw. You demonstrated that you have created capabilities of Nine that you haven't shared with your own VP of Development."

Niko shook his head, his face scrunched up in confusion. "You're willing to lose the government contract and sabotage KnowMe because you were impatient? Because—"

"Actually, the committee is *particularly* supportive," said Harriet. "Your little demonstration rattled them to their core. Typical Rafaelo, try to make friends by intimidating them, by showing off how smart you are and they aren't. Fortunately, I was still hanging around. They called me in, and we had a very frank discussion."

"You set this up," said Niko, glaring at her. "You set this all up. Why do you keep showing up?"

She stood and glared back at him. "Because Niko, you are a mistake. No one should know your name, no one should know you exist, and you should be nothing. Instead, you played people's sympathies in school; you played on people's fears and insecurities to get KnowMe started. Then you conned the public with marvels you claimed were your own, when really they were designed and made by the dozens of slave-labour, glossy-eyed followers you'd amassed, including Sandra here. You have no idea how satisfying it is knowing that I'll finally get to set the record straight."

Niko put his trembling hands behind his back. He looked at Sandra. "Where are you in all of this?"

She'd been staring at the table the entire exchange. She shook her head back and forth. "You gave us no choice. You wouldn't listen. You wouldn't share, you just... you just locked us out." With a sigh, she raised her teary-eyed gaze to meet his. "You abandoned me, Niko. Everything went in one direction, and you ran the other way."

He swallowed hard and nodded, accepting the accusation. "So is this final?" he asked the board chair, licking his lips.

"Yes."

"You have no idea what you've just done," said Niko, his voice sorrowful, his shoulders slumped. "You—"

"Before you go," interrupted Harriet, "We'll need you to surrender all designs and prototypes for NanoCloud Nine, and subject yourself to a zeroing process that Sandra will administer. We know that your new nanobots are more resilient, so we've created a new zeroing device."

Niko stared at her. "You're never going to break me, Harry. I always find a way to beat you."

Harriet walked up to the front and stood beside the door. "No, you won't, Niko. That's one of your many mistakes. You think the cockroach running out of the way of the boot has beaten it. Now, you're out of room, and the boot is going to end you." Her tone was simple and calm, and had an eloquence to it.

Rubbing his forehead, he shifted from foot to foot. "You know that she recently drove a financial startup into the ground and wiped out billions from the market, right? The only benefactor of that was Eversio..." no one was looking at him. "You don't care. She's already spun everything..." He stepped towards the door.

Harriet motioned for him to stop. "Sandra, please zero him."

Niko bit his tongue and stared as Sandra picked herself up and shuffled over, her eyes averting his gaze. In her hands was a crude hand-held device. He didn't recognize the design, then noticed a faint Cloudster logo on a piece of it.

With a flick, he awoke his NanoCloud. The diagnostics screen appeared on his lens-display as it hit full power, and he showed the density at 60%. "Go ahead." He closed his eyes and spread his arms and legs apart.

A moment later, Sandra said with remorseful heaviness, "It's done."

Niko opened his eyes and caught a glance from Sandra as she turned to go back to her seat. He asked Harriet. "Now are we done?"

"Security will escort you out. We'll send any personal effects... And, I know I don't need to remind you but since I'm CEO of KnowMe, I must set an example. You are required by law to surrender any and all property of the company, conceptual, virtual or physical in nature. Good riddance, mistake."

———————————

The board chair smiled as he finally took Harriet's hand and shook it. "I know the other board members have said it, but I mean it when I say welcome aboard. I'm looking forward to great things, Harriet."

"I'll have that ninety-day plan before you know it," she said with a warm smile and wink.

"Talk to you soon," he said as he left.

The door slid closed and Binger turned to the room of mixed KnowMe and Eversio executives. "Well, what a start to the day. How's everyone feeling?" she asked, sitting down.

The KnowMe VP of Finance was about to answer when she noticed one of the Eversio executives crack a smile. "Why's he laughing?" she asked.

"Because at Eversio, we don't care how you feel, you just get the job done," replied the executive.

"Exactly," said Binger.

"Well, I guess there's going to be some cultural changes," said Andre with a smile. "I've done my best to get this place shipshape and professional. It'll be great to have an ally." He leaned back with a relaxed smile.

"Ally?" Binger twitched. She touched the back of her short, auburn hair and smiled. "Let's discuss real cultural change. Over the past several weeks, many of you have got to know members of my executive team. I think it has been key in bringing us to this moment, where finally one entity can go forward, stronger than ever. But to do that," she mused, "we must be ruthlessly efficient."

She looked around the table, where all faces, save for Sandra's, were looking at her and nodding. "Sandra, are you with us?" Sandra glanced up and nodded. "Good, I'm glad. I know you're the oldest and most respected employee here. That's why I'm keeping you."

"Excuse me?" said the VP of Finance.

Andre sat forward, "Yeah, what are you talking about?"

"Well, to be perfectly clear, I no longer require the services of *any* of the rest of you," said Harriet, her expression as detached as if she were talking about the weather.

"Wait, no, hold on. We just—"

Harriet leaned forward on her elbows and raised both eyebrows. "Andre, do you think that because you led a mutiny against your boss, that you get loyalty from me?"

The mousy VP of Team Focus and Development raised a hand. "But the board—"

"Oh please," said Binger, shaking her head. "I can't remember how many times I've heard people like you say *but the board won't stand for it* or *the employees will rebel* or any one of a million other statements that while you desperately wish would be true, aren't. The board has known that I would clean house, both because they know my history, but also because I told them outright. They fully supported my team doing an analysis, and they each had their pick of companies that I control within the Eversio family. From our evaluations, none of you are doing an admirable job, except for Sandra. So she stays, and the rest of you, well, have a good life."

She stood up, as did her executive team. "We'll give you a couple of minutes to talk amongst yourself. Please know that all of your NanoClouds were zeroed a moment ago, and that any attempt to contact anyone at the company, or each other within the next six months after leaving here, will result in a lawsuit by KnowMe. And you can ask any member of my team whether that's an idle threat or not."

Andre glanced at one of the women, who chuckled. He put his face in his hands.

"In a moment," continued Binger, "you'll each receive a tablet with the details of your termination package. You'll have five minutes to accept the non-negotiable terms; if you don't, then please note that my legal team is looking for someone to make into a hobby." She had a professional grin.

"Sandra?" asked Binger.

She stared at her new CEO in shock.

"Sandra, come on."

Everyone glared at Sandra as she grudgingly followed Binger out of the room.

As the conference room door closed, Binger said, "I want you to take me to Niko's office. I want to have a look at Mistake's inner sanctum before I take it apart."

"I heard you call him that in a board meeting. Why do you call him that? He's—"

Binger raised an eyebrow, her eyes narrowed. Sandra sense the peaceful facade cracking. "I know you have respect for him, but you haven't known him for as long as I have. He's one of those people who symbolizes weakness. Weakness that needs to be stamped out."

"How could you say that?" blurted out Sandra, her fists clenched. "I've known him a long time."

"How? Because I've seen the lives he's nearly destroyed, have you? Has anyone here? He doesn't deserve the success he's had. And I'd like to make one thing completely clear. If you have *any* contact with him, any at all, you will regret it on a level you can't imagine. Understood?"

Sandra lowered her gaze.

"Good. Now lead the way."

Arriving at the door, Sandra motioned for Binger to enter.

"Well, well, well, quite the setup. The desk and holo-screen setup is characteristically over the top, but I do have to say that the back wall of photos surprises me. I never thought him as much of a sentimentalist."

Sandra glanced at her, an eyebrow arched.

Binger made her way over to the photos. "I guess some things have changed from the Niko I knew. This photo must have been when you guys founded KnowMe."

"Actually," said Sandra walking over, "the company already existed, and it was my second week."

"Whatever happened to those two guys? They look like developers."

"They stayed with us for a few more weeks, then left. They were contractors and they didn't believe we'd get funding."

"Ah," said Binger, remembering. "I remember that board meeting. Quite the disaster. I'm surprised you stuck around. Who's this kid? Actually…" She started scanning the rest of the photos. "She's in nearly all of them. She looks familiar, very familiar. But I know I haven't met her. Was she in the background of one of our meetings?"

Sandra shook her head. "Maybe you just—"

"Could I have passed her in the hallway?" asked Binger, taking a recent, framed photo off the wall and examining it.

Sandra scratched her face nervously.

Suddenly it was like all the oxygen in the room had been sucked out, and Binger's face went red. "I can't flaring believe it. It's right there, in your eyes. What's her name?"

"I—"

"Don't even *try* to lie to me." Binger grabbed Sandra's hands, letting the picture fall to the floor. "I can see it in your eyes, your hands, the way your head's moving. Answer me or I will ruin you such that no one will ever consider even giving you a coffee as you beg on the streets. You'll lose your marriage, your children, everything. Do you understand me?"

Sandra bowed her head.

"Now tell me," said Binger, composing herself. "Who is she?"

"Her name is Tasslana."

Binger laughed. "Oh, that's funny. That's really, really funny." She slammed the photo down on Niko's desk. "Oh I miss glass, so much less dramatic these days." She glared at Sandra, making the woman take an unconscious step back. "I thought it would be enough to teach Niko *Mistake* Rafaelo a lesson by taking his company and ruining his reputation. But this? There's not enough pain in the world that I can exact on him for this."

CHAPTER FIFTEEN
PRECIPICE

"Is everything okay?" asked the owner of Fillion's walking up to Niko's table in the back corner, away from prying eyes. Mal was a tall, square-jawed man with long bangs. "It's not like you to keep dismissing serving-drones, one after the other. I thought I'd see if you needed the personal touch. Is there anything I can get you?"

Niko put his fingers down and glanced up from the table, flashing a broken smile. "No thanks, Mal. Is it okay if I stay here just a while longer?"

"Hey, you can stay here until we close, and then some. I have some friends coming by later, you're welcome to join us for drinks."

"Thanks, but no," said Niko with a sorrowful smile, massaging his elbow. "I appreciate the offer though."

"You sure you're okay?" he asked, motioning like he was going to sit on the opposing bench seat.

"Yeah. Just in a bit of pain. I'm okay, really."

Mal sighed. "Well, if you need anything, just send me a message. I'm upstairs. Don't hesitate, okay?"

Niko gave him a thumbs-up.

"Alright," said Mal, giving Niko a friendly slap on the shoulder.

Niko stared at his empty message center, shaking his head once again. He'd been certain that Sandra had known her zeroing device would have little effect, and that she'd then meet up with him for them to plan how to fix everything, but the hours had melted by without a hint or sign. *Maybe the look had been guilt or remorse*, thought Niko.

Putting his hands over his face and closing his eyes, Niko felt himself slipping. His chest heaved as he fought to hold his emotional ground. He remembered back in high school, when several weeks after the funeral for his parents and brother, Harriet had turned on him. In a matter of hours one day, she'd turned every single friend and acquaintance against him. No one would take his calls, reply to his messages or even just stop and listen to him.

"I should have listened…"

With a deep sigh, he gave himself a light slap and gazed around the restaurant. "Come on, you need something to focus on. Anything."

He was about to get up when he noticed a little girl with her dad being seated a few tables away. Niko immediately recognized the tell-tale signs of a struggling father: the severely frayed ends of his pants, the discolored nature of his well-worn jacket, his half-tucked shirt, and several days of stubble on his exhausted face.

The little girl was dressed in a beat-up blue jacket and

black pants. Her long hair was badly brushed and in a sloppy pony-tail with a festive gold ribbon. She was excitedly pointing at pieces of memorabilia on the walls, bouncing in a way that made Niko certain this was a special birthday lunch. It felt all too familiar.

He subtly held out an index finger and thumb, and clicked their image. He ran a quick image search, finding as he expected, nothing about them. Tapping his fingers on the table, he smiled. With a quick swipe, he created a new message and attached the picture. He then wrote: *Mal – I'd like these guys to eat 'free' here whenever they want, for however long they keep coming. I'm sending you some money to cover it, plus I'd like you to give them the rest as some kind of scholarship or as winner of some contest. Whatever you want. Thanks, Niko.* A moment later, he sent Mal four million dollars.

With a satisfied sigh, he summoned an auto-taxi and got up, smiling as he passed them.

———————

Niko stepped out of the auto-taxi on to the dark concrete walkway leading up to his manor. Usually, he'd have it drive him up to the door, time ever at a premium, but not this time. He was looking forward to the long walk in the fading sunlight, even if his body was protesting.

He smiled at the hum of the gardening-drones. They darted about, white blurs lost among the flowers and shrubbery. He thought of all the analyses they were doing, checking moisture levels, analyzing soil, and determining growth rates. His head gardener had thought Niko was trying to replace him and had quit on the spot. The assistant gardener had seen it as an incredible new tool and joked that they should go into business together. Niko shocked the man and his family when he did that, making himself a relatively silent partner. For the past few years, the gardener's daughter maintained Niko's property and used it as a testing ground for new features. Every now and then they would catch up. He scratched his chin, wondering how they were doing, if they would be spared what he feared in his gut was coming.

Leaning against a tree, he pushed against the pain in his chest. His eyes hurt, and the idea of taking out his contact lens was tempting. Instead, he quickly wrote a message to the gardener, telling him he was selling all of his shares to them for a dollar and why. There were a lot of these little enterprises he would need to contact. They were fragile little birds who could be crushed in Harriet's vendetta against him. He'd heard of her taking down CEOs and then hunting them until they were left completely broke and broken.

Biting his lip and knowing better, he sent messages to Sandra and his other friends at KnowMe. His simple one-word message of *hello* was met immediately with a response that any and all further communication with KnowMe would result in legal action against him.

Niko felt himself sliding towards despair. It was an old, familiar feeling. He bowed his head and closed his eyes, his fists shaking. Small jolts of pain played about his body, and with each one, it whittled the noise in his mind down to a single idea: no compromise. With a steadying breath, he opened his eyes and listened to the birds. Forcing one foot in front of the other, he continued on his way, his face twitching. He imagined the stranger from the scramjet crash giving him a nod as he refused to give in.

As the house came into view, he was surprised to see a woman there. At first his stomach tightened, fearing that it was one of Harriet's lawyer attack dogs, but the woman was seated on the white palatial steps leading up to his front door and not pacing about.

He kicked himself for not recognizing Tass in her standard Manhattan business attire. With her hair in a bun, wearing a double collar, and white and cream suit, it gave her an almost demure exterior compared to how he thought of her. Nothing could take away her gripping gaze however.

"I think I actually miss your blue hair. The natural dark brown is nice, but... weird."

"You never really know what to say in moments like this, do you?"

He shook his head. "No. I'm not... you know."

"I know," she said standing and smiling. "I was beginning to get antsy sitting here. I figured if I messaged you, you might not come home. But if I didn't, you might go somewhere else."

"Why didn't you let yourself in?" asked Niko. "Your

NanoCloud's fully authenticated."

Tass shrugged. "I don't know. I guess I wanted to see you come up the hill. It reminded me of watching you come home when I was little." She paused, her eyes narrowing. "You should have let me know as soon as you walked out of KnowMe." She curled her lip. "I feel like you've been leaving me out of things lately. Stop that, okay?" She hugged him. "It's me. You don't get to leave me out of anything."

He gently pulled away. "I... ah..." his voice cracking. "I was going to tell you... but... so much is building up lately." He tilted his head up and wiped his eyes. "How did you—?"

"It's all over the news and TalkItNow. How could the board let a viper like Harriet Binger get anywhere *near*—" she said, her nostrils flaring.

Niko raised his hands. "It's my fault."

"No, it's not. It's—"

He rubbed her arms. "No, Tass, it is. If I hadn't..." he choked up. "If I hadn't created the opening, she wouldn't have been able to exploit it. It's... it's that easy."

"No, it isn't," said Tass, her eyes glaring and her jaw forward. "Do you know that she's already making claims that you've violated—"

"Tomorrow. Tomorrow, I'll have my lawyers start to deal with everything. But right now, I'm..." A tear rolled down his cheek. "I just..."

She took his hand. "Hey, you don't need to say anything." She stroked his hand with her thumb.

He shrugged, a few tears quietly escaping down his face. "So... ah," he cleared his throat. "What are you doing here? You could have called or messaged me." He sat on a step and patted the spot beside himself. Despite his best effort to hide his pain, he saw her notice. Mercifully, she let it go.

She sat down beside him, put her arm around him, and lay her head on his shoulder. "Well, when the news coverage about you and KnowMe was interrupted with a severe tsunami warning, I figured it was a sign. I'm not really keen to witness first hand if my building really is rated for more than a level five. I cringe every time the sirens go off. You've got ten minutes to get off the streets and the auto-taxis immediately go to lockdown points and shutdown. I've heard the sea-wall's not going to last long, but no one wants to leave. And I get it, the offers I had from there aren't just for way more money, the types of challenges they offer are unmatched. It's like a death wish."

Niko laughed, wiping his face. "I'm proud of you, standing on your own two feet. You never had to, Toughy."

Tass smiled at him. "You always called me Tough Stuff for a reason."

"Yeah," he said, kissing the top of her head.

She sighed and squeezed his hand. "I couldn't let you face this alone. Not this."

"I'm okay," he replied, a fragile smile on his lips. "Really."

"No, you're not." She wrinkled her nose and sniffed hard. "We're going to fight this or do whatever we need to. We're…" She lowered her gaze. "I love you."

"I know. I love you too." He smiled at her, and turned to the garden. For a while they watched the drones flutter around dutifully.

With a broken voice, he said, "The worst part is that I don't know what to do. I know better than to fight her in her arena. In the world of innovation, she can't touch me. And invention had always bought us the time we needed to figure out how to outmaneuver, until now. But then I failed… I couldn't finish Nine in time. Now, it's corporate and legal warfare, and I've seen better CEOs than me throw punches at her, only to land them on themselves with twice the force. The only person scarier than Harry is her step-mother, Lucinda Feer, whom she's forever trying to earn praise from, Lucinda Feer." He swallowed and shook his head. "I… I don't know what to do."

Tass pulled her hair out its bun and pushed away a fiery reply. "You used to always tell me that if we don't have the answer, change the question. We just change the fight or if she really is this irresistible force, then we just wall ourselves off from her and make NanoClouds irrelevant with something new."

Niko straightened up and pinched her cheek. "I

appreciate that, but this isn't your fight. You have your own life that you need to get back to."

"I might have quit," she said with a smirk.

Niko shook his head. "You're kidding."

"There might also not have been a tsunami warning."

"Tass?" he asked.

She squeezed his hand. "When I saw the news, I quit. To hell with that flaring job. You can't believe what it's like working for idiots. I have to take every idea of mine and break it into ever smaller pieces until they are beyond elementary, and then I'm *still* told that they're too complex!" She shuddered. "I'm surprised I haven't beaten anyone to death with a tablet."

Niko laughed. "Why are you so fiery and violent?"

"It's in my genes. And before you start with any of that talk about keeping your worlds apart, understand that I don't care. I'm part of this world now."

Wincing more from the emotional discomfort than a flash of pain, he said, "Okay. But before you come on this journey with me, there's something I need to tell you."

CHAPTER SIXTEEN
PIECES OF HOPE

Two Weeks Later

Niko nudged his cup of green tea around once again. The cafe was nice enough, but part of him wondered what was he really doing in Burlington. For all the talk he'd excitedly engaged in with Tass about starting a new company on the very Startup Strip that he'd founded, part of him just wondered why he'd bother.

Phoebe had given him a mixed reaction about the idea that he'd be around more. It would test whatever they had going on, if it was anything really at all. Both of them agreed that it would greatly help them keep tabs on what was happening with Niko's body.

Another lawyer message came in and Niko banged his table, making his cup spill and clatter, and several people around him jump. "Why is she doing this?" he muttered. He glanced at the door, half expecting to see Harriet come looking for him. With a wave and swipe, Niko wrote a message to his lawyer asking how it was possible for Binger to be able to preemptively start seizing some of his assets.

"I'm sorry sir, cloud payment only," said the cashier, getting Niko's attention. The man in front of her was in his late-twenties. He had short dark hair and tanned skin, his facial features a clear indication of some Indian heritage. He was disheveled and unshaven.

"But I can't," said the man. "Is your boss here? He always lets me pay by stick. He knows my story."

"Sorry, Sam's on vacation."

"I'll pay," said Niko, standing up and making his way over. He studied the man's expression and appearance. "Down on your luck?"

The man looked away and shook his head. "Like you wouldn't believe."

"Are we good?" Niko asked the cashier after a wave.

"Yup, thanks Mister—"

"Just thanks," he said, cutting her off. He turned to the man. "Join me? I need someone to talk to keep my mind off some things."

"Sure." The man grabbed his coffee and followed Niko to his table. "I'm Arju."

"Nice to meet you. I'm Niko." He glanced over at the cashier who was staring at him. He wondered if she was going to blurt out who he was. He'd managed to avoid anyone noticing him so far. "So what do you do?"

"Software developer. Well, I was. You?" asked Arju,

taking a slow sip of his coffee.

"I'm a tech guy too. I just moved here yesterday. How is this place? Compared to the other coffee shops in town."

Arju looked around. "I don't know, okay I guess. I don't have a lot of choice though. It's the only place with an actual person at the cash, I can't pay non-people."

"So what happened? Developers usually have the latest and greatest. It's almost a mark of social pride," said Niko picking up his tea with both hands, appreciating the soothing warmth on his hands.

"Yeah… do you remember about a year ago there was a Wall Street startup that went live and crashed the market, wiping several billion out of the market?"

Niko's face perked up and he sat back, putting his cup down. "Yeah. I heard that Eversio Investments made a killing on the instability."

Arju licked his lips and nodded. "Yeah, a couple of other people did as well. I can't legally talk about the details."

"Did you work at the startup?"

Nodding, Arju took a sip and looked at the door. "What I can say is, I was the guy who reported the problem. Everyone else went out to celebrate our software going live and our crazy IPO. Me? I went to my desk to figure out what was bugging me."

Niko narrowed his eyes. "So what happened?"

"Our CEO, Harriet Binger—"

"Excuse me?" Niko interrupted. "Did you say Binger was your CEO?"

"You know her?" Arju glanced around, nervously.

"Yeah," replied Niko, crossing his arms. "Go on."

Arju furrowed his brow. "Who are you?"

"I'm just some guy who listens to the news. Go on, you were saying your CEO…" Niko motioned for Arju to continue.

"When everything goes down, she's fine, while all the VPs and directors go to jail, along with most of my colleagues on the development team. My reward for helping the FBI? Banned for ten years from having a NanoCloud."

"Wow, that's severe. And you reported it?"

"And more, but I can't talk about it."

"Out of curiosity, how do they monitor it? You having no cloud."

Arju gestured to the room. "Someone sitting could have a detector, or someone could drive by me. Supposedly I'd get a message if I violated it; I'm allowed one warning. If things go well, they can reduce it to five years, whatever that means."

Niko tapped the table. "Okay, so I get that all of this happened, and you were in Manhattan. Judging by how you talk, you didn't grow up there or here, so why are you in Burlington?"

His face slack with a hint of sorrow, he shrugged. "It's

the only place I've been able to find where people are willing to consider hiring a guy like me, cloudless and with a tarnished record." Staring into his cup, he continued. "I went home to Idaho for a bit... my mom's still there. I applied around and got a job here. I've been here a week and I'm thinking it's not going to work out. They're coming to realize what it means when a guy doesn't have a Cloud, it's a real disability."

"I can't imagine," said Niko. "Wow. And the FBI won't —"

"To quote the agent who worked with me, I should be lucky I'm not in jail because Binger apparently gave them enough to suspect even me."

"That's brutal. So I guess you're starting to look for something new?" asked Niko, leaning in.

Arju bowed his head. "I'd like to, but who's going to hire a guy like me? I mean, you can't even have me go through the most basic, standard hiring process. No auto-authenticate, no banking encryption key set to my genetic fingerprint, nothing."

Niko stroked his beard and sat back. "I hadn't realized that NanoClouds had changed the world so fundamentally. I'm sorry."

"For what? You didn't do this to me," said Arju, shaking his head. "I hadn't realized how hard it was being permanently zeroed. I mean, zero NanoCloud, zero jobs, zero hope. Imagine if something went wrong with

NanoClouds or they went away? The world would be crippled."

Niko's eyes widened. "I hadn't thought about that either. I guess we've got to hope that KnowMe just keeps doing the right thing."

"Yeah, not likely. They just turfed the founder, Niko Rafaelo. You know, he's actually one of the reasons I got into development."

"Huh, small world," replied Niko. "Listen, I'm trying to get a startup going here. You sound like someone who needs a second chance, and I'd be happy to give that to you. When the time comes, want me to call you in for an interview? No promises."

"Sure," replied Arju.

"What's your last name?"

"Cartier. Arju Cartier."

Niko immediately kicked off a scan to collect all the information he could on Arju. Standing up, he stuck out his hand. "Nice to meet you, Arju."

Arju raised an eyebrow. "A bit old school?"

"I believe in making a personal connection with people."

"Ah... yeah, okay," he said shaking it awkwardly. "Thanks for the coffee. See you around, I guess."

———————

Tass dropped her travel bag and took in the barren office space. The walls had signs of a business long gone, and the flooring hinted at a place that hadn't seen renovation of any kind in over forty years. The early afternoon light tried to be kind, but dusty windows did little to help. "Here?"

Niko turned around, nodding. "Here," he replied. He had his trusty brown trench coat on.

"Those antique blue jeans and the black turtleneck, you're hunting for some inspiration?" she asked, coming up beside him.

"Maybe a little. Or maybe it's laundry day."

Tass started walking around, mapping out how to break down the empty space into useful work areas. "Laundry day? Did I miss another lawsuit from Binger?"

Niko bit his lip and nodded.

She turned to look at him, not having heard a reply. "What happened?"

"More of the same. Like I've said before, she's a gladiator in this space. I don't know how she gets lawyers, or judges, to side with her, but we'll win out. It'll just be expensive, and long."

Tass put her hands down. "I think we can get twenty-two people in here comfortably, with three conference rooms and a decent sized lab area. Of course, it begs the critical question."

Niko nodded. "I found a developer we should interview."

"Great, but that's *not* the critical question. What are we

going to do?" she asked. "Getting a bunch of people together and doing random crap, burning through money, is a strategy that I'd prefer not to try. Particularly with someone else burning through money at the other end."

Niko stared at her and smiled. "Where did you learn to be so cut and dry?"

"Is that curiosity or —"

"Well this is a crap-hole, isn't it?" boomed a voice from the front door.

Tass spun around, recognizing the voice. Her arms waved excitedly for a hug from the short, stout man with a thick beard who came barreling towards her. "Oh my goodness, how the flood are you?" she hugged him tightly.

"You watch that mouth, Tassy," he joked, stepping back. "And I've been fine. Now let me look at you, I haven't seen you in forever and a day." He stroked his beard.

"It's Tass these days," she said with a red cheeked smile. "I can't believe you're here."

"I brought all eight volumes of The Yellow Hoods, just in case we need to remember old times. Though, you're going to need to sit beside me. There's not enough real estate on these legs of mine for a tall woman like you. I can't believe it, you all grown up."

Folding her arms, she narrowed her eyes at Niko. "What's he..." she stopped and turned back to Flint. "What are you doing here?"

"Someone called and said that they might have room at

a startup for an old, washed-up developer who could still crack through the toughest stuff around. One Felip Lintman, a.k.a. Flint, reporting for duty," he said with mock-salute to Niko.

Niko saluted him back.

"But you're retired," said Tass with a frown. "You always talked about doing that. I mean, when we were your tenants way back, you were working like a madman as a software developer buying every piece of property you could. Wasn't the whole goal to retire early?"

Flint sighed and scratched his beard. "It was, and it worked, for a while. I lost properties in a flood, two to riots, none of it covered by insurance. Then when my wife got sick, I needed every penny I could get my hands on. When we were down to our home, I finally took a call I'd been avoiding. It was him." He pointed at Niko. "He covered everything, and in so doing, bought her another two years of life." Flint sniffed and shook his head, shaking off the sentiment. "And when I woke up from my heart attack two years ago, guess who was at my bedside? That man there."

Niko smiled. "We couldn't have gotten through my college years without you. And Tass wouldn't have half the tech skills she does, if it hadn't been for you babysitting her."

"Ha, babysitting. Does he still think that's what I did?"

Tass made a zipping motion over her lips.

"Good," replied Flint with a wink.

Pulling her hair back into a renewed pony-tail, Tass glared at Niko. "Why didn't you tell me that you were helping out Flint? I'd have loved to be a part of that."

Niko's eyes darted around, he bit his lip. "It wasn't that big of a deal. I just helped him out a bit."

"Helped me out," Flint laughed and stared at Tass. "He pulled your old landlord out of bankruptcy and set me up nicely. Then when I had a heart attack, he'd paid all the bills and then some." He wagged a finger at Niko.

"Huh, and he didn't say a thing to me." She thought for a moment, her expression sliding along with her shoulders. "Wait, this was a couple of years ago? Ah. I wasn't much into listening then, was I?"

Niko waved off her concern. "You had a life and were angry, and when we finally got everything back on track, it slipped my mind. Which reminds me, there's something I keep meaning to talk to you about." His jaw was clenched, his eyes narrowed.

"Oh?" she replied.

"Over dinner." Niko tried to smile and turned to Flint. "Are you sure you're up for some crazy work? Real startup hours, all the benefits of no sleep, and frustration on a heroic scale."

He pointed a finger at Niko. "You better have something worth moving to this place for, or so help me, I'll be sticking you with my bar tab! I'm eager to see if twelve years of hobby coding have kept me sharp enough."

"So are you going to tell us what we're going to do already?" Tass asked Niko.

He scratched his nose. "We're going to crack the cell communication protocol." He looked up after a moment of awkward silence.

"Crapsters, he's gone mad," said Flint. "And I really loved that apartment. I shouldn't have let it go."

"He's pulling our leg." Tass shook her head. "That's mumble jumble idiot talk. What are we really going to do?"

Niko laughed. "No, we're *actually* going to create a startup to figure out how to communicate with cells. I even defined a metric for it, I call it protocol harmony. We're starting with a value of zero percent."

"And this is to do what? Tell cells that they aren't alone in the universe?" asked Flint with a laugh. He ran his hand through his thick head of brown hair. "Talking to cells..." He grumbled and stared up at Niko with a stern grin. "Mind you, when you wanted to rent my apartment and told me you were creating nanobots, I thought you were mad then, too. That one didn't turn out too badly."

Tass stepped back, shaking her head. "I get the premise is distinct enough from what KnowMe does. It avoids some of the initial lawsuits and the press turning against us right out of the gate. But even with a nanobot layout that was obviously only designed for cell-communication... I can't believe I even just said that half seriously... There's something you're not telling us."

Niko sighed heavily, his face twitching with pain. He started massaging his hands. "I know the idea is a long shot."

"It's not why you want us here," remarked Flint, stroking his beard. "It's been a long time, but I recognize that look."

Tass took a step towards Niko. "Something's wrong." She put a finger on his chest and glared up at him. "There's something you feel you need to do and you don't want to ask for help."

"I can't. Several parts of it are illegal, if not all of it," replied Niko.

"Good thing you aren't asking, then," said Flint.

"Flooding good," added Tass.

CHAPTER SEVENTEEN
NOT OF A KIND

Six Weeks Later

Phoebe locked her truck and, with hot coffee in hand, made her way to the front doors of her building. The crunch of the early morning snow amused her, as two days before it had been hot enough for shorts. February in Burlington was fun, random weather.

She stopped in her tracks and stared at Niko leaning against the front doors.

"I'd heard you've been in town for a few weeks, and I was wondering when you'd finally surface. I figured it was best to give you your space, and let you get settled. I'd have called eventually."

"I know," replied Niko.

"It's good to see you."

"It's good to see you, Phoebe," he said, wincing as he rolled his shoulders.

She frowned, then let it go. "Anyone back at KnowMe talking to you?" she asked, as they started walking into the building.

He shook his head. "No, and every few days, there are less and less people who I thought of as friends and acquaintances who will. Binger's doing what she does best, isolating someone, in this case me. She announces a new lawsuit against me every few days, and wastes no opportunity to feed it to the press in tasty, bite-sized pieces. No one notices the ones she doesn't actually file, or does and then removes. She's a master of misinformation. Not a surprise though, she learned from the best of the best, her step-mother, Lucinda Feer."

"I saw a photo of the KnowMe offices on TalkItNow. There were corporate nanny-drones in the background. I can't imagine being monitored for everything I did, every transmission I made or received with my NanoCloud, everyone I spoke to."

"I hate those things," said Niko. "You know how many times a new board member would suggest we employ them? It's the norm, it improves efficiency... Every time I'd do my rant and either they would leave, or they would let the issue die. People can't thrive if they have to watch everything they do; I know I can't. Sometimes genius needs to happen in a vacuum."

She shook her head and laughed, stopping them in the heart of the building's lobby. "So is this a social call or did you want to do more testing? Because I've been through the previous results several times, and I don't see anything that should be causing what's happening to you. I don't care what you think your nanobots are doing, there's no evidence." She looked at him in the eyes. "I'm thinking you need to go get some real medical tests done." Holding on to her string necklace, she sighed. "I think that you might have Creeger's. The skin reaction and swollen joints, the white cell count, it's consistent. Have you had any spiking pain?"

"It's *not* Creeger's," he answered with a glare.

She stared back at him. "I understand it's not likely, but you need to accept that you might be wrong. So what are we doing? Onwards with more tests until we have something impossible or will you go to get help?"

Niko stood there, staring at the floor, his arms pulled in like he was cold.

"Hey, I just remembered, there's something that's been really bothering me," said Phoebe. "Why haven't you destroyed your NanoCloud? You think it's harming you, so why not get rid of it? In my old company, there was a special lab where they zeroed everyone when they walked in. They even double checked afterwards."

He sighed heavily and kept his focus on the same tile. "I've tried. It keeps coming back."

She noticed his hands were trembling. "Okay, maybe it's not Creeger's."

Niko played with the wrist-watch. His forearm muscles were already sore from its weight, and his skin irritated from its presence. He stopped himself from removing it, as he knew if he did, he'd quickly pull up his lens-display and then be lost in his work.

Over the past few weeks, he and Phoebe had gone to the movies and spent time together, all the while running more tests and analyses and he got his startup, Spero, off the ground. She'd been surprised when that morning, he'd formally asked her on a date. She'd been even more surprised by his claim that Tass was okay with it.

He'd arrived early at the restaurant to meet with the head chef and double check that they had everything for Phoebe's three favorite dishes, in case she wanted one of them. The owner had come to meet Niko in person, overjoyed to meet the celebrity genius, and offered him the chef's table in the kitchen, away from prying eyes.

A police-drone came whizzing up to the restaurant and started methodically patrolling the perimeter. A chill ran down Niko's spine. He could just imagine someone in the middle of eating, and watching their companion gunned down. Despite his best efforts when at KnowMe, he'd been unable to get any action by government to change its stance on what they called *immediate justice for semi-hostiles*, and had been threatened with a lawsuit for raising the idea of an investigation into how many people had been the victim of a software or data error.

He noticed several staff members and patrons taking his photo. He offered a half-hearted smile and wave. Within minutes, he found the photos on TalkItNow, with chatter and speculation piling up.

For all the damage that Binger was doing to his public reputation, it wasn't having any effect on the gossip. He hoped, at the very least, it meant that the Pieman's Fare would be booked solid for a few months.

Niko fidgeted with his tie and pulled at the shoulders of his suit as an auto-taxi pulled up and Phoebe stepped out.

"I was wondering if you were going to drive," he said taking her hand.

She chuckled. "Um, no. I love my old truck, but this isn't the type of place I drive to. Have you seen how much they charge for parking? It's more than I make in a month."

"Oh," he said, smiling awkwardly.

"Billionaires don't usually notice little things like cost, unless you're buying a country or something," said Phoebe, smiling as Niko frowned. "I'm just teasing. But I do have to say, Niko, I didn't know you could actually wear a suit, let alone that you owned one."

"I think I've worn one for an interview or two before. I have a few of them, scattered around the world. I only managed to bring this one with me."

Phoebe stopped and looked him over. She straightened his tie and brushed some dust off his shoulders. "How old is this suit?"

"Remember when I had that personal assistant? I think she bought it for me," he replied with a nose wrinkle.

"Was that the woman who was aggressively trying to be your girlfriend?" asked Phoebe.

"Yeah, that one."

"She was such a flooder. How did you ever manage to get rid of her? Didn't she threaten you with a lawsuit or something?" asked Phoebe, walking slowly with him towards the restaurant's entrance.

"We should probably go in," said Niko.

"Tass?" asked Phoebe.

After a moment, he nodded.

She pushed her hair back. "Now I'm actually feeling sorry for that psycho. What did Tass do? It had to be more than scramble her schedule, set alarms for every ten minutes throughout the night, and fill her message center with colorful, youthful expletives."

"She just hacked the woman's NanoCloud into streaming everything she said to the police. It was low grade audio, but you have to hand it to her, that was amazing. It only took a few hours before the woman ranted something about wanting to fake a baby, marry me, and then kill me."

"Okay, I don't feel so bad," said Phoebe.

Niko was about to step into the restaurant when she pulled him back gently.

"What?" he asked, looking about. "Camera-drones?"

"No. Is this a real date?" she asked.

"Yes."

"For real?" she asked again. "No working on the side, just two people, out to enjoy each other's company to see where the relationship might go?"

"Yes."

She glanced at the ground and then at him, a near-patronizing smile on her face. "Well, in that case, then there's usually one part that's happened by this point that you've missed."

Niko stared at the ground mumbling to himself as he went through everything he could think of.

"Niko."

"One sec, I'm just going through my checklist for the evening."

"Niko, you're over-thinking this. By this point, both parties have usually remarked on the appearance of the other party. Now, that said, I don't need a compliment but I figure some protocol would be a good idea," she said with a cheeky grin. "And for the record, you look very handsome in your suit, even if you're acting like a twelve-year-old going to a wedding." She waited, shaking her head as he just looked at her nervously. "Now, it's your turn."

"Oh, right." He stepped back, holding Phoebe by the hands. She'd given her hair a wave, and had a rare touch of red on her lips and cheeks. Her smoky grey jacket and pants were accented by her white shirt, red cuffs and red shoes. "You look beautiful."

"Well thank you," she said with a nod.

"But you always look beautiful."

Phoebe sighed, hanging her head and chuckling.

"You're one of a kind, Niko. Come on, let's get to our table."

———————◡———————

Phoebe walked over to refill her cup of coffee, only to realize that the machine needed another thirty seconds. She looked at the time shown on the wall-mounted holo-screen and shook her head, it was only five thirty in the morning.

She leaned against the counter and glanced around the basement laboratory. She and Niko had agreed it was best to have a separate space, with its own equipment, for their work. It had a wheeled chair, a gesture pad in front of the holo-screen, several analytical machines lined up against one wall, and a counter with a sink and beverage machine. Initially the lab had been cold and stark. She was touched to come down one Monday to find that Jay and a few of the others had painted and decorated it. Since then, it felt more befitting a billionaire's secret hideout. In particular, she liked the oversized penny and dinosaur painted on the opposing wall.

The door creaked open and familiar footfalls started down the metal stairs.

"Niko, what are you doing here?" she asked, pouring her coffee after the machine chimed its completion.

He was dressed in a rumpled shirt and loose pants, his coat already in hand. "Last night at dinner, I kept thinking about the last set of test results. Something's bothering me about them."

"Yeah, me too," she replied, staring at her coffee. She

carefully took a sip and glanced up at him uncomfortably. "I came here right after dinner."

"I'm sorry about the lawyer call. I had to take it. I ended up being on that for an hour," he said, walking over beside her.

She moved over a few feet and set the machine for Niko's favorite tea. "I know, but it wasn't just the lawyer. It was Tass' call regarding the interview candidates for your startup, then Tass' call regarding something about the new condos, and then the first lawyer call. It just kind of ruined the mood." She hugged her coffee and leaned against the counter, her face obscured by her hair.

Niko rubbed his blurry eyes. "I'm—" He stiffened.

"How's the pain?" she asked, coming over and taking his hand, then quickly letting it go. "Was it in your arm again?"

"It was just a sharp spike. Nothing big," he replied opening his eyes and glancing around.

She stood back and studied his face. "You only get those when you're exhausted. Did you even try to sleep?"

He squirmed, stepping over to the holo-screen to see what she had been working on. "I had a conference call with my new lawyers," he said, plunking himself down in the wheeled chair, audibly relieved to be sitting.

"What happened to the lawyer that called you last night?"

Niko scratched his forehead. "He was actually telling

me he couldn't work for me anymore and what my options were."

Phoebe's face fell and she closed her eyes. "I'm so sorry."

"It is what it has become, as some fatalist probably once said."

She smiled.

"It'll be okay," he lied, staring at the screen and biting on his thumb. "Anyway, the conference call was a knowledge transfer and then listening to the strategies offered by the new guys. Binger's coming at me with a vengeance. She's claiming that I still have NanoCloud Nine technology, plans and designs that I didn't hand over."

"But, that's true."

He glanced at her, his eyes fierce. "No one knows that. And if I give her any of it, she's going to have it on the market in six weeks. We won't be able to get a lick of media attention, even if we could prove Nine was outright killing people. She would just suck all the oxygen out of the room."

She kneeled down beside him. "Have you thought of just going public?"

"With what? We don't have anything; never mind that I'll be opening up myself to all types of libel suits." He sighed heavily. "I'm trapped, Phoebe. I'm trapped."

"So what are you going to do?" she asked, taking his hand.

He shrugged. "The lawyers are preparing something they're calling a firebreak defense, but I'm not confident it's going to work. The idea is that every attack to seize my assets becomes increasingly more expensive for her. The lawyers think that at some point her business sense will kick in and she'll do the cost versus benefit analysis and stop. They have no idea who they're dealing with, which is exactly what Binger wanted me to end up with." He took in a sharp breath and steadied his emotions. "I've pushed more than half of my remaining wealth into the fund that's fueling Startup Strip. I'm going to empty out as much as I can from some of my wealth management companies so that if and when Binger gets to them, they're empty."

"But won't you own shares in those startups?" she asked, standing.

"The lawyers are pretty certain we have a way whereby we can donate my shares to schools, unions, and charities, without Binger being able to reverse the transaction. But if anyone could, it'll be her."

Phoebe took a moment and thought it all through. "How much are you going to be left with?"

He looked at her and licked his lips. "By the end of the week, I'll have maybe a hundred million safeguarded, if I'm lucky. And it won't last. She's going to come for it."

"What did you do to get her so flared up?" asked Phoebe.

Niko glared at her and shook his head.

"I know, it's a separate world of yours. It's not right though, Niko."

He shrugged, his fingers dancing on his lips. "If there's one thing that I've learned in corporate life, right has nothing to do with anything. Justice is simply a matter of which end of the blade you're on. I always tried to do the right thing with KnowMe. While there were moments that I enjoyed being the leader, it was nothing compared to the discovery and invention."

Phoebe stepped on to the gesture-pad and started going through the latest set of test results and images. "Wooo."

Niko looked up at her and then over at the screen. "What? Wait, what is that? It looks like a blob on a tether."

"Huh," said Phoebe, her eyebrows arched in amazement. "Niko, that's from yesterday's skin sample."

He stood up stiffly. "But we already checked that."

"Around three this morning it occurred to me that we were looking for things we know, like skin cancer and the like. So I decided to run an analysis on any features that couldn't be explicitly mapped to things from your first skin sample we took months ago." She left the gesture pad and went right up close to the holo-image. "This is unbelievable."

Niko gently pulled back his shirt sleeve and carefully ran his fingers along the skin. "Do you think that's why it hurts and feels rough?"

Phoebe shrugged. "Probably. I don't know. Let's see

what the breakdown is."

They carefully went through the data and then stood, silently, glancing at each other. "Do you understand what this means?"

"I've broken the laws of nature?"

"What? No. Well, maybe. If this really is related to a leukocyte, then you've somehow managed to form a mutant white cell thing on the outside of your body."

"How is that possible? And what's the tether?" asked Niko.

"I think it's a tendril," said Phoebe, bringing up a different set of test results.

Niko stared at his forearm. He couldn't see anything. He looked up at the screen again. "How didn't we catch this before?"

Phoebe rubbed her eyes, and yawned. "When you first came in, we checked for a variety of anomalies. As you can see in these results, we didn't see anything like this."

"Huh." Niko stroked his beard.

She pulled up one of the tests from the day before. "I think what you and I both noticed yesterday was that your white cell count was different than two days before. It could have been a virus or something, but you'd been pretty consistent for two weeks and then it changed."

Niko paced about. "Is it possible we just missed it the first time? That I had this before any of my Cloud Nine work?"

Phoebe took a sip of her coffee. "I was pretty specific for the type of unknowns I was searching for this time... so maybe? But my gut says this is new. Have you been doing anything different lately?"

Niko's eyes narrowed and he lowered his head. "No," he replied, turning to stare at the screen.

"You know," she said with a chuckle. "You've kind of made a liar out of yourself."

"How so?" asked Niko.

"All that stuff about the human architecture being limited, and then here you are, showing it isn't."

He stepped onto the gesture-pad, his face blank. Silently he started consuming all the new data. Phoebe watched in wonder. Then, all of a sudden, he stepped off and said, "I can use this." He grabbed his coat and left.

CHAPTER EIGHTEEN

THE
INTERVIEW

Two Months Later

"Do you really have to go?" asked Arju's mother as they stood on the porch of her Idaho home. Though a thin, wiry man, Arju was bulky compared to his petite mom. "The week's gone by so quickly. Why don't you just move back here? It doesn't have to been in town, just somewhere within a few hour's drive would be nice. I hardly ever saw you when you worked in Manhattan for that horrible company, and now with you in Burlington, it's honestly not much better. Don't make me go old school and arrange a marriage or something."

Arju laughed and kissed his mom on the head. "That would so completely shock me, I think I might actually comply. And I know what you're saying, the company I moved to Burlington for let me go, but... I just can't leave yet Mom. I came back here for another quick recharge but I need to go back there. I'll find something, I hope. If I can't find something there, then I'll have to throw in the towel on this software career and look for something else. Anyway, I promised Dad that I'd push myself to be the best and I haven't done that yet. I hide at home."

"Your dad didn't say that to haunt you, and you know it," she said, her head tilted in disapproval.

"It doesn't... it inspires me, come to think of it. Sometimes when I'm trying to figure something out, I think of the talks we had in those last days. Seven-year-old me sitting on the edge of his bed, him laying there with the machines working their failing magic." He sniffed back a tear. "I'm sure something's coming. Anyway, you didn't send me to a top college for nothing."

She laughed, straightening his jacket and checking his hair. "I didn't *put* you in that school, you earned it. You, Will and Davis, all three of you, from elementary school right through to college, cheering each other on. It breaks my heart to think of what happened to them. Anyway, going to that school made you able to do so much. You could do anything; it doesn't have to be software."

"What else can I do, Mom?"

Glancing around, his mom wondered and then snapped her fingers. "Open a restaurant. You can cook. You'd be the boss, so you decide who needs a Cloud or not. Cooking is a good way to meet a nice girl. You do like girls too, don't you?"

"Yes," he said with a smile. "And I know you're just

trying to say you love me."

She hugged him. "I am."

Arju caught sight of the auto-taxi coming down the lane. "Thanks for calling it for me. I love you too."

He took several steps towards to the taxi and halted. He dropped his bag and started fishing about in his pants.

"Arju?"

"It's my phone," he said, annoyed. "I hate that infernal piece of archaic junk." Tapping on it, he held it up to his ear. "Hello? Yes, this is Arju. Uh huh. Niko? Yeah. Really? When? Okay. Yeah, I can be available first thing." He hung up and stared at his mom in utter shock.

"Arju, is everything okay?" she asked, approaching slowly.

He laughed nervously. "Ah... Remember that guy I told you about? The one from the coffee shop?"

"The one who paid for your coffee? Yes."

Arju put the phone back in his pocket. "Apparently that was Niko Rafaelo. The Niko Rafaelo."

His mother frowned as she thought. "Wait, no. No, how —"

Arju laughed.

"Really?" she asked, her eyes wide.

Arju nodded.

"I can't believe it," said his mother. "You were talking with him? You've been idolizing that man since you were little." She grabbed his hands and they laughed together. "What did he say? Did he want to hire you? It's karma, you know it."

"Hang on," he said, letting her go and taking a breath. "That was the Director of Team Development. They want to interview me."

"When?" she asked, grinning from ear to ear.

"Tomorrow morning. Well, actually, first there's a phone interview in about an hour. But assuming that goes well, then they want me to come in tomorrow."

She picked up his heavy duffle bag. "Then get out of here!"

"Thanks Mom," he said, giving her a kiss on the check and dashing off.

"Go change the world," she said watching the auto-taxi take off.

———————

Arju stared out the window of the bullet train at the blurred landscape. A chime sounded, and the windows darkened. He glanced around at the newbies, curious how they would react. It was different each time he traveled across the country.

Curious children asked questions, and parents replayed what they'd heard as facts: that this was for their protection as they went through the abandoned, flare-scarred states. Arju wondered how much of it was true.

Suddenly the train's calm and soothing voice cut

through the chatter. "Please prepare for emergency deceleration in five, four, three, two, one."

Arju lurched forward against the shoulder straps as the train quickly came to a standstill. He watched four people go flying, smacking painfully into other passengers.

"Lockdown commencing in five, four, three, two, one." There was a chain of loud clamping sounds that started in the distance, ran through Arju's train car, and faded off in the other direction.

Arju turned to the bald, olive skinned woman beside him. "Has this ever happened to you before?"

She ignored him, lost in her virtual world.

He tapped the arm of his chair and watched everyone else. Some were gesturing, some were cursing, and some were staring at the walls and ceiling. Arju worried about what they knew that he didn't.

"Does anyone else have a connection online?" yelled a man leaning over the back of his seat.

"I just lost mine. What's going on?" asked a woman.

"I don't know," said the man stepping into the aisle. "Hey, do you have a connection?" he asked a fellow passenger, and then the one beside them, and then another.

Nervous conversations broke out throughout the car.

"How do we get in contact with an actual person?" asked the bald woman beside him. "I can't get connected to anything."

Arju shrugged. "I think everyone should sit down," he

said to her.

"Why?"

"Because a bullet train doesn't clamp down unless there's a flaring good reason."

The woman squinted at him and turned to look at her opaque window. She closed her eyes and put her ear up against the glass.

Arju shook his head. People were weird. One more reason he loved working in the realm of technology.

"There's a sound," said the woman. "Do you feel it?"

Before Arju could answer, a thundering boom went through the cabin. Then came a deep bass vibration that Arju felt in his teeth and bones. The train car, however, didn't budge a hair.

"What the heck is that?" yelled a man. Despite being only a few seats away, he was barely audible.

Kids started to cry, and when a second boom came, some started to scream. Arju closed his eyes and gripped the arms of his chair for all he was worth. He rocked himself back and forth, thinking of home.

As quickly as it had all started, the sound melted away. Arju watched everyone glance about and ask each other if it was over. He refused to relinquish his grip on the chair until he heard the train's voice.

"Lockdown conditions cleared in five, four, three, two, one." The sound of clamps releasing started in the distance, and ran through, just as it had before.

"Partial speed resumption commencing in five, four, three, two, one."

Smooth as silk, the train started moving again.

Everyone rushed online, their fingers flying and their whispered audio commands filling the train car with a rumble of anxious questions. Arju straightened up, listening hard for a hint of what had happened. All he heard was frustration as there were apparently no answers.

"Hey the windows are clear," said someone happily.

Like everyone else, he let go of his fear and stared out the window, quickly lost in thought. When the familiar landscape of Vermont appeared, he pulled out his phone and thought back to the phone interview he'd had just before getting on the train.

It had been routine for the most part. He'd found it strange, almost creepy, how interested the woman interviewing him had been in his lack of NanoCloud. She'd asked everything from how it affected his professional performance, to how he felt standing in an elevator. The oddest part had been learning that not only did the interviewer share his love for young adult books, but that Niko Rafaelo had a first edition set of The Yellow Hoods on his shelf in the office.

Arju felt the shift in the train's speed and glanced at his fellow passengers. Everyone was starting to get ready to disembark. Before he knew it, he was outside the Montpelier train station getting on the bus heading home to

Burlington.

He tried researching Spero on his phone, but all he could find was the essential corporate presence information. Even on TalkItNow, there were little more than whispers. There was plenty of news about Harriet Binger and her blaming Niko for bad earnings and making excuses about why they would need to consider delaying the next NanoCloud release.

Closing his eyes, he remembered when Binger had walked into the Manhattan startup he was working for, took control, and then a year later, drove it into the ground so hard it caused a partial collapse of the financial markets. Yet when the FBI was done, it was Arju's friends and bosses who went to jail, and Binger walked away with her reputation relatively intact.

Arju hoped that at Spero he could do something meaningful, and finally be rid of the guilt he carried around for having had a hand in people losing their life savings.

The auto-taxi stopped and Arju stepped out with a skeptical squint. He took a sip of his morning tea in its steel travel mug and glanced about.

He'd been to plenty of startups in and around Burlington, particularly on the strip, and all of them had huge in-air holographic signs fighting to get your attention. Some went so far as to paint the outside of their offices, or even the entire building, loud colors.

What stood before him was a very plain, boxy, grey-beige building with three floors. There were a few unkempt bushes, several empty flower beds, and the four standard parking spots with a mess of bicycles and foot-scooters. He pulled out his phone and double-checked he was at the right location. It said he was right where he was supposed to be.

Taking in a breath of fresh morning air, he walked up to the dirty, windowed steel door, and squinted at it. Etched in the glass of the window was the name Spero. Peering through the window, all he could see was abandoned office space. "Maybe it's the second floor?" he muttered "Maybe I should have stayed home."

Grabbing on to the door handle, he noticed it felt wrong. He ran his hand along the handle. While it looked dusty and dirty, it shone in the sunlight. A cheeky grin appeared on his face as he realized the entire door was just painted that way. He pulled it open and was surprised by the noise and a sight of people milling about and workstations of all sorts. He closed the door and looked at it again. The window showed an empty space, and the surrounding area was quiet enough that he could hear birds chirping.

"I think I like this place already," he said with a grin and entered the Spero office. On one side of him were hooks for coats, with a mat below for boots, and cubbies above. Along the other wall were wheeled contraptions of all sorts. He felt like he'd just stepped into an adult kindergarten.

"Excuse us," said a short haired, dress-wearing figure in a deep voice, with a tablet under their arm. A stream of others was following them out the door.

"Where are we going?" said the woman immediately following her.

"JenJen's!" said a tall, thin man behind them. "Best food and they have a real workspace."

"Sold," said the dress-wearing leader who was already out the door.

After they'd vanished out the door, Arju turned back to look at the clearly not empty space. There were offices with doors along the periphery, with open areas defined with tape or old style cubicle walls, some of which were hip height while others stopped just short of the high ceiling. He saw some people on gesture-pads, while others were seated at desks with keyboards and gesture sensors, which brought a smile to his face. It seemed that every permutation of ways to program over the past sixty years was either in use or on display.

He watched as people huddled together, brought up holo-screens and collaborated on ideas right there. No formal need to book a meeting, no issues of personal space. He'd read about companies like this, but his experiences to date had been anything but.

"How does anyone get anything done here?" he mused, glancing about.

"By harnessing the chaos," said a tall Asian woman heading out the door. "Interviewing?"

"Yes."

"Good luck," she said, and was gone.

He smiled. "Unbelievable."

"Hi Arju," said a woman with an Irish accent who seemed to appear out of nowhere. She was dressed in a short-sleeved red shirt and black pants. "I did the phone interview with you. Okay, let's get going. The others are already in process."

"Others?" replied Arju nervously.

She motioned for Arju to follow her as she weaved in and out of people and workspaces. "We like to organize our interviews in clusters, it's the best use of our team's time. One big day of distraction every two weeks, instead of pecking away at their time every day, disrupting their schedules." She pointed at a door. "You're in that conference room. Have fun."

Arju entered the conference room. His face fell as he looked about the rather ordinary room. He walked around the old wood table to the far end. The chairs were standard though well worn, likely from a going-out-of-business sale.

The only thing of note was a small, state of the art holographic projector. Arju immediately recognized the model and was tempted to turn it on. His fingers twitched with excitement. He started imagining himself manipulating in-air models and then his shoulders slumped. He didn't have a NanoCloud, and it wouldn't be able to detect his presence.

"Hello!" boomed a voice from the doorway.

Arju jumped back and shook his head.

"Did I scare you?"

Arju stared at the small, stout man with the thick salt and pepper beard. He had a tablet stuffed under one arm. "A bit, yeah."

"Huh, honesty, that's a promising start. My name's Felipe, but everyone calls me Flint," he said getting into a chair. "Sit down, unless you're planning on standing for the whole interview." He waved his tablet awake. He grumbled and tapped it several times, each time more annoyed than the previous. "Come on you flaring thing."

Arju looked about and then leaned forward. "Would you like a hand with that?"

Flint glanced up at Arju and then back at his tablet. "Come on, it was right there!"

Slipping out of his seat and around the table, Arju came around to stand behind Flint. Just as he arrived Flint yelled, "THERE! Okay. You can go back to your seat, thanks, Arju. You'd think I'd done enough of these interviews I'd remember them by now."

Arju returned to his seat.

Flint checked his chunky wrist-watch and shook his head. "She's almost never late." He slapped his own face.

"Tired?"

"We've had a few late nights," Flint replied. "Namely, all of them since I started. It's fun though, wouldn't give it up for the world. I can't remember, did I introduce myself?"

"Yes, you did, Flint."

"Good." He looked around waiting.

The door opened and in walked a woman whose gaze immediately made Arju shift in his seat. She was in her late twenties, with electric blue hair in a high ponytail that flowed down her back, and eyes that took her prey apart and analyzed the pieces. Her face was steely and she was shaking her head, muttering.

"Sorry, Flint," said Tass, sitting down. "I was reviewing the synaptic connectivity code and had to give that flooding developer a piece of my mind. Worst flaring code I've seen since I was a kid."

"Gone?" asked Flint.

"Oh yeah, he's walking for the bus as we speak," she replied, sitting and turning to Arju. "Good news, there's a job opening."

Arju swallowed hard.

"Oh, did you do the fake tablet problems thing already?" she asked.

"I did," said Flint with a smile.

"He was faking?" Arju shook his head in disbelief.

"And how did he do?" she asked.

Flint stroked his beard. "Offered assistance, then came all the way around. Respected my personal space but very eager to help. Consistent with what we heard about him."

Arju shifted his gaze back and forth them. "What's going on?"

Tass glared back at him. "Job interview. Why? Were you here to buy groceries?"

Before Arju could react, Tass and Flint burst out laughing.

"She does that. Oh, I love it," chuckled Flint. "I bet you were halfway to a heart attack."

Arju sighed, bowing his head, nodding. "Did you really just fire a developer?

Tass nodded, her lips curled.

"This is Tasslana," said Flint, "but everyone calls her Tass. She's Niko's right hand, the director of all things technical, and often a pain in the—"

"Thank you, Flint," she said, elbowing him. "Flint's like the uncle you never had, never wanted, and can't live without."

Arju leaned back, a relaxed smile on his face.

"Ready for some questions?" asked Tass.

"Sure," he replied.

Leaning forward and with a wicked smile on her face, she said, "Then let's get started." She waved at the holo-projector and the room came to life with models and windows. "I think this would be a good one." She circled a set of them and pulled them towards her.

Arju stared at Flint, confused. "I thought you guys didn't allow NanoClouds."

"We don't," he replied.

"But then how is she doing that? Is it the bracelets?"

Tass smiled and looked at Flint.

"Fifteen seconds," said Flint.

"Not bad, but you did give him a nudge."

Flint shrugged. "I like him."

"Well, let's see if he holds up."

For the next hour, they gave Arju ever more complex technical puzzles to solve.

Tass' bracelet hummed. "Alright, that's it for now. Niko's free, I'm going to update him. Can you check on the build? I want to make sure that because you and I have been in interviews all morning, that the junior developers don't forget we need all their code checked into the vault and working."

"I'm on it," said Flint, hopping out of his chair. "Someone will be back shortly, Arju."

They left, and Arju slumped in his seat. He'd kept a brave face, but he hadn't been so certain about his answers to the last few challenges they'd given him.

Several minutes later, there was a knock on the door and it slid open.

"Hello Arju," said Niko walking in. His hair was short and neat, as was his beard, and both had splashes of gray in them. His eyes were fierce and surrounded by dark circles. "I'm glad you came in."

Arju stared at him in disbelief. "You're really...ah... ah."

"Having a fan moment?" asked Niko, sitting down.

Arju nodded like a kid getting ice cream.

"It's okay. We'll just chat for a while, it'll pass." Niko smiled, leaned back and crossed his legs. "I've spoken with some of your former professors, they spoke very highly of you. Apparently while not the top of your class, you had a reputation for being very innovative. Tass and Flint said they saw signs of that with the puzzles they gave you."

"Ah, thanks." Arju stared at his hands and rubbed them together. "I hear that a lot, but I don't see it. It's just…" he looked up at Niko, "it's just how I see things. Does that make sense?"

"Yes. I'm the same way. It's not that we see the regular way and the other way, we just see the other way."

"Exactly," said Arju.

After several minutes of chatting, Niko's mood suddenly soured and he stood up. "I have to go. I look forward to hearing how things turn out." He offered his hand.

Arju scrambled out of his chair and shook it.

"Oh, and anyone who's got a grudge against Harriet Binger is a friend of mine. If she ever comes your way, you contact me, regardless of whether or not you're working for me. Understood?"

"Ah, yeah," replied Arju, his eyes wide.

"Good."

Niko turned to Tass and Flint, his face steely. "Flint, Tass, please wrap things up with Arju in terms of the offer and take him out for lunch. Don't go to JenJen's."

Tass nodded.

Niko grabbed his coat and walked up to the auto-taxi that was ready and waiting.

Stepping out of the taxi, Niko double checked for any new messages from his lawyers, but there were none. He opened the door and shuffled up the steps into the much-loved restaurant, JenJen's.

It's 1950's decor was quaint but looking a bit rough around the edges. Like many on Startup Strip, he'd taken advantage of them being open around-the-clock and their great food. It was a startup favorite because each booth had voice dampers for privacy and holo-screens with gesture sensors in the table for working. It was ideal and well thought out, unfortunately the owners didn't seem to have their hearts in it anymore.

Niko waved at the drone greeter. "Hey Kitty. I'm meeting someone," he said sharply, walking passed it. Arriving at the table, he glared at the woman waiting for him. "What the flood are you doing here, Harry?"

Harriet Binger swiped her lens-display clear and smiled at him. She was dressed in a dark suit with a red coat. "Please sit… Niko. Let's try to be civil for a minute. You know, this kind of reminds me of —"

"Of nothing. What are you doing here?" he asked, his fingers twitching.

"Sit," she commanded, her thin lipped smile fading. "I want to make you an offer. Maybe we can avoid any more unpleasantness. Or, I can raise the temperature. Does anyone over at your quaint little startup know that you're going to be out of money soon?"

"I'm fine," he said, plunking himself on the bench seat opposite her. "You overestimate your own power."

"Actually, I don't think I do," she said, pulling on one of her silver earrings. "I've done this many, many times over. I think I have a fair assessment of what I'm capable of."

He glanced over at the voice damper.

"It's on, please. I'm not an idiot," she said.

"No, you're just evil."

"You're one to talk, Mistake... I mean, Niko." She moved her hands along the table top as if smoothing it out. She took a breath and then renewed her smile. "Ready to listen?"

"I'm all ears," he replied, putting his hands on the table.

"By the way, siphoning your money in the startups along here, and the trusts and charity endowments, was reasonably clever. They won't likely hold up, but it was a nice try."

Niko didn't react.

She put an old leather portfolio on the table and carefully removed a photo from it. "Do you recognize this? It came from your office. I noticed that this woman was in lots of photos." Her cheeks were going red, the skin on her face tightening. "So I dug into it a bit. Imagine my surprise." Her measured tone gave way. "How *dare* you?"

"We're done," replied Niko, getting up.

"No, Mistake. No, you sit and listen," she said pointing sharply at him. "I still have an offer to propose."

"Whatever it is, the answer is no," he said turning to leave.

Harriet got up and grabbed Niko by the arm. "How dare you?"

"How dare I what? You even said it, Harry. I was a mistake. Why don't you run back to Lucy and beg your stepmother for some attention like always? That's why you took KnowMe, isn't it? Made too much of a mess with that last startup? A bit too obvious to the world?"

"Shut it," she snapped, glaring at the people who were noticing them. "What I want—"

"Is irrelevant, it's not going to happen. Unleash whatever you want, I'm not giving you anything. I don't listen to threats, and I know better than to trust you with anything."

As Niko walked away, she yelled, "I'll wipe you from history!"

"Do what you have to, Harry," he said, leaving.

CHAPTER NINETEEN
CRACKS

Three Months Later

"And there we go!" said Arju swiping at his holo-screen to kick off the compile of his code.

The developer next to him stepped off his gesture-pad and peeked over. "Already?"

"I'm on fire tonight," said Arju standing up and stretching. "But it only really counts if it passes all the automated tests, otherwise… it's just a lot of wasted time."

"This morning I thought I had an actual positive acknowledgement from a cell. Turned out to be a loop back."

"So you were answering your own acknowledgement request?" asked Arju.

"Yup," said his colleague, rubbing his bald head. "I went from my arms in a V for victory to wanting to hide in the bathroom."

"I've been there," said Arju. "I just don't tend to stand on my desk when I do it."

"So you saw that."

Arju pointed at the proximity of their desks. "You're lucky I didn't have a NanoCloud, otherwise a picture of that would have been all over TalkItNow,"

"Oh, and we're in business," said Arju, tapping the button to kick off the automated tests. "The compile was clean."

"You're a machine," said his colleague.

Arju smiled, his eyes slightly narrowed.

"I meant that as a compliment."

"Yeah, I know. It's just… at the startup I was at that Eversio bought, compliments like that were usually a sign of jealousy, and then something bad would happen."

"Oh, sorry."

Arju shook his head. "It's not you, it's me. My best friend became like that. Kind of… I don't know. Anyway, doesn't matter. We're a team here, right? And there will be plenty of credit to pass around when we can actually talk to a cell, or even just to the simulator properly. I'm happy to have my piece of it," he said rubbing his face vigorously.

"That was unexpectedly eloquent," replied Flint as he walked passed and disappeared into Tass' office.

Arju looked at his colleague. "Ace?"

"Haha, no, I'm heading home," he replied, picking up his coat. "It's ten. I'm heading over to join some friends from other startups. You should come along."

Putting his hands up, Arju shook his head. "I'm going

to call my mom, and then look at what's next on my to do list." An alert popped up on his screen. "Huh, did you see this? KnowMe has just announced the release date for NanoCloud Nine. They're going to skip Eight altogether." He scrolled through the article. "I wonder how Niko feels about that?" he said glancing over at his office.

Since joining, Arju had been in a few meetings with Niko, but mostly he'd seen him in his office, slaving away, each week looking more exhausted than the previous. Tass had become increasingly more protective of Niko's time. Whereas anyone used to be able to walk into Niko's office and talk, now they were usually intercepted by Tass or were told that Niko was out of the office. The mood around the office had definitely been changing, and tension was rising.

Arju got up and walked around the partially deserted office, thinking about their upcoming important major milestone. He stopped outside of Niko's office, tempted to go in and ask what they were really trying to achieve because like many, he was beginning to quietly wonder if the goal was impossible.

"Lost in thought?" asked Flint.

"Huh? Yeah," replied Arju. He looked at Niko's closed office door. "He's not looking so hot lately."

"Oh, he's a brick. Don't worry about him. He's dealing with a hundred and fifty problems, half of which are thanks to Binger. That woman needs a hobby."

Arju shook his head. "I don't understand how half of

what she's doing is legal."

"It isn't, or rather, wasn't," said Flint, motioning for Arju to follow him. "She's got an inside track to the senate and has been getting little laws tacked on here and there. Got a budget bill that needs passing? How about allowing this along with it? Got a civil rights clarification needed? How about a little something for Harry? Binger and that whole Eversio crew, evil to the core if you ask me." He opened the antique fridge and handed Arju a can of Ace, and took one for himself. "It's disgusting, but she's the second best there is at that."

"Who's the best?"

"Her step-mother, Lucinda Feer." Flint opened his can and took a swig. "That woman is a third generation billionaire tyrant. Highly disciplined, apparently brilliant, with the kind of stare that can melt hope. Married Binger's father after she took over his company. Harriet was a kid I think. Binger and her step-mother have this competitive relationship. They look all smiles on the outside, but you can see it in their eyes whenever they are in public together." He took another swig of Ace.

"Why does Binger not leave Niko alone? I mean, she got KnowMe."

Flint shrugged. "I don't know, and frankly, it's none of any of our business. She probably wants to get at Niko's best ideas, the ones he keeps in the sea vault."

"What?" asked Arju, laughing.

"Oh, it's serious. In a lake in Switzerland or something, I don't know. The lake's part of a nature reserve that he sponsored years ago, at the bottom of it is a sealed shipping container with all his brilliance that was off the books from KnowMe."

"Seriously?"

"Ha! No, but it sounded good, didn't it?" said Flint with a wink. "Now, ready to give a couple more hours to see if we can talk to that flaring simulator properly? That milestone's scaring the beard off of me."

"Yeah, I'm good," said Arju, putting his empty can in the recycler and listening to it deconstruct the can as he walked away.

Arju stretched and let out a mammoth yawn. Waving his workstation off, he stood up and gazed, blurry-eyed at his colleague's clock. "Two in the morning is an *honorable* time to leave." He rubbed his face and gave it a light slap. "No amount of Ace is going to help now." He yawned again. "We will connect to you later, simulator. So close, yet so far," he said, staggering to get his coat. "Maybe a week of four-hour power-sleeps is a bad idea."

Grabbing his coat, he slowly started making his way for the door.

"You're a flaring bastard!" yelled Flint, storming out of an office and spinning back around to wave his fist at the person inside. His face was beet red, spit was flying out as he spoke. "You have no place here! You're a backstabbing bastard! This isn't just a company, it's a freaking crusade! Do you know that we're trying to save lives here? You're what's wrong with humanity, you flaring flooder!" He stomped back and forth, huffing and puffing.

Arju stood stunned, never having heard Flint angry before. He glanced at the name hovering over the door: Malcolm. It took Arju a moment to realize it was their VP of Finance. He then scanned the other office names, including his own. There were no last names.

"You're fired, Flint!" yelled the deep voice from the office.

Flint pointed a finger. "Oh no, I'm not! Niko hired me, and only Niko can fire me. And trust me when I say I'm taking this to Niko. You unscrupulous bastard. Once he finds out what you're doing, he will nail you to the wall! Never mind Tass! You're a worthless piece of garbage!"

There was an awkward moment of silence.

"Get in here, sit down. You're misunderstanding all of this."

Flint stood his ground, fuming. He made momentary eye contact with Arju, and then stepped back into the office.

The door slid closed.

Shaking his head, Arju went home.

———————

Phoebe looked up from her holo-screen as her door opened and her right hand walked in. "Morning Jay, what's up?"

"Ah," he scratched his head. "I'm not sure how to say this, but I found Niko Rafaelo nearly passed out at a door near the back. He doesn't look good."

"Geezes. Take me to him," she said, grabbing a bag off the credenza behind her.

"You aren't surprised?" asked Jay, leading the way.

"You know I've been shielding you from what's going on, but it's not good. Lots of things to discuss one day, but it's not today," she said as they raced out the back.

Niko was leaned up against an outside wall, several feet from the back entrance.

"I've got it from here," she said, her stomach tight as she saw Niko muttering, fighting for consciousness.

"I assume that you're going to be busy for the rest of the day. I'll clear your schedule."

"Thanks, Jay. And sorry for dragging you into this."

He grinned. "Hey, we're a team, right? Plus, you're the one who convinced me to call that woman back after the disastrous first date. Dawn and I still owe you for that."

She nodded and turned to Niko, kneeling down beside him. "Niko? It's Phoebe. Do you know where you are?"

He opened his eyes wide and glanced about. "Had an idea... needed to check something. I think the Meta-Captains are burrowing... when we want to zero them... into my skin... burrowing."

"What? Look, Niko, you cannot keep doing crazy hours and running yourself into the ground. You're falling apart," she said, her eyes welling up. "You need to listen!"

"Want help getting him downstairs?" asked Jay.

She nodded and they took Niko under the arms and hauled him to the lab.

"Having a bad week," said Niko. "Binger again. I got to solve this. Spray worked…"

After carefully getting Niko down the stairs, they put him in the chair and Jay left. "I haven't seen you in a few days," Phoebe said to Niko. "But I know you've been working, I saw the reports and logs showing up in the vault."

He squinted at her, slumped in the chair. "Well, you didn't answer me about another date, so…"

"Very funny," she replied, scanning about. "I really need to get another chair down here. What happened with Binger? You were mentioning her upstairs."

Niko pulled himself up and leaned forward, putting his elbows on his knees. "Would you mind getting me a glass of water? My throat and skin feel dry."

"Sure," she replied, stepping over to the counter. "You were saying something else about Captains?"

Making sure not to be seen by Phoebe, Niko did a few new gestures and connected his NanoCloud with the analysis systems around him. With another swipe, he kicked off a series of processes, the machines momentarily blinking their compliance.

Phoebe walked over with the water in hand. "What are

you doing? You know our agreement, you're not supposed to be using your NanoCloud, it just makes things worse. Is this why you're looking so terrible? Your skin's looking pale and blotchy, and I'd swear your hair's looking—"

"Thinner?" he asked, stopping and staring at her. "A bit's fallen out."

She handed him the water and paced about, running her hand through her hair. "I know what you're going to say, but I have to say it. We need to get you to a hospital."

Niko finished the water and shook his head. "You know they can't do anything for me, and once I'm there, I'm a sitting duck for Binger."

"By the way, I know you've been sneaking into the lab to work on things. We also had an agreement about doing this together."

He sighed, lowering his gaze. "You know?"

"Of course, I know," she said pinching his bearded chin. "You're many things, Niko, but physically sneaky isn't one of them."

"I didn't want to worry you."

"You know, I genuinely believe that. But I also know that you're doing more than burning your candle at both ends, you've dipped it in rocket-fuel and thrown it in the oven. Even if you didn't have all of this," she said pointing at his fragile frame, "you'd still be looking beat up. You need to take care of yourself. You need to slow down."

He bit his lip and shook his head. "I can't. I'm not

done."

"But Niko—" She stopped, seeing the look in his eyes. "I know. I've just never seen you like this, and I don't like it. I wish things could be quiet and simple," she said taking his hand.

"I do too, sometimes," he said.

She kissed him. "I just want to help."

Niko smiled, his face slack with exhaustion. "I just need you to keep doing what you're doing. It means a lot to me." He squeezed her hand.

"So what was your idea?" she said, wiping her eyes and standing. "A new test?"

Niko's face hardened and he gripped the arms of the chair.

"What just happened?"

"I need to get to the office, now," he said standing.

"Niko, you're in no condition—"

"I just got a message from Tass, Flint's had a heart attack."

CHAPTER TWENTY

CRUMBLE

Arju was standing outside the door of Spero when Niko's auto-taxi pulled up. "Flint's already been taken to hospital," said Arju as Niko stepped out.

Niko let the taxi leave. "Where's Tass?"

"In her office. She's waiting for approval from the hospital to visit," he said, sniffing back his tears.

Niko rocketed off, and Arju followed.

"What happened?" asked Niko as he entered Tass' office. He was blinking hard to keep his eyes dry. After the door closed, he leaned against it. "Tass?"

She was sitting with her arms crossed, staring a hole in her desk. Her steely face was puffy and tear streaked, her blue hair down and a mess. Her head had a subtle shake back and forth. "I should have seen the signs. He pulled an all-nighter, *again*. He wanted to see me first thing and when I finally got around to seeing him, he dropped. He just…" she wiped her nose with her sleeve like a kid. "He just dropped, bang." She gestured at the spot she was staring at. "Right outside my door…"

"It was like the life was just sucked out of him," said

Arju.

"It's not your fault, Tass," said Niko.

She hit the desk with her fist. "He can't go! He can't. I..."

"Shh," he said, coming around and rubbing her arm. "You remember why his wife used to say that he was a dwarf?"

She frowned at him, wiping a tear with the back of her hand. "Because he was twice as dense."

Niko laughed. "She did say that, didn't she?"

Tass nodded. "You know that she used to bring us cookies when I helped him with his coding contracts? Who has a kid help them?"

"No one, but you didn't code like a kid."

"He can't die. I won't allow it," she said, her eyes welling up again.

Arju scratched his stubbled face. "Everyone just stood there... She screamed and I called the ambulance... He mumbled something but..." he shrugged... "I don't know what it was." He looked up at Tass and Niko. "I'll give you guys the room."

"Thanks," Tass replied.

Arju walked back to his desk, avoiding the spot where Flint had dropped. He sat, arms folded, staring blankly at his holo-screen until his workstation neighbor waved in front of him. "Hey."

"What was that all about? Because the old guy dropped

dead?" asked the workmate. "He shouldn't have been here. I mean, old guy drops and she floods. I thought she was made of steel. My respect for her is gone," he said, taking a sip of coffee.

Arju scowled. "Firstly, he's not dead. He had a heart attack or whatever. Secondly, did you just say you lost respect for her because she got upset that a life-long friend had a heart attack? Are you an idiot?"

His workmate pointed at his fellow developers who were gathering around. "Look, I think it's just a sign of what we can already see. We're going for an early lunch. This place is going down, and two of the new startups are picking up the lunch tab. Why don't you come with us? We could be over there making some serious money by this afternoon. And these startup founders, they're real steel man. None of this weak woman crap—"

Arju punched him in the mouth, knocking him backwards. Standing over him, Arju glared at the others. "What the flare's wrong with you? All of you? We're supposed to be a team, that means when one of us falls, all of us—"

"Arju. Tass' office. Now," yelled Niko, his head peeking out of her door.

As the workmate got to his feet, rubbing his jaw, he said, "Offer still stands, but you owe me a beer."

Stepping into Tass' office, he found Niko slouched into a chair, his face barely able to hold an expression. Tass offered Arju a modest smile and motioned for him to shut the door and sit. "Can you please tell him what you told me?"

"That the ambulance took Flint to Hickman Weis Memorial hospital?" he asked frowning.

"No. I already told him that. The argument you overheard."

"Oh," replied Arju. "Of course, right." He forced his gaze to meet Niko's. "I was here until around two this morning. I was about to leave when I heard Flint having an argument with someone in Malcolm's office."

"Someone or with Malcolm?" asked Niko.

"Honestly, I don't really remember. I was exhausted and I don't want to say I'm sure when I'm not. I mean, I wasn't planning on coming in until lunch today, but I had an idea that woke me up, so I came in. I think I can get the protocol harmony to finally break through the eighteen percent barrier."

Niko stared at him coldly.

"Sorry, I guess it's not that important right now."

Niko shook his head.

Arju continued, "I don't know what they were talking about. It was really heated, though, and whomever Flint was arguing with threatened to fire him."

"Anything else?" asked Niko, leaning in.

"I walked outside then came back in and waited for about ten minutes to see if Flint was going to come out of the office. It sounded like things were slowly calming down, so I left."

Niko closed his eyes. His face twitched, and his fingers fluttered.

"Are you okay?" asked Arju.

Tass snapped her fingers at Arju.

He looked up to see her glaring at him, shaking a finger at him sternly.

When Niko opened his eyes, his face transformed, twisted with anger. "This day keeps getting better and better." He rubbed his forehead with his fingers. "If dealing with Binger has taught me anything, it's to double check what I think is already secure. I need to talk to Malcolm."

"Let me do it," said Tass.

"No. Once you get the okay from the hospital, go see Flint. Arju, I need you to be an example to the others. Get back to work." He stood up, steadying himself with the wall. He patted Arju on the shoulder. "Thanks for everything you did and are doing. I might not show it, but I appreciate it."

"Sure."

After Arju left, Niko leaned on Tass' desk, his head down. "I just got a message from the lawyers. Binger's team just took out the entire firewall defense. She's frozen almost every dollar I have."

Tass leaned her head back and laughed. "So to top it all off, we're running out of money."

"Yeah," he said, tapping the desk. "I meant it when I said that I've learned a lot from dealing with Binger. She is resourceful, ruthless and remorseless. I'll be in my office, dealing with the lawyers and this mess. Hopefully there's something we can do. If you don't hear from the hospital in an hour, go over and make some noise."

Tass scoffed. "An hour? They've got fifteen minutes."

After a late, solitary lunch, Arju walked back into the office. His heart tightened as he realized it was nearly deserted, a few nontechnical people were present but clearly polishing their resumes.

He'd been tempted to join Tass at the hospital when he saw her drive past in an auto-taxi, but felt he'd just get in the way. Instead, he felt he could help by making sure they hit the upcoming milestone. He'd completed his own work already, but he was certain that Flint hadn't, as he'd heard him complaining about the upcoming deadline shortly before he'd fallen.

Waking his system up, Arju connected to the development vault and tried to find what Flint had been working on. "Okay..." he said scratching his head, unable to find any code associated with Flint. After several more searches, he shook his head and stood up. "You were working on something," he said, staring at Flint's closed door office. He wished he could somehow hack into Flint's account, but the systems were tightly secured for good reason.

A thought then occurred to him, and sitting back down, he searched for Felipe, and found a deleted development project that had recent activity. There was no documentation or description, just code and a holographic model and objects. The latest change was from that morning.

After two failed attempts to opening any of the files or objects, Arju got up and walked around the office, his hands behind his head. "What were you doing? You always complained about our deadlines. Were you lying?" He watched as one of the few remaining employees ended a call excitedly and jumped up. She threw a guilty glance at Arju as she ran out the door.

Returning to his desk, he looked at the holo-screen. He thought back to his first days at Spero, how Flint had clearly taken a liking to him. They'd chatted many times about life and their love of creating things. Arju glanced at Tass' office, certain that whatever Flint had been up to, she'd been in on it.

Leaning forward, Arju decided to try the special testing account that Flint had made him use in those first days, and to his surprise, it worked. A special screen opened, requesting him to authenticate himself. He frowned, not having seen something like that before, but without hesitation waved his hand back and forth in front of it. A message appeared: *I figure this is you, Arju. You shouldn't be here. I know you've been suspecting something lately, and sorry I've dodged the questions by being a flooder and extra blustery, but there's a good reason. I trust you, so I'm assuming you're looking at this for a good reason. Just tell me when you do - Flint.*

A cold sweat ran down Arju's back as he stared at the date and time, it was from that morning, ten minutes before everything had gone wrong.

———————

Two Weeks Later

Arju roused as a firm hand landed on his shoulder. Raising his weary head, he squinted at the world. His arms felt numb at first, a familiar side-effect of having fallen asleep at his desk. He'd barely gone home for more than a few hours each night since Flint's funeral.

"I need to see you, in my office. Now," said Tass, heading off.

"What time is it?" he asked, standing up and yawning.

"Six thirty in the morning. Time to rise and shine," yelled back Tass.

Arju rubbed his face and stretched. "I'm coming." He walked in.

"Close the door," she said, pulling up something on her holo-screen.

He glanced out into the office and then back at her. "None of the early birds are even in yet. Well, the ten of us developers who didn't abandon ship. Why—"

"Just close the door," she insisted.

He complied and sat down, his brow furrowed. "Isn't it

a little early for you?" he asked.

"Before Flint's death? Maybe. But in case you hadn't noticed, in the past ten days, this is my usual time."

"I guess we're both glued to the place."

She grimaced and stared at her desk. "Your commitment makes this particularly difficult." She looked up at him. "Arju, you're fired."

"What?" said Arju, standing bolt upright. "What the flood did I do?"

With a swipe of her hand, she rotated her holo-screen display to face him. "You've been accessing Flint's project since the night he had the stroke. I was behind on my reviews of the audit logs and finally got to it last night. Guess what I found?"

Arju put his hands up. "I was just trying to finish what he was working on. And he left a message for me, he knew that I'd try and he said he trusted me."

"Do you have any proof?" she asked.

He glanced about the room, rubbing the back of his neck. "No, but how else could I have access to it? I'm no security expert, not even at Flint's level, never mind you." He wiped the fresh sweat off his face. "Listen, I knew how much the upcoming milestone meant to him. I just wanted to succeed. I wanted him to come back and see it, and when he died… I just stayed here. I can't go to funerals… they freak me out, so I just stayed right at my desk. I've been pulling double duty, doing his stuff and my own stuff. Has anyone noticed that I managed to get cell communication protocol harmony up to thirty percent? No, because it's all a sham."

Tass' eye twitched and she placed her hands flatly on her desk. "What are you talking about?"

"I only leave here to shower, change my clothes, remind myself that there's a thing called weather, have a nap and then I'm back. I didn't understand his code at first, but I'm finally starting to. He was trying to find a way to hack the communication protocol for NanoCloud Nine nanobots. And it didn't make sense at first; I kept wondering, why the heck would he be doing that? Then I noticed that the code didn't all have the same style. After a while, I realized there were three styles, and it finally clicked last night."

Tass looked at him, her face giving nothing away, her breathing nice and even.

"Say something." Arju glared at her. "I'm not losing my mind. I figured out the latest bit of his code, and I finally fixed the last bug he was working on."

Tass licked her lips and clasped her hands. She stared at Arju until he sat down, wiping his sweaty hands on his pants. "Anything else?"

He nodded. "Every few weeks I've wondered: what were we really trying to do here at Spero? I started to think I was paranoid, but then something happened a few weeks ago, and you, Flint and Niko began working ridiculous hours, and you guys were always stressed. At first, I thought it was Niko's health, which was getting worse but it didn't seem that desperate. After I got into Flint's code, I wondered if all of the cell communication stuff was a front, a facade to hide what you guys were really up to, I mean, even though there kept being these magic nuggets of code that showed up every now and then."

"Wait, magic nuggets?" asked Tass.

"Yeah," said Arju, squinting at her. "You know, the bits of black box code that show up every few days, usually resolving something really important. Wait, you don't know about that? I thought it was just my code, but a few of the other guys had it happen too. We usually got a jump in protocol harmony either because of it, or shortly after it."

Tass rubbed her forehead and then shooed away the idea. "Someone was playing code hero, doesn't matter."

Tass folded her arms and leaned back. Her eyes narrowed.

"Am I still fired?" asked Arju.

"I don't know yet," she replied, wiggling in her chair. "How's your mother?"

Arju's eyes went wide. "Are you threatening me?"

"No. I asked how is your mother?" she repeated, leaning forward on her elbows.

He frowned and glanced around. "She's out of the hospital. The tornado was pretty serious, and happened all of a sudden, but she's okay."

Tass played with her fingers. "She was having surgery,

wasn't she?"

"All done. She's stable. Why are you asking?"

"Because if I pull you into this, you are going to need to be one hundred percent focused. One hundred percent, no excuses."

"I'm in," said Arju.

"You don't even know what I'm asking."

"Doesn't matter."

She chuckled. "Niko figured you'd be here. He told me at the hospital, when we were waiting to find out if Flint would have any chance of coming out of his coma." She rubbed her face and let the exhaustion show. "You know, before interviewing you, Niko really looked into you. He spent over an hour with some of your old professors, your summer job employers. He even spoke to your junior high informatics teacher. He had a hunch about you."

"Wait, this was all a test?"

Tass shrugged. "I'm beyond caring. Sometimes Niko works in ways that I know make sense to him, that they are justified in his mind and if I could see it from his perspective I'm sure I'd agree. But when I look at things from the outside, sometimes they just make me mad."

"I want in."

Tass scratched her head and gazed at a wall. "You understand that if what you think was happening, that it would be illegal? And that involving yourself could open you to legal prosecution? The property you're mentioning,

NanoCloud Nine, is the rightful property of KnowMe."

"I don't care," he replied. "If you guys are doing this, it means there's either something wrong with Nine or you're trying to hit Binger back. Either way, I want in."

"Okay," she said, nodding.

"I have one question."

"Go ahead."

"Is Niko dying?" asked Arju, his hands shaking at the prospect.

She closed her eyes and raised her hands.

"It's his NanoCloud, isn't it?"

She shook her head.

"Why doesn't he just zero the bots?"

She slammed her open palm against the desk. "Because he can't! It doesn't work." Her chin trembled and her eyes opened, the tears seemingly held in place by force of will.

"Can't or won't?" asked Arju.

She rubbed her temples. "He's tried, many times. He made them so robust that they learn and adapt and more. *Somehow* they start increasing their density, I don't know how or why."

"So he's dying..." said Arju, exhaling audibly. "Woo." He ran a hand through his hair. "That's not fair." His eyes welled up. "That's not—"

"You want to know what's not fair? That piece of garbage Malcolm, who was arguing with Flint, he betrayed us. After the doctor declared Flint wasn't coming back, I began going through every scrap of log and message we had. Yesterday afternoon I finally figured out exactly what Malcolm had been leaking to Binger. I'm surprised Binger hasn't brought the roof crashing down on us yet, but it's coming." She made a fist and focused on it. "He said everything we wanted to hear. He was part of the team, he wanted to get to the bottom of everything too, but it was him. We should have just pulled the trigger on getting rid of him the second we suspected him. When Niko confronted him last night with the evidence, he actually admitted it. He didn't care. He actually gloated about having sabotaged our attempts at getting more money." She hung her head.

"But... you just offered to get me involved. Are you saying it's over?"

"I'm saying that we've got a very short runway in order to make things matter. I need someone who's one hundred percent loyal and focused, or just get out."

"Where do we start?"

CHAPTER TWENTY-ONE

CLOUDED

Niko leaned on the old knotted cane Tass had given him, standing in the middle of the empty Spero office. When he'd walked in with Tass and Arju, there had been the last of the sixteen employees waiting for him, all of them fuming.

Malcolm had sent a message to each of them that morning. It had told of a wave of patent infringement and other lawsuits that Binger was going to be bringing down on Spero, and how each employee could be held responsible for their involvement, unless they left immediately.

Niko had started with fact and reason, telling the group how Malcolm had only leaked documents of no consequence. As they railed against him, he'd bowed his head and closed his eyes. He was thankful that Tass' investigation had shown Malcolm had entirely missed their secret project. The group had left in chunks, until finally the office had fallen silent and Niko had opened his eyes, squinting at the light.

He laughed, shaking his head. Binger had found a way,

one more time, to take something away from him. But in failing to take Tass, Phoebe and Arju, she'd given him an even more devoted team.

He stared at the front door, thinking of the anonymous tip they'd received about what lay on the other side. With everything ready, he turned out the lights and stepped outside.

There, waiting for him, was a woman in an expensive suit. Immediately upon seeing him, she called him out, "Doctor Niko Rafaelo." She held out a silver token.

Niko put both trembling hands on his cane and leaned on it, glancing at the token and then at her. "Yes?"

"This is your legal notice," she said, holding out the token again. "We will be accessing all of your vaults and searching through all of your code, documents, messages and other property for evidence of copyright, patent and intellectual property infringement. We will be starting in," she glanced inwardly, "ten minutes."

"You have no grounds," said Niko, taking the token. "My lawyers will have this thrown out in five minutes."

"The token will give you access to the affidavit by one of your developers as well as a former vice-president. You can talk to your lawyers, but you'll find it ironclad."

He winced as a wave of pain hit. "Anything else?"

"Ms. Binger will be sending you a message with one last opportunity to accept her offer. If not accepted, I've been told your remaining assets will be seized and criminal charges will be laid against you and your two remaining employees, Arju and Tasslana. If you are willing to give a verbal acceptance of the offer right now, the search will be withdrawn."

"Have a good day," said Niko, hobbling away, the sounds of an auto-taxi quickly approaching. He stopped and turned back to her. "How long is your access to our systems for?"

"Fifteen minutes," she replied.

"I assume it's a fully automated search."

"Yes," she confirmed.

"Good," he said, sighing and getting into the auto-taxi. "Very good. Take me to JenJen's."

"Phoebe?" said Niko walking up to the booth at JenJen's. He glanced at Tass and Arju, dumbfounded.

"Tass sent me a message that I should be here. We chatted outside, and I think... I *think* we have a starting point, after all this time." Phoebe glanced at Tass, who nodded. Phoebe tried to lower her shoulders, but they rose back up. "I guess you're not going to be keeping your worlds apart anymore."

"These ones, no," he said, sitting and tucking his cane under the table. "Tass?"

"When I was going through the logs, I found you'd been connecting to Phoebe's institute. You must be exhausted these days, because I found an *open* connection and used that to find all the test results data you had."

Niko's face went white.

"I closed all of them, and double-checked before we left to come here. Binger's not going to find anything." She looked out the window. "Why didn't you tell me about all those tests? I knew you were doing something, but all that data might have been helpful if I'd known earlier."

"I'm certain you spent time with it. Was it useful?" asked Niko.

She shook her head.

"There's your answer," said Niko. "Too much information. It's distracting."

She glared at him. "Feels more like you want to control all the information, have a feeling of power."

Niko's face fell.

"Hey," said Phoebe.

"It's okay," replied Niko. "You're angry."

"Yes," said Tass.

Phoebe looked at her. "Do you really believe that?"

"No. But I have to ask, is there anything else I need to know?" Tass stared at Niko, her cheeks flushed, her brow furrowed.

"No," he replied, glancing around for a server-drone. "I loathe how there aren't any people to take your order. No one to talk to."

"There hasn't been in years," said Phoebe. "It's one of

the reasons I don't like coming here."

Arju leaned forward. "Hey Tass, you said you've been getting tips. Is there anything to let us know what Binger's going to do next?"

Tass shook her head.

"Did you figure out who your anonymous tipster was?" asked Niko.

She shot him a sideways glance. "Of course."

Niko smiled.

"I'm guessing her guilt finally got to be too much," said Tass.

"Niko, I know you aren't going to like this, but you need to stop being the middleman. Your condition is deteriorating, and we need to get moving on figuring out what's going on and how to stop it," said Phoebe.

"Yeah, we can't have a single point of failure," added Arju.

He nodded. "Ahh," he said as a jolt of pain hit him. Looking out the window, Niko collected his thoughts. "I wish Flint was here. He'd have a good wisecrack or something."

"Niko, Tass said you can't just zero. I don't get it. Why?" asked Arju.

Niko glanced at Phoebe. "In Phoebe's lab we tried. The tests showed that it did very little. My last update to them, before I lost the ability to update them any further, made them too robust. Whenever I try to zero them, the remaining Meta-Captains quickly start building or repairing nanobots into new Meta-Captains or regular nanobots. Then promotions happen, and new Captains are in place. We need to see if we can overwrite the Meta-Captains' programming and get them to stop, which was what Flint was going to do after he finished the piece you fixed up," he said.

Phoebe noticed Arju's expression, Tass caught on to it too. "I'm not quite following," said Phoebe, earning an appreciative glance from Arju.

"There's a hierarchy among the nanobots," Niko continued. "Regular nanobots are either Workers or Captains. For NanoCloud Nine, I created Meta-Captains. The Captains are just workers who have been promoted by the other nanobots to help keep things organized, efficient and focused. They also relay important messages to other Captains, to allow for larger coordinated actions. Rather than having different physical structures, these are just roles that different nanobots play."

"You introduced that in NanoCloud Four, right?" interjected Arju.

Niko smiled guiltily. "Three, actually, but it wasn't really used until Four."

"The app vendors weren't ready," said Tass. "People paid for an upgrade that they didn't really get the full benefit of." She looked at Niko.

"That wasn't my call."

She quickly added, "It was his first big fight with the board of directors."

Niko scratched his beard. "Anyway, in NanoCloud Nine, I've increased the power level and signal strength for all of the nanobots by a hundred times."

"Wait, what?" Tass stopped the conversation cold. "You never told me that." She put her head in her hands. "Might as well have strapped a phone tower to your back..."

He glanced at her, and then continued. "I did more than just introduce the role of Meta-Captains; they are an entirely new physical structure. They are three times the size of other nanobots, and extremely resilient. I also revamped the design of the regular nanobots, so that among other things, it allows them to be disassembled and reused by Meta-Captains. If no Meta-Captain is present, the Workers will form a proto-Meta-Captain, which can then clumsily build a real Meta-Captain, and then the entire cloud starts to truly rebuild. The increased size of the Meta-Captains came along with a dramatic increase in the amount of microbial matter that they needed to consume. And they are the backbone of the increased communication network. And that network's protocol emulates real cell communication."

Arju burst into laughter. "You had me for a second there."

Niko raised an eyebrow.

"The part where you made it sound like you gave

yourself cancer or whatever you have on purpose. That." Everyone looked at Arju. "What, you're serious? That's crazy. Flaring suns, did you give yourself cancer?"

Niko turned to Phoebe. She straightened up and answered. "Cancer? No. We've checked several times. What's happening to Niko is different. The nanobots are very organic in behavior and structure. They're screwing with his body. It's almost like they're being treated like an alien invader. But there's something else."

Massaging his hands, Niko leaned back. "I thought about bringing down the output levels when I had everything working properly, but the last bit of code that I uploaded unintentionally sealed them. Every time I resprayed, instead of the newer nanobots updating the older ones, the opposite happened, part of the commandeering capability I'd added."

"Have you thought about doing a chemo-radiation type thing?" asked Arju. "I mean, zeroing is one thing but what about outright nuking them?"

Niko glanced at Phoebe.

"We actually tried that," she said. "At first, they seemed to be gone, but then they came back and... Niko's compromised immune system only made things worse." She lowered her gaze. "I'd insisted, and..."

Tass was shaking her head. "There's something you're not saying. I've seen a few of the tests you had Flint run, and there's something else about Meta-Captains you're not mentioning."

Phoebe sighed and frowned. "One thing about them is that they orbit a lot closer to the skin. We've actually found them burrowing into it. They consume the dead skin and other waste. It's a superior power source for them, and they've adapted to it."

"Meaning?" asked Arju.

"Meaning that they can rebuild faster; they can actually pass the limits on bandwidth and signal strength that I'd set."

"Flood me," said Arju, wiping his face with his hands. "It sounds like you made them nearly impossible to zero."

Niko nodded. "We zero them, a few of them are missed or are burrowed in my skin, and then they start rebuilding the whole NanoCloud."

Tass' finger started to go up, and then she backed off.

"Then there are the Leukos, which are a different problem," said Phoebe.

Arju put his hands up, motioning for everyone to stop. "Wait, hang on. Niko, why didn't you just have all of us at Spero focusing on this stuff rather than wasting our time trying to talk to cells?"

"It *wasn't* a waste of time." He paused, glancing around the table. "It was vital research." He scratched his head, tossing loose hair aside.

Tass tapped the table. "Which I still don't completely buy. I still feel like you're holding back."

Arju nodded at Tass.

Phoebe leaned forward, her elbows on the table. "Niko's body has had a reaction to Nine. He's developed these white cell derivatives on his skin I nicknamed Leukos. I figure they're likely trying to fight off the Meta-Captains. Whenever the NanoCloud density increases, their numbers start going up. The more of them there are, the more likely they seem to change, to mutate. I've never seen anything like it before. Other than looking weird and being related to what's happening to him, they seem harmless."

Tass shook her head in frustration. "I don't understand. How can his body be having a reaction to them?"

Phoebe was about to say something, but Niko stared at her.

"It's really disturbing… Sorry," said Arju.

Niko glanced at the voice damper for the millionth time, confirming it was on. "I can't go to the world announcing that what Binger's going to release is going to harm people, maybe, in some inexplicable way. Never mind not having the data, I don't have their design. What they're proposing might be very close to what I've built, or it might be nothing more than marketing polish on what's already there. But I'm not going to just sit by and watch nanobots become a banned technology again because it did some great harm to humanity."

Tass reached out and took his hand. "*We're* not going to let that happen. We're not going to give the world an excuse to recoil in fear again." Tapping her fingers hard on the table, she stared at Niko. "You should have told me everything. Everything. Not just bits and pieces."

Niko bit his lip and nodded. "I should have... but I'm not good at that. And I didn't want... I didn't want you to fear you were going to end up alone in this world. I know how that just shakes you apart..."

Tass went quiet, and she dropped her gaze.

"He was trying to keep his worlds separate, like he always does," said Phoebe, rolling her eyes.

Tass glared at her.

Arju raised his hand. "I need to ask. So, for the record, we *have* been violating KnowMe's intellectual property then? The NanoCloud Nine protocols and stuff, they actually own all of that, don't they? Doesn't that mean that some of Binger's lawsuits have merit? Technically speaking. And if that's the case, why aren't we panicking that they're searching everything we have connected to the Spero office?"

Tass leaned in. "Because an automated scanner won't find a thing. A human one might, and that will likely come next. Legally they need to do an automated one to validate the evidence given by those that betrayed us. If the same messages or documents are found, then it'll give sufficient grounds for them to be able to bring in an army of people to go through everything. But I wiped out *everything* I could that should be able to validate or substantiate their claims, without making it noticeable. Now it's just a matter of time to see if it worked."

"That was illegal," said Arju, his brow furrowed.

She folded her arms. "Do you have any better ideas?"

He stared at the table.

Tass handed each of them a silver token. "Anything you need to do, use this vault."

"The underwater one?" asked Phoebe.

"One of them," answered Niko.

Tass frowned.

"What about the stuff at my lab?" asked Phoebe.

"The data's already been moved," said Tass.

"When?" asked Niko.

A small, devilish grin crossed Tass' lips. "As soon as I got the tip that Binger was coming. Come on, I've got tools to help me with data cleaning and logs, I had to do something with my time," she replied, yawning. "Geezes, I just realized we've been here for what, over an hour and we haven't ordered anything. I need coffee."

Niko laid his swollen knuckled hands on the table.

Everyone stared quietly for a moment, none of them having realized how bad things had become. His skin was red and scaly.

"I didn't mean for this to happen," he said, "or to drag any of you into this. I want you to know that I've prepared documents that should protect all of you in the event that things go wrong. And—"

Phoebe interrupted him. "Don't bother with the 'if anyone wants to leave' speech, it's pretty clear we're all in."

"So what do we do now?" asked Arju.

"We order a quick lunch and then get back to trying to crack the code before Binger brings our world crashing down," said Tass.

———————————

Arju closed the Spero door and stomped the snow off his sneakers. The office was empty, other than Niko sitting at Arju's desk, and all non-essential furniture and equipment had been sold off over the past two days. It had been a trying few days since the team meeting at JenJen's.

Arju's workstation was accompanied by Tass', as she'd moved her things to work side by side with him. "Good morning, though I have to say, we have the weirdest weather here, sometimes."

Niko slowly and painfully rose, freeing Arju's chair and grimaced. "I'm always surprised how quickly the weather can turn here. The temperature will probably bounce back fast enough that the trees will keep their leaves. Nature seems to like reminding us that we know nothing." He was wearing sneakers, loose dark pants and a sweatshirt. His bearded face was thin and slack. "How's your mom doing?"

"She's doing better, thanks," said Arju, hanging up his coat on one of the hooks by the front door. "Where do you sleep at night?"

"Pardon?" laughed Niko, swallowing a pill and dropping his pillbox. He tried to bend down to reach it, but Arju got it for him.

"Where do you sleep?" he said. "I just read on TalkItNow that the last of your homes was seized. That's the condo here in town, and that was a few days ago. So where have you been sleeping? Are you staying at Tass'?"

"You are resourceful, aren't you?" replied Niko. Scratching the back of his neck, he nodded at his office.

"You've been sleeping here? Really?"

"Go look," said Niko. "I forgot to pack everything this morning. Some mornings when you've been in early, I just wait for you and Tass to go grab your coffee, and then I come out."

"Why? Does Tass know?"

He shook his head.

"And what about Phoebe? Aren't you guys—"

Niko looked away. "We had a few dates, but for some reason, it just fell apart. Every time we seem to start getting closer, things drift apart. It doesn't matter anymore. The only thing that matters is cracking the code and making a connection. Anyway, I'm not good at handling people and emotions, especially when there's something to discover," he said with a weak smile. "How about I share what I've learned since you left eight hours ago? I didn't sleep much, I don't anymore."

"Sounds good. Let me get you another chair though," said Arju.

Niko sat down. "Alright, I think I found an opportunity in the communication protocol between Meta-Captains. A classic man-in-the-middle type of attack."

"Using what?"

"A compromised Captain."

Arju raised a curious eyebrow. "I'm listening."

For the next twenty minutes, Niko walked Arju through his ideas and what he'd been doing.

"Okay," said Arju standing and stretching. "I've got to let that soak in, and then I'll see where I can go with it. Feels like we're trying to push a cow through a moving needle though."

Niko laughed. "A what?"

"My mom says stuff like that. She blames her mother… never mind. It's a mixed heritage thing, I think."

Niko shrugged and carefully reached for his cane. With clenched teeth and a shaking body, he brought himself to standing. "Well, with that passed on to you, and you knowing the secret of my office, I'm going to have a nap. Make sure you store everything—"

"On the vault that Tass gave us, yes, I know, you've been repeating that every day. I've got this. Get some rest."

An hour after the door to Niko's office slid closed, a rush of cold air alerted Arju to someone's arrival. He waved his screen off and sprang up. "Oh. Hey Tass."

She stared at him suspiciously as she took her coat off. "Too many cans of Ace already?"

"What? No. No, no, none so far."

"That's called a yes in my books," said Tass, taking off her boots and putting on her bright sneakers. "Where's Niko?"

"Ah…" Arju glanced at Niko's office door and then back at her.

"He still thinks no one knows that he's sleeping here?" she said, shaking her head. "I worry about him, a lot."

"Yeah," replied Arju, rubbing the back of his neck.

She stepped onto her gesture-pad and brought her holo-screen to life. "Alright, did he say anything?"

"He thinks he's found something in the Captain communication protocol. A chink in the armor, so to speak. Looks plausible."

Tass shook her head. "We've been down that road before, and it feels like flailing. I don't know if he's trying to throw us off course so he can hide what he's really up to, or if he's just getting that desperate." She rubbed her frowning forehead. "Maybe he's actually ten steps ahead of me, and I'm not seeing it yet."

"Do you want me to work on this, or do you want me to keep sneaking through his medical results and the logs? I'm guessing your feeling that something's off didn't go away last night any more than mine did," said Arju.

"Let's give him the benefit of the doubt. Show me what

he showed you and asked you to do. We did our poking around already. Unless he's got all of his data in another vault—" and she paused, thinking. "But he doesn't have the energy for that, so never mind. We should focus on cracking that protocol."

"Okay," said Arju, bringing it up.

Ten minutes later, Tass told Arju to stop. "Go back to that latest test log. There. That's a false signal response. We had that before. This is a random goose chase. He doctored the logs." She pounded the desk with her fist. "What the flare is he thinking?"

"Wait, I thought that too at first. When I couldn't find anything we'd missed with the initial tests and everything, I went back to one of the things that has always been bugging me, the zeroing. He did another zeroing two weeks ago according to Phoebe, right?" He brought up the records from the zeroing logs.

"Okay. I don't see anything interesting in these logs," said Tass.

"They looked normal to me too. You can see where the zeroing started, the reports of worker deaths, here are the Captains, and here are the first Meta-Captains. Here we have attempts at destabilization and promotions to Captains and Meta-Captains. The number of messages and requests grows quickly, then plateaus, then calms down. Everything looks like you'd expect for them resisting a zeroing, right? Final density ends at twenty point zero, zero percent. I mean, everything looks textbook normal. The ID numbers and everything are unique and—"

"What's your point?" snapped Tass, her leg bouncing with anticipation.

"I can't tell you what, but the data looks off; I just can't put my finger on it." said Arju.

Tass took control of the holo-screen and started going through the data again. "You're right, there is something off. No, not off. This data looks familiar."

Arju got up and paced about, his hands behind his head. "I don't get it."

"I need to look at this properly," said Tass, swiping the data over to her station and standing back on her gesture-pad. With swift, sharp gestures she started pulling the data apart. "Damnit, I know this data. Why?"

Crossing his arms and leaning against a wall, Arju said, "I compared it to several other random logs we have or that I found regarding NanoClouds online. I got nothing. I know I was grasping at straws."

"Shh!" Tass stepped off the two-foot black pad, closed her eyes, and covered her eyes with her hands. "Is it the IDs? Why do I know this?"

"Maybe it has something to do with the training exercise you had me do when I interviewed?" proposed Arju.

"What was that?" asked Tass, pointing at him with her eyes wide open. "Repeat that."

"The training exercise."

Tass snapped her fingers. "That exercise's data is from a sample set of fresh nanobots being deployed. It's the reverse of what we're looking at." Her face went red. "That's a complete fake!" She stormed over to Niko's office and smacked the door sensor. Nothing happened. "Open the door, Niko!" she yelled. A second later, she brought up the holographic emergency code panel, and forced it open.

Niko was lying in a heap, on top of a sleeping bag and bean bag chair. His cane was in the corner. "Niko? Wake up," she said shaking him. "Niko?" She felt for a pulse. "Wake up!" She shook him vigorously. "Arju, call Phoebe, now!"

"What about calling emergency?"

"Call Phoebe, now!" She pulled Niko's upper body into her lap and lightly slapped his face repeatedly. "Wake up! Wake up! Come on, Daddy. Wake up!"

CHAPTER TWENTY-TWO

#

Arju waved his apartment door closed and flopped on the mattress that permanently inhabited the middle of his living room. It had been delivered months ago and never made it to the bedroom. He thought of his mom and the look she'd give him for still living out of boxes.

He'd spent the past several hours walking around aimlessly, awaiting updates from Tass or Phoebe. Phoebe had freaked out when he'd called her, and then she'd called her friends at the hospital and emergency to make sure Niko would get special care. While the ambulance was on its way, he'd had to stand there, watching Tass come apart, her anger and steely resolve increasingly giving way to sorrow and despair.

Forcing himself up, he put himself in the shower, hoping it would help him sleep better. He leaned his head against the wall and let the hot water beat down on him. After a while, he stepped out, sure that he'd probably scalded himself but unable to tell. He felt numb, inside and out.

Toweling off, he sat on the mattress and stared out the

window at the Startup Strip in the distance, its bright holographic signs pushing back the darkness of night.

It seemed like each new startup had to outdo the others with a bigger and better animated holographic sign. Some of them seemed like fifteen second movies, rather than logos. He could tell which of the startups were the ten that Niko had funded, as their signs were more subdued. Arju found that funny, given how he used to love watching Niko on stage. The real man had proven to be a lot more complex and down to earth than he'd imagined.

Arju checked his phone for a message from Tass or Phoebe. Nothing. He tossed it aside and lay back, staring at the ceiling and wondering what he was going to do when it was all over. Soon, no matter what happened, Spero wouldn't exist and in all likelihood, Niko would be gone, and then what? He was the soldier who was tired of war, and the idea of being involved with software turned his stomach.

His thoughts drifted to his dad in his final hours. For weeks he'd been a prisoner of the master bedroom, surrounded by machines of all sorts. Every few minutes, his dad had squeezed his hand and asked Arju to promise him two things: to follow his gut and to take care of his mother.

An uneasy sigh escaped Arju, and he rolled back to stare at the ceiling. He remembered all the meetings he and his mother had had with the doctors and specialists, everyone trying to figure out how to treat his father's ever growing white cell count. It was years before the disease was classified and the path to a cure started.

Now, mutant cousins of those very same cells were going to rob Arju of Niko, and possibly threaten the world. He'd never imagined software being so stressful, the stakes so high.

He crawled over and picked up his phone. He scrolled back and forth aimlessly through his meager contact list. He didn't feel up to calling his mom, not yet.

The phone glowed red, a reminder that he once again hadn't properly charged it. He tossed it into the charging tray by the door, knocking his wallet-card out and on to the floor.

Staring at it on the floor, he flirted with sleep. Denied at every turn, he finally picked up his wallet-card, tossed it in the air and caught it repeatedly.

After a while, he got up and got dressed. Grabbing his coat, slipping on his sneakers, and taking his phone, he headed out the door.

The air was wet and cool, the snow nearly gone. He listened to the gentle whizzing of the police-drones scouting somewhere above.

He pulled out his phone and retrieved the wallet-card after it landed on edge in a pile of slush. "Wow, that would have been impossible to see," he said picking it up. He walked and played with it in his hands. He called Tass.

A tired, grumbly voice whispered, "Arju, it's three in the morning."

"Sorry, I couldn't sleep. I just... I have an idea rattling around in my head that I have to get out. Are you still at the hospital?"

"Yeah. I think this chair has to be a hundred and fifty years old. It's like I can feel all the sleepless nights of those who have sat in it before me," she replied.

"Listen, the zeroing log that we saw has been really bugging me. I've got a hypothesis." He held up his wallet-card. "Something's that right in front of us."

"I think the reason for the log is pretty obvious," snapped Tass. "He's a stubborn jerk who lied to our faces because—."

"No. Look, I know you're mad at him, and I'm not going to pretend to understand all of it." Swallowing nervously, he continued, "What if that was a log for an actual deployment of an even newer version of Nine? I mean, maybe he really did do a zeroing a long time ago, but what if he's been faking the rest, instead using them as opportunities to deploy a new version."

There was silence on the other side of the phone.

"So... um... woo." Arju straightened up. "What if trying to have us crack the protocol code wasn't about breaking in, but about making it stronger?"

"You mean like hardening it? Find all the weaknesses so that he could make it ironclad?" said Tass.

"Yeah, exactly!"

"That part of your hypothesis is a definite no. I've

looked at the code, and trust me I've done a fair amount of that type of stuff over the years, but I don't think that's what he was doing. Though… though now you have me wondering if he's been doing something else." There was the sound of a door closing and then shuffling.

"What are you doing?" asked Arju.

"I'm heading to the office. If he's been deploying improved nanobots like you're thinking, then he'd potentially have been changing the communication protocol. And if he's been doing that—"

"Then what are those changes?" finished Arju.

"And do they have anything to do with the cell communication work that I thought was a waste of time. I need to look at all of this stuff… What time is it? Geezes. Okay, grab some cans of Ace and meet me at the office. OH FLARING SUNS."

"What?" asked Arju, stopping and looking around the empty streets.

"I just got a tip that Binger's coming tomorrow. We're running out of time."

———⌒———

Arju ran from the front door of Spero right up to Tass's workstation.

She glared at him, and then pointed at his feet. "We're not savages."

He glanced down at his snowy sneakers. "Sue me."

"Well, this is a new Arju. I'll keep this one," she said,

her mood slightly improved. "I'm bringing the logs up now."

Shifting from foot to foot, Arju asked, "So Niko's your dad? Why do you call him Niko?"

"Oh flood, more questions that we need to empty out of your head?"

"Sorry, I just… I can't concentrate otherwise. It eats me up."

"I know. It's fine," said Tass. "Hey, listen, earlier on the phone. Sorry for biting off your head."

"Well, you left the neck, I'm thankful for that," he quipped.

She gave him an appreciative smile. "Calling him Niko just kind of happened. I mean, everyone around him called him Niko. When we were at home, just us, he was Dad. Outside, he was Niko. It also kept the worlds separate. Also, given there's only seventeen years between us, it kind of helps sometimes," replied Tass. "Questions done? Can we move on?"

"One more?" asked Arju, wincing.

Tass glared at him. "Seriously?"

"The tips. Where do they come from? Any chance we can find out why Binger's coming?"

"Nope. We got our last one," said Tass, turning back to her holo-screen.

"Are you sure?"

Tass nodded. "It'll be in the news in a few hours. Sandra

Gomez and anyone else who was ever loyal to my dad has been fired, effective immediately."

"Sandra Gomez, as in the VP of development?" asked Arju, his eyes going wide. "Crapster."

"You know who she is? Really?" asked Tass, raising an eyebrow.

Arju stared at her in disbelief. "Of course! She always took the stage after Niko. He'd do the big stuff, and then she'd give the details. Then he'd come back right at the end with that *one more thing* line of his. They don't do those anymore, since Niko's gone, but I remember her. I thought she was part of how Niko got pushed out."

"She was, though in her mind she said she was trying to snap my dad out of his funk. Thankfully, regret makes you do dangerous things," replied Tass. "She's been like an aunt to me since KnowMe started. I hadn't heard from her in a while, until the first tip showed up. It was from an anonymous account at first, but I figured it out. She got the message out to me tonight just before Binger had her NanoCloud disabled."

"Woo, that's some heavy-handed firing," said Arju.

"Yeah, she instituted some of the military protocols. Really extreme stuff. And she did it in the middle of the night, too," said Tass, scanning the logs and shaking her head as she tried to analyze them.

"Who's replacing her?" asked Arju.

Tass stopped and looked at him. "I don't know."

"Wait, no transition plan? That doesn't sound smart. Won't that have crippled KnowMe? Isn't that bad for business? That sounds like a temper tantrum," said Arju. He expected a quick reply out of Tass, but instead, she stood there thinking. He sat at his workstation and woke it up, glancing at her every few seconds, waiting for her to come out of her pensive trance.

She scratched her neck, lost in thought. Her gaze scanned about, from him to Niko's office to the ground and back. "It's personal, it's got to be. Why else do that? And so much to the extreme? She knows he's dying, but… there's got to be something else. What could make her so mad?"

"Maybe we can use that against her?" asked Arju, hopeful.

Tass stared at him blankly. "I have no idea." There was an itchy thought at the back of her mind. She pulled up the latest tip message from Sandra. "Damnit. Look at the geo-stamp, the time zone. Binger's not coming tomorrow morning, she's coming *today*. We've probably only got about six hours until she's here." Tass' face went pale, her eyes distant. "She knows, that's why she's doing all of this."

"Knows what?" said Arju.

Shutting down her workstation, she waved off Arju. "If anything happens with my dad, call me." She snatched her phone off the charging tray on Arju's desk.

"Where are you going?" he asked, chasing after her as she grabbed her coat and put on her boots.

"I have a stupid idea. A stupid, stupid idea, but I've got to try it. You handle this stuff. I'm going to try and beat Binger at her own game." She grabbed Arju by the shoulders. "Don't give me that confused puppy look. You are the smartest programmer that I know. If anyone can figure out what's happening, it's you. Solve it."

She kissed him and ran out the door.

CHAPTER TWENTY-THREE

TICK TICK TICK

Phoebe sat at her kitchen table, staring out the bow window at the final minutes of night.

She patted the head of her old golden retriever. Glancing down at the head in her lap, she smiled at him. He'd been at her side since she'd come home from the hospital and hadn't made a sound. A fresh pot of coffee was brewing on the counter filling the kitchen with the promise of pending comfort.

It meant a lot to her that Tass had called her in the moment of need, and it made her feel horribly guilty. Guilty at knowing the person she blamed in many ways for why Niko and her would never be together, truly did accept her underneath it all, she'd just never dug deep enough.

Phoebe closed her eyes, remembering Tass' broken voice and words that erupted feelings in her that she'd forgotten were there: *Phoebe, my dad's unconscious and I don't know what to do. Please help.* She still couldn't imagine the words coming out of the child she'd known, or woman she knew now.

She put her head in her hands and let a few eager tears

escape. Unlike with Flint's death, she was able to bypass all the mandatory quarantine rules and have Niko taken to a special section instead.

Seeing Niko's fragile body at the hospital, and holding Tass' hand, had been surreal. She wasn't sure what would come next, but she swore to herself she was going to be different. Laughing, she looked up and sniffed back the tears. There was a supportive sound from her lap and she laughed again. "Come on Bugsy, let's get you a healthy treat." She got up and went to a dog house cookie jar, and took out one of her homemade treats. Crouching down, she gave him a good scratch and the cookie. With a heavy sigh, she felt steady again.

A notification showed up on her lens-display that the coffee was ready and she shook her head. "Even if you go, you'll never be gone, Niko," she said, thinking of the hundreds, if not thousands, of moments a day that Niko would touch her life.

Bugsy stood up, went to the bow window, and started growling.

"Really Bugsy? Someone's coming at this hour?" she asked filling a cup of coffee.

Headlights shone and then an auto-taxi stopped in front of her house.

"What's he doing here?" she wondered, making her way over to the front door. "Be good, Bugsy," she commanded at her growling companion. "Hey Arju, a bit early, isn't it?"

"Sorry, my phone's dead and Binger's just had everything shut down at the office. No connections, no vault access, nothing. I think she actually had the whole block taken down," he said, out of breath.

"Like I told you at the hospital, go home. There's nothing we can do anymore," said Phoebe.

"Actually, that's why I'm here. I think there is."

She put a hand on his shoulder. "Arju, listen to me. You are loyal and devoted, and that's wonderful. But I'm sure some part of you thinks you can clean your conscience of what happened at that financial fiasco, which you can't blame yourself for."

"No, it's not that. Can I come in?" he asked, his big brown eyes hopeful.

"Sure, come in," she said. "Bugsy, come on." She gave him a nudge with her knee.

Arju stomped his sneakers on the mat and took off his coat. "I think that Niko's been increasing his NanoCloud density on purpose, and been working on newer and newer versions."

"What?!" snapped Phoebe, nearly spilling her coffee. "What are you talking about?"

"Got any more coffee?" asked Arju, his nose picking up the scent.

"This way, and then you are going to explain everything," said Phoebe leading him to the kitchen.

"Nice house."

"Thanks. Growing up, we lived in a bungalow. It's the only one in the area. Kind of reminds me of Dad, as if work wasn't enough."

"Oh," replied Arju, sitting down and rubbing his hands together anxiously.

"Cold?" asked Phoebe, pouring the coffee.

"No, just... don't know what to do with myself." He saw Phoebe pause with the mug. "Black, thanks," he said, his arms outstretched.

She sat opposite him and cuddled her coffee. "You think Niko's been doing this on purpose? That's crazy. What would make you think that? Never mind, I don't want to know."

"What? You don't want to know?"

She shook her head and stared out the window. She sighed and said, "No, I don't."

Arju was beside himself. "Why?"

"Is it going to change anything? All these months and months of helping Niko, and he's been creating the problem all along? Or making it worse?" She shrugged. "I mean, that's—"

"Betrayal, I know."

"No," she said, leaning back and taking a sip. "I was just about to use that word, but you know, it's wrong. That's not Niko. He's driven, and he breaks his universe up into these worlds, and he doesn't like them to touch because so many times in the past, that means someone trying to stop him from doing what he sees as right or necessary. And I guess the other bit is, while my medical training's a bit rusty, I know when someone's time is up. I saw it with my dad, I see it in Niko now."

"But don't you at least want to hear—"

"No, I don't," she interrupted. "I want to remember him how he was. I want to push the version of him that I saw tonight out of my mind. That wasn't him, and what I'm going to take away from what you've said is that he had something he wanted to do, that he felt compelled to do." She took a slow sip of her coffee and carefully put the mug back down on the table. "I wish he'd been willing to share all of it and bring me along, but there's no point in getting upset about that, is there? Can you understand?"

Arju stared at the floor for a while. "Sort of… I should go," he said fiddling with his phone. A minute later, new headlights appeared outside.

"Are you going back to the hospital?" she asked, her expression a mix of sadness and concern.

"I got a message on my way here that he's conscious, and I… I can't just let things end how they are."

"Careful, Arju. Sometimes we go hunting for answers we don't really want." She wiped her tears and stared out the window.

Niko stared at the beige walls of his small and simple

private hospital room. Since regaining consciousness, he'd done nothing but frustrate the doctors and nurses. Twice they'd come to zero him, only to find that his nanobot count didn't change. One doctor had accused Niko of somehow resisting it consciously, and threatened to sedate him and do it without permission.

Looking back at the tubes and simple machines wired up to him, he shook his head. It was all so primitive and barbaric. How little things had truly changed in a hundred years.

He grimaced as he brought his red, welted arms above the covers. With a wiggle of his index finger, he brought his lens-display to life. A moment later, he was connected to the machines around him and the hospital network. Pulling up his chart and the medical notes, he got up to speed on the plans the staff had for him. "Sorry, I can't let you do that," he muttered, changing them.

Gritting his teeth in pain, he reached over to the bedside table that had a basket with some of his belongings. He smiled as he found a silver token and made himself comfortable again.

An hour later, there was a knock at the door. Niko looked over at it and smiled as Arju walked in.

"You're awake!" he said with a big grin.

"Hey Arju," said Niko, his voice creaky and weak. He put something under his pillow.

"I thought Tass would be here. We were working

together on something, and she had to go. I finished up and… did she drop by?" he asked, pulling up his phone. "No messages from her."

"She came by. She's hoping to be back a little later."

Arju pulled up the chair and sat down. "Wow, she wasn't kidding when she said that this felt like a hundred years of discomfort."

"Hundred and fifty, at least that's what I think she said." He resisted laughing, his face tightening as pain shot through him instead.

With his hands between his knees and staring at the ground, Arju sighed heavily. He licked his lips and then looked up at Niko. "I don't know how to say this, so I'm just going to say it. I know you've been lying about your zeroing tests and that you've been giving yourself new nanobots."

Niko stared at him, poker faced.

Arju fidgeted. "Am I right? You don't seem surprised."

"I'm just listening," said Niko, shifting uncomfortably in the hospital bed. "You know, if there's one thing that I've learned about you, Arju, it's that we share the same tenacity for a problem. Even in the final moments before everything is lost, you won't give up."

Arju frowned at him. "Okay…"

"Did you crack the Captains' protocol code?"

Arju stared at the floor and shook his head. "That's the thing. Tass and I, we put our heads together and after she left, I finally realized what you were doing. Well, what I think you've been doing. You've been trying to get the nanobot communication protocol closer to actual cell communication. It was hard to figure out, but I did some error comparisons—"

Niko smiled and looked up at the ceiling. "You looked for the pattern of what had failed with both. Clever."

"So I'm right? Because if so I might be able to help."

Niko coughed and reached for his water. He took a calming few sips. "You found similar errors, and so…"

Arju shook his clenched fists, and continued, "I wrote a middleman that did error recovery. This allowed me to see what was going on and play with it as the data went by."

"Why?" asked Niko, his breathing becoming more pronounced.

"It lead me to see the differences between the cell simulator and the actual cell data you had in the vault from Phoebe. I thought I saw a pattern, so I tried using an alternating direction encoder. It encodes messages one way up to twelve bytes, then reverses it. It seemed like I was on the right track. That's why I need to know, so I can help."

"Probably an organic efficiency issue…" said Niko, grabbing the side of his bed as he writhed in pain for a moment.

"Geezes, Niko. Tell me. Let me help!"

Niko gazed at the ceiling, shaking his head. "Stupid, I should have seen that. Did you get it working?" His fingers fluttered, his eyes darted about.

"I think I got most of it assembled, but I couldn't try it. Binger shut down the whole office. Listen, we need to stop what you're doing with the nanobots so your body can help. With the protocol work, I think we can save you by working together with Tass but we need—" He stopped as Niko's face went red and cold, his eyes narrowed. "What's wrong?"

He glared at Arju. "Binger's coming. She's in the hospital."

"How do you know?"

"A camera just told me. You have to get out."

"A camera? How—"

"You better go," he said, wincing in pain. "If she sees you here, she's liable to make an example out of you. Have a life, go."

Arju stood up, shaking his head. "Just tell me if I'm right! Don't just die. You can't just do nothing and die, not when I can help. I couldn't help my dad, but let me help you."

There was a knock at the door.

"You better go," said Niko.

"Was this all a joke? Did you leave all of these clues as breadcrumbs for me to follow? Niko," said Arju, standing at his bedside, staring at him, his eyes full of broken hope.

"Not exactly," replied Niko.

"I'm done with software and people like you," said

Arju, storming out.

"I couldn't have you stop me," whispered Niko, shifting pointlessly to get away from another wave of agony. "And I couldn't have done it without you." He pulled up a diagnostics window on his lens-display. "I wish you could understand."

CHAPTER TWENTY-FOUR

HARBINGER

The nurse stepped into the room, "You called?" His voice was soft and clear. He was wearing the standard issue beige robe, from head to toe.

"More water… please. And, I believe I'm due for my next round of medication," said Niko weakly. The magic cocktail's effectiveness was wearing off faster with each iteration. His lungs felt like they were changing to stone, forcing him to consciously move them back and forth. His pinky fingers started twitching, a sign of the returning tremors. He clenched his fists and glanced about, wondering how much time he had before the lightning pain that shot up and down his nervous system would start again.

The nurse waved in the air, bringing up Niko's medical file on his lens-display. "You're a precise man, you've got the medication timing down to the minute. It's almost like you have a NanoCloud on you," said the nurse laughing.

"I know the rules," said Niko with a tired grin. "Anyway, you zeroed me thoroughly."

"Standard procedure, even if you are the creator of

them. Sorry."

Niko closed his eyes and shrugged.

"I'll be back in a minute," said the nurse.

As the door slid closed, Niko waved in the air, bringing his lens-display to life. The various windows and tasks stood at the ready. He sighed heavily as he thought of Arju, emotion at the edge. Arju had looked so angry and disappointed when he'd left, and for the first time in a long time, Niko had felt the pangs of guilt and regret, but he knew he didn't have the time needed to sort everything out. *Best to leave it as a partial mess than a complete one*, he told himself.

Checking his NanoCloud's health, density and other stats, he moved on to rummage through the new code in the vault. A moment later, he pulled up Arju's work.

As the door opened, Niko relaxed, thankful for the breather as the nurse handed him the pills and water. While he took the medication, the nurse opened a panel beside the bed and checked the various bags of fluids.

Niko touched the nurse's arm gently. "I just wanted to say I appreciate all your help."

"Oh, well, you're welcome," he replied with a smile. "Let's see. All these bags look good for the next few hours. I'll come check you at the end of my shift." He stopped, frowning.

"What is it?"

"Well, it's kind of funny, I guess. I just got a low

NanoCloud density warning. Right here, beside the man who made it."

Niko chuckled. "I wish I could offer you a spray can, but... I'm all out."

The nurse chuckled. "You focus on you, which it doesn't take a genius to figure out you don't do much of. I'll get resprayed at the nursing station, we have a steady supply. Call if you need anything."

"Thanks." As soon as the door closed, Niko raised his hands and flexed the fingers. His hands were red and blotchy, his knuckles swollen and discolored. With a forceful exhale, he immediately went right back to working, a whimper of pain escaping as the first of the nervous system jolts arrived. His face shone with sweat.

The door opened again, Niko lowered his arms and stared at the doorway.

"Thought I might as well bring you a pitcher. I'll just put it on the side table," said the nurse, coming in and stopping. He looked Niko over. "You really should try to sleep; you're looking a bit flushed."

Niko nodded and closed his eyes. The door touched closed and then immediately reopened.

"Bracing for impact?" asked a sharp female voice.

"Hello Harry," he replied, opening his eyes. He tapped an index finger against his other fingers together.

"Compulsive counting? Are you nervous, Niko? That'd be new." She waved the door closed and stood at the foot of the bed. Taking in the room, she shook her head. "I'm disappointed, Niko. I mean, unless I've financially crippled you even worse than I thought, shouldn't you be in something a bit more becoming a former celebrity? I'm fairly certain I'd left you enough. After all, I am a surgeon when it comes to taking someone's life apart." She stared at him, a flash of surprise and concern was quickly replaced with the wry smiled poker face Niko was used to.

She was wearing a crimson three-quarter-length coat, and dark crimson pants. Her subdued white, double collared shirt brought attention to her piercing green eyes.

"You don't usually wear your hair loose," remarked Niko. "What's the special occasion?"

Gripping the edge of the bed, she stared at him, her predatory eyes cold and calculating. "I'm visiting a dying… old friend," she said, straightening up and folding her arms. The edge of her mouth twitched with anticipation.

"How bad is it for him?"

"Well, let's see. His company is gone, his friends deserted him or were legally barred from communicating with him; which reminds me, did you know that Sandra Gomez was arrested? Turns out she was leaking information to someone. It couldn't be proven to whom she was leaking information, but it didn't matter. She'll be sued into oblivion. Poor thing, has a family and everything."

Niko's face went red.

"But why would you care? I mean she *did* betray you

after all. Part of the club that brought in the coup." A Cheshire grin spread across her face. "You know, I came in here ready to have an out and out argument from the first moment, but I'm *so* happy we're doing it this way. I get to feel your pain so much longer, Mistake." She sat on the edge of the bed. "Did you see the technical specifications we released about Nine? I think we did pretty well on figuring out what you were up to. There were enough old designs, plus the prototypes that we collected from the day you did the hearing... it'll have quite the punch."

Niko stared at the bed.

"Oh, you didn't see them? Maybe that's because we just released them. I'd share them with you, but I know the rules about patients and NanoClouds. I think it's important that hospitals abide by those rules, and given how hard up they are for funding these days, I was quite proud of our decision at KnowMe to provide brand new zeroing devices to all the hospitals in this area."

Rubbing his sweaty face, Niko sighed. "I bet you like the idea that it's Sandra's handiwork under it all, that stripped away my cloud."

"You know, I do."

"Harry, whatever your Nine is, if it's based on any of my work, you can't release it. People will get sick, like I am."

She chuckled. "Oh please, Mister Melodrama. Always thinking of yourself. You know, I *actually* worried about that early on, so had my people look at the designs we went through, and run simulators against the levels of radiation, etc. There were absolutely no health concerns raised whatsoever."

Niko glanced up at the time on his lens-display and then back at Harriet. She stared at him, her eyes studying him. Niko raised a finger and waved it back and forth. "You really are easy to play, Harry. Always so paranoid." He laughed, wincing as he did so.

"Oh shut up," she snapped. "I came here to offer you one last chance.

He elbowed his pillows to get more comfortable, his eyes welling up in pain as he did so. "Your people are simulating Nine, I've lived it."

"So you admit to having my property on your person? Well, that makes things a lot easier," she said, clicking an index and forefinger. "Oh, sorry, that's not a picture, but rather ending the recording I needed. Wonderful new feature we've added in Eight."

"I didn't say that," snapped Niko.

She brushed her hair back. "You're really bad at this game, aren't you? One mistake after another. And then comes the part where I had my team reduce the power levels by thirty percent, just in case there was something we missed. We're now covered from a press and liability perspective because even without any evidence, we took precautions. Happy?" she asked. "Not that I care."

Watching her like a hawk, Niko reached out for his water, his arm shaking. With heroic effort, he got it mostly to his mouth. His face relaxed as he embraced the cooling sensation. "What are you really doing here, Harry? I don't believe that you came here to get a quote from me that would let you rob me of what little I have left. You've never needed real cause or reason to sue someone into oblivion. You just break whatever laws you fancy and pay off whomever you need to get the justice you want."

She smiled. "Laws don't really apply to people like me. No one can touch me."

"Lucy could."

Harriet glared at Niko. "Really? Are you trying to sow some seed of suspicious in me? Make me fear that perhaps one day Lucy might betray me? Please, if she was ever going to it would have been long ago," she said waving him off. Her eyes opened wide in mock-surprise.

"Or is it that you want to remind me that there's someone more powerful than me?" she asked. "Oh, wait, maybe that's just how I let it appear. If anyone came after me, there would be dire consequences. Your company's stock would drop like a rock, for one. And if there's anything Lucy hates, it's losing money. She'll protect me until her dying breath, not that I need it." She poked him in the ribs. "Was that fun? Dying man's last attempt at wounding someone? You're so petty."

Niko reached out and grabbed her arm as he shook in

pain, his face contorted, his teeth clenched.

She shook him off and stood up. "Are you done?"

He sighed in relief as the wave passed.

Harriet leaned against the wall, her arms behind her. "According to these doctors, you've probably only got a few hours left, though it could be minutes. They don't really know. But before you're out of moves in the grand game, I'm going to offer you one last chance to make the world a better place. A way to make some amends for your wrongs to me."

Niko growled. "Wrongs to you? Ha. You know, that look in your eyes takes me back to high school. Were you trying to impress your step-mother when you stole all my friends, turned the teachers against me, and did your best to run my life into the ground? Was Lucy impressed or was she upset that you didn't break me? Did she even notice?"

Harriet scowled at him, her cheeks going red. "You have some nerve. You should have never taken away what was *my* decision. And you had it up on your *wall* in your office for all the world to see. Parading it around for everyone to know how I had been weak for a few hours. A disciplined life, threatened because you made it your life mission to mock me. Do you know how horrifying it was to see her in those pictures?"

"What's wrong with you? She has nothing to do with you, and you never wanted anything to do with her."

"I wanted her not to exist! Of all the mistakes I have

made in my life, Niko, none was greater than feeling sorry for you that one night. One late night of thinking you were a normal guy, that maybe the entire world around us was wrong. I get pregnant, and you return back to being your loathly Mister Hyde. Of course, I ripped everything I could from you, I couldn't have anyone know. That embryo was to be cleansed and repurposed. And you weren't even supposed to know about it! I bribed that doctor enough for him to buy a car! That *thing* you've raised—"

"NO!" yelled Niko sitting up, his abdominal and back muscles feeling like they ripped. "You do *not* get to say that about her. You gave away your egg. You forfeited every right you had. Do you know how I found out? I showed up to do drone repair, one of the many part time jobs I had. Do you know what it was to see the haunted look on that doctor's face? He wouldn't say a thing, he just looked at me and hung around in the background. When I went to leave, he glanced at a screen and then walked off. I came over to it. Imagine my surprised when I saw my name listed in some embryo's history as the initial genetic donor, along with yours."

"You should have left it alone!" yelled Harriet. "You should have accepted your place! You had no right, Mistake."

"I had every right! That's what the law of Seven Day Redemption is exactly for. I had nothing to distract me, nothing else in my life because of you, and so I used my inheritance and fought through every decision and moment. *You* made it possible. I was forced to switch schools, I sold my parents' house, I had nothing to focus on except for the artificial womb and then Tass when she arrived. And to think, you've hunted me every now and then for sport, and you never even knew that I had a daughter."

Harriet came right up to Niko's side, her face twisted with rage. "Every time I hear your name, every time I see your face, it reminds me of that sickening weakness that lives inside me. And then there was her, doubling that. A living, breathing symbol that infects my world." She shook with revulsion. "The *one* reason I haven't outright destroyed you, Niko, is because I've looked into who Tasslana is. I've spoken to the simpletons she worked for in Manhattan, to her professors at college, and despite having you in her DNA, she's me in many regards. I think I can reform her, help her get over the you in her makeup."

Harriet leaned back and sighed. "I know how much you must feel for her. I know how much financially you care for her, because I have my finger on the trusts you left for her and Arju. With a flick, they will be penniless, and so I offer you this opportunity to call her. Bring her here, give your… blessing… and I will embrace her as my own."

Niko glanced upwards for a second.

"Stop doing that! Stop pretending that you're important, that you have a NanoCloud, that you matter!" She smashed her fist against the wall. "The only thing that you can do that matters, is stop this woman you forced to exist from being an abomination."

Panic flashed on Niko's face as his eyes darted back and forth and his breaths became shallow. He clenched his teeth as another wave of pain hit. After it passed, he ran one hand along the back of the other. "I can't feel it… AH!" he screamed as a sharp jolt ran through his back. He slumped in his bed, his eyes half open, his head soaked in sweat. "Protocol harmony is ninety-one percent," he mumbled.

"What are you… never mind. Look, Niko, you're falling apart." She pulled out a shiny, red cellphone from a coat pocket. "Call her, bring her here. Tell her who I am and that you want her to know me, and I will accept that as an apology for everything you have done and been." She placed it in his hand. "Just do it, Niko."

He stared at her. "You know, I never wanted to admit it, but she *does* have some element of you. She knew I couldn't be you, I didn't have enough time," he said weakly.

"You could never beat me, not with all the time in the world," retorted Harriet with a chuckle.

"Tass sees solutions that I can't, or are too ruthless for me to consider. She's beautiful, technically brilliant, has immense business savvy, and a great sense for the battlefield."

Harriet smiled. "I guess we'll get along then."

Niko shook his head and dropped the phone to the floor. "She's the center of my universe and my safety line back to the world of the sane. And to her, I'm the same. You aren't after discovering a daughter, this isn't about me making amends with you, you're after a trophy for Lucy. If there's one thing that a near-trillionaire like Lucy Feer can't force into this world, it's a granddaughter. And there's nothing in this world that could make you give her one. I'm not handing Tass to you."

Harriet walked up to the panel beside Niko's bed and waved at it; it unlocked. "Call her," she said, opening it. "Bring her here and do as you're told."

He frowned. "How did you open that?"

"Oh please," she said, swatting away his surprise. "Money and influence, well planned and well played, trump everything."

Reaching out, he placed a gentle hand on her forearm. He closed his eyes, his brow furrowed. "No more…" he mumbled.

She stared at his hand, curious. A relaxed smile slowly appeared on her face. She removed his hand and closed the panel. "So the threat of a hastened death, that's what it takes to humble the great Niko Rafaelo? I thought taking KnowMe and devastating your public image would do it, but no. I guess it means you're human after all." She recognized him gesturing with his other hand. Gradually, her expression shifted to a frown. "Niko, what are you up to?"

He gradually opened his eyes, a sense of peace on his face. "You lose, Harry."

She cracked a smile and then laughed. "Why, because you said so?"

"No, because Tass just did."

"What are you talking about?" Her expression went steely.

He smiled as his body started to tremble. "I told her who you were shortly after you took away KnowMe. I almost believed that you'd managed to take her away from me as well, but I gave her the space she needed and she came back. I didn't argue with her when she visited earlier, when she said there was only one way to beat you. There was no point. She had her mind made up. She was determined to take everything from you."

Harriet shrugged. "I don't believe you. I don't know what you think she could have done, but there's nothing."

"I just got a message from Tass that she's finished her meeting with Lucy."

Harriet shoulders dropped, her face went white. "I don't believe you. Lucy's office is on the other side of the country, anyway."

"You forced the sale of my scramjet, but we still get free rides on it. The benefit of having helped some of these startups hit it big, is that a few of the owners didn't mind shelling out a few coins to help me out."

Harriet rubbed her chin and took a step away, before turning back to stare at Niko. "Lucy would never see someone out of the blue. I can't even see her without an appointment."

"That's what I thought. But there's something about a woman with blue hair and demons behind her eyes, with an impossible story about being Lucinda Feer's long-lost granddaughter that can capture the imagination. Apparently Lucy couldn't resist."

Harriet laughed and sighed. "You know, I needed that. I needed to know that despite everything, your spirit was still in there." She walked over to him and stroked his forehead. "I would have heard, Niko. I would have received a message or call, and yet…"

"I did."

"You did what?"

Struggling, he brought his hand up to his eye and tapped it, the lens-display flashing blue momentarily before becoming transparent again. "You would have got the message, but you don't have a NanoCloud anymore, do you?"

Narrowing her eyes, she shook her head. "I used the codes to open this panel. What are you talking about?"

"How about now?" asked Niko, erupting into a coughing fit. His face went red as he fought for air. He stared, teeth clenched, at the water.

Harriet swiped the air, and then again. "So you zeroed me somehow. That's cute." She shrugged and looked at Niko flail and swat at the water. Picking up the glass, she smiled at him and then dropped it to the ground. "I want you to die hearing this, Niko. I want you to know that I will rip apart the trusts you have for Arju and Tass. I will ruin it all and still have Lucy's favor. You think your little game has done anything? You've just inconvenienced me, claimed an afternoon of mine, maybe."

She turned and walked to the door, glancing back at him. "And whatever parlor trick you did to my NanoCloud, enjoy that glimmer of victory as you fall into the darkness." She waved goodbye as he continued to cough, and left.

The nurse arrived a few seconds later. He refilled Niko's cup, hauled him to a sitting position, and helped him drink. With the fit subsiding, he eased Niko back against his pillows. "I'll get you some clean sheets and a new gown."

"I'm okay," croaked Niko.

"You're soaked." The nurse's eyes filled with sorrow. "You can't feel much, can you?"

"Just pain," he whispered.

"I'm sorry," said the nurse. "You should rest. I'll stop any further visitors."

Niko grabbed the nurse's hand. "No. Please, if my daughter comes back, no matter what, please let her in."

The nurse nodded.

Exhausted, he slumped into his pillows and clicked his index finger and thumb together. "I created that recording feature, Harry," he whispered. Rallying all of his strength, he reached under his pillow and pulled out the silver token and activated it.

With hands in his lap, he closed his eyes and let his tongue search his mouth for moisture. Opening his eyes, he stopped and stared at the brown string bracelet on his right wrist. He smiled at the three beads, and then glanced about the empty room, unable to remember Phoebe visiting.

His breathing was shallow and labored, each one more painful than the last. Slowly flicking a finger, he awoke his lens-display. "NanoCloud density is up to five hundred and thirty-one percent. It might be enough," he whispered. Fighting his swollen joints, he brought up a developer window. "Protocol Harmony is at ninety-eight percent. That's not good enough." He closed his eyes and shook his head. "I need to…" he frowned. "What do I need to do? Getting so hard to think… I just… I just need to rest for a minute… just a minute."

CHAPTER TWENTY-FIVE

GOODBYES

One Week Later

"Few people know that when the solar flare burned the middle states, Niko almost abandoned his dream. Imagine that for a moment. There would have been no NanoClouds, no hero bringing about an era of innovation, no one reminding our broken nation that it could heal. We would have stayed in the shadow of the past, instead of rising and casting our own." Phoebe took a steadying breath and smiled. The crowd waited patiently.

"I got to know Niko," she continued, "right after The Flare. He was so passionate about this vision he had. And each and every day he was urged by those in authority to drop it. His life would have been so much easier if he had, but he wouldn't, he couldn't. That's not... wasn't Niko." A sorrowful laugh escaped. "Not at all."

She gripped the sides of the old podium and stared out at the enormous crowd. There sat captains of industry, heads of startup companies, press, politicians, and friends. She still couldn't believe she'd been asked to give the first speech.

She pushed her long, curly, black hair over her ears, revealing more of her beautiful square jaw and the sadness that soaked her from soul to face.

She looked at the front row. She smiled at Tass, a younger woman with a topknot of dark hair. For so long, the two women had acted like rivals for Niko's attention. Why had it taken Niko's death for them to be able to find common ground?

Phoebe glanced at the silent camera-drones as they floated about, broadcasting the funeral to hundreds of millions of people around the world. She closed her eyes and took in a breath of the warm and welcoming summer air.

"For days, the news had been filled with stories about the raw power of the destruction, about those who had been evacuated from the coasts decades before or who had escaped the Great Quake of California, having once again lost everything. It didn't matter that the best minds had seen it coming over a year ahead of time, and that everyone had been safely removed, because it was yet another opportunity to tell tales of destruction and despair. It almost tipped Niko over the edge.

"But somehow," she said, glancing at the woman with the topknot, "he held on to his dream. It was a privilege to see it first hand in the early days, as that almost extinguished spark of innovation became a roaring fire. And then, to be there at the end, despite his broken body, to see his passion and fire still burning as brightly. There won't ever be another Niko Rafaelo." She shook, tears streaming down. "Thank you."

She paused, staring out at the crowd. "I loved him," she said staring at Tass, "I wish I had let myself, instead of finding excuses to keep turning away." She kissed her hand and waved it in the air. "Goodbye Niko."

As she was leaving the podium, Tass got up and hugged her. In contrast to Phoebe, Tass' eyes were tearful but her face was steel. Slowly making her way up to the podium, she took a silver token out of her pocket and clutched it tightly with one hand. With a swipe, she awoke her NanoCloud and with a wave, connected herself to live stream on TalkItNow and the world.

She put on a brave smile for the camera-drones, her hands trembling. Catching Phoebe's gaze as she took her seat, Tass tapped the three-bead necklace. With a fast exhale and her voice on the verge of breaking, she started. "We had a complicated relationship, my father and I. When most people say that, they mean it negatively. They mean that there was some good, and a lot of bad, and they don't want to speak ill of the person. I mean that I was saved by a seventeen-year-old boy who had no support and no idea of what he was doing, other than he felt it was the right thing to do." She licked her lips and hit the podium with her clenched fist, surprised at herself.

"Ah…" She glanced at Phoebe, cracking a smile and now understanding how impossible Phoebe's task had been. "I was more than a pain, as a kid." She wiped a tear, laughing. "To be honest, I was unrelenting. I saw his kindness and gentleness, his awkwardness and vulnerability, and thought they were weaknesses until one day someone at school said something to me. I was seven years old, I think it was recess. I left school right there and then and walked home. And when he opened the door, I hugged him and bawled. I bawled and apologized because... because it wasn't..." she wiped her face and laughed.

Staring up at the sky, she shook her head and focused herself. Turning back to the crowd, she laughed once again. "I'd thought this was going to be pretty easy." The crowd chuckled. "But... but it's not."

She tapped the podium with her fist and stared at it. "I became so impossibly protective of him that I made things difficult for everyone. Things were complicated because we were complicated people, and neither of us were particularly touchy-feely but we had our moments. And stupidly, somewhere along the lines I stopped calling him Dad. I thought of him as my friend, as my mentor, and in some arrogant ways, as a peer. And he let me. And I am so thankful I got to be there for his final moments, because..."

She grit her teeth and dug her fingers into the podium, then pounded it with one hand. "Because laying there so frail, I couldn't help myself but hit him with question after question, getting more and more angry with each one. He let me fire and fire until I was empty, and then motioned for me to come close. I lay on the bed, cuddling him, trying. He kissed me and reminded me of when I was seven, and I bawled all over again. He said that it was okay, because people like us, we are forces of nature, and nature has no limits. That we must go forward or nothing..." her chin quivered and she covered her face with her free hand, "and then he stopped..." She broke down. A moment later, Phoebe retrieved her from the podium.

Arju sat on the couch, watching the holo-screen with disbelief. He'd been glued to it for the past twenty minutes as the news had broken.

"Move over," said his mother, placing her own spin on curried nachos on the coffee table.

He scooted over and leaned back. "I can't believe it."

"I can. These things should happen to bad people," she said, reaching for a nacho. "Oh, I forgot the lemonade. I'll get it."

Arju put his arm across her. "No, I'll get it, Mom," he replied. "You've spoiled me since I arrived. I really appreciate it. I couldn't get out of town fast enough."

"Did you tell anyone you weren't going to the funeral?"

Arju stared at the floor. "I... I couldn't."

His mother tapped his arm. "I understand. All that emotion, you've got to have some time. Now, in terms of this helpful gentleman who showed up at my house, I'll tell you this. Whatever you've done with my son, no worries,

I'll even help you hide the body."

"Very funny," he said, getting up. Stepping into the kitchen, he heard his phone chime from its perch on the counter.

"Is that another job offer coming in? They won't stop," said his mother. "And that reminds me, we need to get you a NanoCloud. I booked you a bootstrapping appointment, they have them every other Thursday. Can't have you walking around without one now that you're not working for Doctor Rafaelo anymore. People will think you're a luddite."

Arju laughed, returning. He handed his mother a tall, icy glass. "Are you *ever* going to tell me the secret ingredient you put in this?"

She shook her head. "You'll stop coming home if I do," she joked.

"Never."

They turned their attention to the unfolding news story for a while.

"Did you even interview at any of those companies sending you job offers?" asked his mother.

Arju shook his head. "Apparently I have a reputation along the Strip. I think the first one came in twenty minutes after the news broke that Niko had died. Two had courier-drones track me down on my way to the bus station on my way here."

"You know, maybe you should wait for one of these

companies to become a huge success, and then accept their offer, retroactively."

"Mom, it doesn't work that way, you know that. You were a startup maven once," he retorted.

She took a sip of her lemonade. "Doesn't mean you can't hold them to the impossible promises they like making."

Arju shook his head at the screen. "I can't believe Binger's going to jail. I mean, wow… One second she's breathing down our necks, and now this."

"Do you think Niko's daughter had anything to do with it?"

Arju shrugged. "I don't know. Last time I spoke to her she ran out of the Spero office with some idea."

"You should have gone to the funeral, at least to talk with her," said his mother.

"I couldn't. It's just… I'm so mad at him, you know?"

"You were mad at your father too."

"Yeah, but that was different. I just… I just need some time."

"Maybe you should throw yourself into some work. Accept one of the more fun offers and kick-start things," she said getting up.

"Where are you going?"

"I might have baked something when you were out this morning," she said.

He hung his head and waved over the sensor to turn off the screen. He leaned forward, and rubbed his unshaven face. "To be honest, I don't want to go back. To software, I mean. I like Burlington, it feels like home... I think even with all that's happened, I want to be there." He smiled at the tray of brownies she set down. "Does that make sense?"

She patted his knee. "Just don't become a lump on my couch like your cousin—"

"No worries," he leaned over and kissed her.

The screen turned on with a message about a letter having just been dropped off by courier-drone.

"I'll get it," said his mother. A moment later she returned. "Something from a lawyer firm of some kind." There was worry in her voice.

Arju took it and stared at it.

"Who would know you're even here?" asked his mother.

Arju shrugged and waited for her to be seated beside him. Holding his breath, he opened it and mumbled through its content.

His mother's eyes welled up, and she grabbed her son's arm excitedly. "I can't believe it."

Arju was speechless. "And there it is," he said, taking out a small credit stick and handing her the envelope.

"I can't believe it," she said squeezing him. "Is it empty? Wait, what's this?" She took out a small piece of paper.

Taking it, Arju choked up.

"Does it make sense to you?"

"It's Niko's short hand," he said, his voice cracking. "It's compressed and encrypted, but we used it at Spero... after Flint died... Let me read it." He bowed his head, tears dripping down.

She rubbed his back and hugged him. "What does it say?"

"He... he said he was sorry. That he wished he'd had the time to explain everything to me." Arju covered his face with his hands. "I should have gone to his funeral. I'm—"

"Hey, shh. It's okay. He didn't want you to stay mad," she said smiling.

Arju sniffed and rubbed his face. "Yeah." He carefully put the credit stick and official letter down on the coffee table and stared at them.

"What are you going to do with all that money?"

He took a sip of his lemonade and shook his head. "I have no idea. No, that's a lie... I have one. Are you up for a little trip?"

CHAPTER TWENTY-SIX

EPILOGUE

"Hi and welcome to an unexpected episode of *Big Sit with Eleanor DeBoeuf*. I know all week we've been sharing bits and pieces of what you could expect. Those of you on TalkItNow have been so excited, I know some of you wanted to just explode. We are all tremendous fans of author Angela B. Chrysler. Unfortunately, she'll be with us next week." Eleanor put her hands together, bowed her head and stared at the floating camera-drones.

"When I called Angela," continued Eleanor, "and told her who we could put on the show today, she told me we had to do it. Then before I knew it, she'd called our guest from next week, Cyn Schneider, and called me back with a wonderful idea. So, next week, for the first time ever, we'll have a double episode."

She stared off at her producer. "I can't believe after all these years we've never done that. Leave it to these brilliant authors to bring some imagination to the table." She laughed and brushed her white hair back.

She walked over to her big chair and smiled. "Have I got you curious? Well, let's go through recent events: Niko Rafaelo passed away, former Wall Street darling Harriet

Binger was arrested, and the enigmatic Lucinda Feer turned evidence against her own step-daughter. Not only that, but we've seen Lucinda Feer out in public with the leader of the New Founders Party. Potential presidential ticket next year? I don't know, but Feer's scathing testimony about her step-daughter's flagrant breaking of laws in pursuit of a personal vendetta against Niko Rafaelo checked a lot of boxes for me. However, that's a different story." She picked up her logoed mug from the side-table and took a sip.

"My guest gave a speech that brought us to tears when she gave her final goodbyes to her father. Showing the cunning from her maternal donor's side, and the brilliance from her father's, she managed to snag control of KnowMe. What's that?" she asked with a smile. "Did you miss that announcement? Maybe that's because it's being announced here first. That's right, my guest is none other than Tasslana Rafaelo, daughter of Niko Rafaelo, grand-daughter of Lucinda Feer herself, and the new CEO of KnowMe. Please, join me in welcoming Tass to the show."

Nervously, Tass walked on stage. She was dressed down for an executive, her hair a brilliant blue and the brown string necklace barely visible under her double collared shirt.

Eleanor waved her over and surprised her with a hug. "I was so sorry about your father," she whispered.

"Thanks for coming to the funeral. It meant a lot to me." Tass wiped away tear.

Eleanor nodded to the seat and turned to the camera-drones. "Now you might be wondering, Elly, what are you doing hugging? You're not a hugger. Well, this woman is a well-deserving exception." She glanced at Tass. "I guess I'm one of the few who knew that he had a daughter, as I actually met her years ago, right here. When I did my first interview with Niko, she sat on the floor, off in the back. A mop of crazy colored hair and hacking away at our systems when she wasn't devouring books by the handful."

"When I shared with our crew who was going to be on the show, they scoured the country and found the original interview chair. They spruced it up and told me this morning. So Tass, you're not only in your father's old shoes in leading KnowMe, you're in his chair."

Tass smiled and rubbed the arms.

"Now, I'm sure I'm not alone when I say, we want to know everything about you. But first, there's a rumor I'd like to address. I've heard you don't sleep much, maybe two or three hours a night?"

Frowning, Tass glanced about. Slowly she shifted to a smile. "Rumors are funny things. People see what they want, I guess. Since my dad's death…" She made a fist of her trembling hand, and slowed her speech, "I've been working a lot more."

Eleanor nodded. "One of the biggest questions on everyone's mind is about NanoCloud Nine and KnowMe. I heard that you've canceled the release, which was to take place soon."

"Actually that's not quite it," said Tass, leaning forward.

"The product that Binger was going to put forward was a mess, and my first job as CEO is to rebuild our reputation. One part of that is making sure that the Nine we bring to the world is something that respects my father's legacy and ambitions, and shows that I can make it my own."

"I heard that you personally made sure that Sandra Gomez, KnowMe's former VP of Development, was cleared of the charges. Something about falsified documents and purgery?"

Tass nodded. "I won't get into the specifics, but I will say that Lucy brought the evidence to the table. I did offer Sandra an opportunity to come back, but at this time she'd rather be at home with her family."

"I can imagine." Eleanor took a sip and cradled her mug. "So, you're a rookie CEO taking over a major company, but you've got a board that has made it pretty clear they are completely behind you, and the stock is up significantly already. The real question is, are you the inventor-type, like your father?"

Tass stared at the floor, rubbing her hands together. "I spend every waking moment when I'm not at the office, continuing his research right from where he left off." Her chin trembled. "Sometimes when I'm working, I feel like he's right there with me."

Six Months Later

Tass waved her lens-display off as she stepped into the

newly renovated JenJen's restaurant. Outside, a small team of security milled about, annoyed at her imperative that she enter the restaurant alone. True privacy was one luxury she could rarely afford these days.

Her hair was short and tinted blue. Long, thin silver bar earrings hung on either side, framing her face and fierce eyes. Peeking out from her cobalt-blue long coat was her low collared white shirt and silver pants. A few customers turned their heads to check who'd just come in. She performed a gesture that got her some curious looks for its uniqueness. An impish smile crept across her face as she saw the signs of frustration as some customers tried and failed to get a picture of her.

With a satisfied sigh, she took a moment to appreciate the new decor. It was fresh and inviting, with plants and a waterfall in the background. Among the wall to wall startup company patrons, were a number of late night couples on dates or hanging out after some event. It was nice to see a healthy mix.

She glanced up at the high ceiling and was impressed to find not a drone in sight. Scanning the room, she noted that every table was serviced by a person, from taking the order to clearing the dishes. It gave off a grounded vibe which she liked. She was certain her father would have loved it even more than he had the predecessor.

She flicked a finger over her wrist, the time projected in the air above her sleeve. She shook her head. "Two in the morning already? That scramjet keeps screwing with my sense of time."

A well-dressed man finished talking and laughing with some customers and hustled over to greet her. "Sorry about that. Table for… oh, hi."

She smiled. "Hi Arju. You look… grown up."

He glanced down at his suit and styled shirt, and chuckled. "Would you believe my mother picked it out for me?"

"Honestly? It's a bit of a relief to hear that. It'd scare me to learn that you had this whole side to you that you'd kept hidden." She glanced about. "I really like what you've done with the place. The plants, the earthy feel… I think it's more JenJen-ish than ever, which is odd but you know what I mean."

He nodded.

"How much of this is you, and how much of this is your mom?" she asked.

Arju turned about and scratched the back of his neck. "About half and half? She still lives back home, but visits about every other week or so. It's been fun, having a project to share. She's also approves of my girlfriend."

"Oh? That's a great development. Where is she?"

"She's working, speaking of development. You know how it is, startups and critical milestones."

"Isn't it always the way? Well, next time maybe. Nice to hear that life's treating you well." She took in the elegant appearance of the renovated restaurant one more time. "I think you put my father's money to good use."

"Thanks," said Arju. "I actually had a good deal left over, and donated some to the schools in the area. I got some of the now no-longer startups to chip in too."

"You're a good guy, Arju," said Tass with a warm smile.

"Thanks. I've got a chef's table in the kitchen we can use to catch up if you like. Also, it has extra anti-everything, so you won't have to worry about privacy. Like you said, more JenJen-ish than ever."

"Well, I always worry these days. Life with Lucinda Feer is interesting," she muttered as they walked through the restaurant.

The smells were delightful, and the dishes Tass saw being plated were colorful and imaginative. "I can't believe you're feeding *that* to people who will just as easily scarf down a half-burnt burger."

Arju laughed. "They love it. Customer satisfaction is up thirty-seven percent since I took over, and profits too."

As they arrived at the table, Tass locked her eyes on Arju. "I was surprised I didn't hear from you after he died. No calls back, no reply messages, nothing."

"Ah," said Arju uncomfortably. "I made a decision, for good or bad, to just cut myself off from everyone and everything. There was just too much."

"I understand," replied Tass. "Still."

"It wasn't personal, Tass. At first I was angry, and then I just didn't know how to say anything to you, and then you were this jet-setting world-class CEO. Plus, I didn't want anything to do with technology anymore."

"After I got the executor's letter, I brought my mom here for a visit. We were walking up to JenJen's, intending to have lunch here, when we saw the two owners fighting. I made them an offer, they accepted, five minutes later I owned the place and wondered what I'd just done."

"Huh," replied Tass, sitting down, her hands in her pockets. She glanced at the state-of-the-art kitchen. Seeing an all human staff working diligently was like a scene out of an old movie. "No robotic assistants, no drones delivering anything, it's amazing. So old school."

"I'm proud of that," said Arju, glancing over his shoulder. "I found a great head chef… but that's a different story. I like the new hair style and look. I'm guessing the sharper image is part of the job."

She stared at the table. "There was a lot I had to accept in taking over KnowMe and having Lucinda Feer take over as chair of the board. I'm living and learning what some of that really means. I now understand a *lot* more about what my father meant about how hard the job was and why he wanted to just explore and invent instead of run the company.

"I don't know how long I'll stay in the job, but there are a few important things I need to do before I consider anything else."

"Are you happy?"

"Enough, yeah," she replied with a smile. She put an arm up on the table and leaned in. "The most terrifying thing yet is tomorrow. It's part of the reason I came here, I needed to see a friendly face. I'd heard a rumor that you had taken over or were the manager or something, so I took the risk to come down.

"Tomorrow, I'm going before that senate committee, the one that had once roasted my dad. My stomach's in knots. I'm told that things will go well, but you never know. It's all par for the course, I guess."

Arju leaned back and sighed. "Good luck, but I'm *so* glad I'm not anywhere near that world of madness anymore. Food is simple. People need it. They will come back if they like it. My job is really about making people happy."

Tass fidgeted in her pocket. "I like that. You know, I've received so many letters from people praising my father since I took over KnowMe, since the world learned he had a daughter. Of the hundred or so I've read, they all tell of how my father had an impact on their lives. I wonder what it was that he really did to affect them."

"He gave all of us permission to believe," said Arju.

Tass relaxed and smiled. "I like that. Whenever I'm feeling lost or doubting myself, I go to a room I've dedicated to the letters, and just pick one out of the pile. I can't believe so many people wrote on paper and sent them. Sometimes I take a cup of tea and sit there, pull one out at random from the pile and read it."

Not sure how to reply, Arju stood. "How about I order some things to eat?"

"Hey Arju, are you really happy doing all of this? Do you miss any of what we did?" she asked, ignoring his question.

Arju narrowed his eyes. "The excitement was fun, I suppose. But you know, I'm happy now. I think I've found my place in the universe."

"I'm glad," she said getting up. "Sorry I can't stay, I just needed to see a friendly face… and I wanted to tell you, all of it mattered. Everything, it meant something."

Her words weighed on him. He smiled at her. "Thanks."

Stepping out of the restaurant, she looked up at the moon and smiled. "I think you're right, Dad. He needs this, he's happy."

"Excuse me," said her head of security as he walked over. "Do you want to head straight to DC? Or should we check you into a hotel? I noticed that no one had booked a reservation. You do have enough time to get some sleep."

She shook her head. "No need. Let's find a good place to grab some breakfast in DC, and then we'll tell the world about Nine."

THE END

THANK YOU
FOR READING THIS BOOK

Reviews are powerful things. In addition to sharing your thoughts and feelings about the book, your review lets the rest of the world know that there are people reading the book.

Many people don't realize that without enough reviews, indie authors are excluded from marketing and newsletter opportunities that could otherwise help them get the word out.

So, if you have an opportunity, I would greatly appreciate it!

Don't know how to write a review? Check out **AdamDreece.com/WriteAReview**. Where should you post it? Your favorite online retailer's site and GoodReads.com would be a great start!

PLAYLIST

Every now and then I get asked what albums I listened to when writing a book. Well, in case you were wondering, here you go (in random order):

Terminator: Genisys, the soundtrack
Tron: Legacy, the soundtrack
This is War, by Thirty Seconds to Mars
August and Everything After,
   by The Counting Crows
25, by Adele
Everyone Else Is Doing It, by The Cranberries

Enjoy,
Adam

ABOUT THE AUTHOR

With a best-selling young adult series, *The Yellow Hoods*, well underway and a successful episodic series, *The Wizard Killer*, I decided it was time to share my deep love of science fiction with *The Man of Cloud 9*. It allowed me to pull from my over 20 years of experience in software, from leading teams at a Silicon Valley startup and working on huge projects at companies like Microsoft.

Like many people, I wrote and wrote but did practically nothing with it. Maybe I would be an author some day. Then two medical events, one after the other, made me change my priorities. With the amazing support of my wife and kids, I kicked off a serious indie author career, and the response has been amazing.

I live in Calgary, Alberta, Canada with my awesome wife, amazing kids, and lots and lots of sticky notes and notebooks.

I blog about writing, life and more at **AdamDreece.com**.
Join me on Twitter **@adamdreece**, on
Facebook at **AdamDreeceAuthor** or
send me an email **Adam.Dreece@ADZOPublishing.com**

ADAM DREECE BOOKS

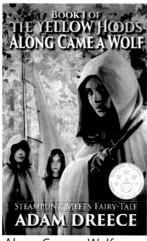

Along Came a Wolf
ISBN: 978-0-9881013-0-2

Breadcrumb Trail
ISBN: 978-0-9881013-3-3

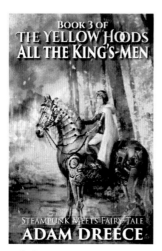

All the King's-Men
ISBN: 978-0-9881013-6-4

Beauties of the Beast
ISBN: 978-0-9948184-0-9

Watch for Book 5, coming Spring 2017